PRA

"I had planned on an early night but couldn't put this book down until I finished it around 3am. Like her other books, this one features fascinating characters with a plot that mimics real life in the best way. My recommendation: it's time to read every book Tammy L Grace has written."
— *Carolyn, review of Beach Haven*

"*A Season of Hope* is a perfect holiday read! Warm wonderful and gentle tale reflecting small town romance at its best."
— *Jeanie, review of A Season for Hope: A Christmas Novella*

"This book is a clean, simple romance with a background story very similar to the works of Debbie Macomber. If you like Macomber's books you will like this one. The main character, Hope and her son Jake are on a road trip when their car breaks down, thus starts the story. A holiday tale filled with dogs, holiday fun, and the joy of giving will warm your heart.
— *Avid Mystery Reader, review of A Season for Hope: A Christmas Novella*

"This book was just as enchanting as the others. Hardships with the love of a special group of friends. I recommend the series as a must read. I loved every exciting moment. A new author for me. She's fabulous."
—*Maggie!, review of Pieces of Home: A Hometown Harbor Novel (Book 4)*

"Tammy is an amazing author, she reminds me of Debbie Macomber... Delightful, heartwarming...just down to earth."

— *Plee, review of A Promise of Home: A Hometown Harbor Novel (Book 3)*

"This was an entertaining and relaxing novel. Tammy Grace has a simple yet compelling way of drawing the reader into the lives of her characters. It was a pleasure to read a story that didn't rely on theatrical tricks, unrealistic events or steamy sex scenes to fill up the pages. Her characters and plot were strong enough to hold the reader's interest."
—*MrsQ125, review of Finding Home: A Hometown Harbor Novel (Book 1)*

"This is a beautifully written story of loss, grief, forgiveness and healing. I believe anyone could relate to the situations and feelings represented here. This is a read that will stay with you long after you've completed the book."
—*Cassidy Hop, review of Finally Home: A Hometown Harbor Novel (Book 5)*

"Killer Music is a clever and well-crafted whodunit. The vivid and colorful characters shine as the author gradually reveals their hidden secrets—an absorbing page-turning read."
— *Jason Deas, bestselling author of Pushed and Birdsongs*

"I could not put this book down! It was so well written & a suspenseful read! This is definitely a 5-star story! I'm hoping there will be a sequel!"
—*Colleen, review of Killer Music*

"This is the best book yet by this author. The plot was well crafted with an unanticipated ending. I like to try to leap ahead and see if I can accurately guess the outcome. I was able to predict some of the plot but not the actual details which made reading the last several chapters quite engrossing."

—*0001PW, review of Deadly Connection*

DEADLY PURSUIT

DEADLY PURSUIT

COOPER HARRINGTON DETECTIVE NOVELS
BOOK 6

TAMMY L. GRACE

LONE MOUNTAIN PRESS

DEADLY PURSUIT
A novel by
Tammy L. Grace

Deadly Pursuit is a work of fiction. Names, characters, places, and incidents either are products of the author's imagination or are used fictitiously. Any resemblance to actual events, locales, entities, or persons, living or dead, is entirely coincidental.

DEADLY PURSUIT Copyright © 2025 by Tammy L. Grace

All rights reserved. No part of this book may be reproduced or transmitted in any form or by any means, electronic or mechanical including photocopying, recording, or by any information storage and retrieval system without the written permission of the author, except for the use of brief quotations in a book review. For permissions contact the author directly via electronic mail: tammy@tammylgrace.com

No AI Training: Without in any way limiting the author's [and publisher's] exclusive rights under copyright, any use of this publication to "train" generative artificial intelligence (AI) technologies to generate text is expressly prohibited. The author reserves all rights to license uses of this work for generative AI training and development of machine learning language models.

www.tammylgrace.com
Facebook: https://www.facebook.com/tammylgrace.books
Twitter: @TammyLGrace
Published in the United States by Lone Mountain Press, Nevada
ISBN 978-1-945591-79-2 (paperback)
ISBN 978-1-945591-78-5 (eBook)
FIRST EDITION
Cover by Elizabeth Mackey Graphic Design
Printed in the United States of America

ALSO BY TAMMY L. GRACE

COOPER HARRINGTON DETECTIVE NOVELS

Killer Music

Deadly Connection

Dead Wrong

Cold Killer

Deadly Deception

Deadly Pursuit

HOMETOWN HARBOR SERIES

Hometown Harbor: The Beginning (Prequel Novella)

Finding Home

Home Blooms

A Promise of Home

Pieces of Home

Finally Home

Forever Home

Follow Me Home

Long Way Home

Come Home for Christmas

CHRISTMAS STORIES

A Season for Hope: Christmas in Silver Falls Book 1

The Magic of the Season: Christmas in Silver Falls Book 2

Christmas in Snow Valley: A Hometown Christmas Book 1

One Unforgettable Christmas: A Hometown Christmas Book 2

Christmas Wishes: Souls Sisters at Cedar Mountain Lodge

Christmas Surprises: Soul Sisters at Cedar Mountain Lodge

GLASS BEACH COTTAGE SERIES

Beach Haven

Moonlight Beach

Beach Dreams

WRITING AS CASEY WILSON

A Dog's Hope

A Dog's Chance

WISHING TREE SERIES

The Wishing Tree

Wish Again

Overdue Wishes

One More Wish

SISTERS OF THE HEART SERIES

Greetings from Lavender Valley

Pathway to Lavender Valley

Sanctuary at Lavender Valley

Blossoms at Lavender Valley

Comfort in Lavender Valley

Reunion in Lavender Valley

Remember to subscribe to Tammy's exclusive group of readers for your gift, only available to readers on her mailing list. **Sign up at www.tammylgrace.com.** Follow this link to subscribe at https://wp.me/

P9umIy-e and you'll receive the exclusive interview she did with all the canine characters in her Hometown Harbor Series.

Follow Tammy on Facebook by liking her page. You may also follow Tammy on book retailers or at BookBub by clicking on the follow button.

"Her absence is like the sky spread over everything"—C.S. Lewis

1

Late Friday afternoon when Erica got home from a double shift at the hospital, Alyssa's car wasn't in the driveway of the house they shared. She went about changing her clothes and pouring herself a glass of sweet tea.

She eyed the sink. Alyssa had a habit of leaving her tea cup in the sink each morning, and it wasn't there. It wasn't like they kept close tabs on each other, but she should have been home by now.

Erica took her glass of tea and wandered back to the refrigerator and the calendar they kept attached to it. She eyed the date, April twenty-sixth. There was nothing written on the square block. The day before, Alyssa had written Trivia Night.

With a tap of her finger on the calendar, Erica frowned. She'd gone to bed early last night and didn't remember seeing her roommate since hearing her leave early yesterday morning and only glimpsed her hurrying to her car.

Did she come home last night? Erica rushed to Alyssa's room and opened the door. It was neat and tidy, as usual. It was hard to tell if she'd been there since she was a stickler for making her bed each morning, no matter that she left the house at five o'clock.

Erica went back to the kitchen and plucked her cell phone from the counter. She scrolled to Alyssa's name and tapped the green button. It rang but went straight to voicemail. She left a message asking her to call as soon as she could and disconnected.

Something didn't feel right. As she waited for a return call, she connected to social media and looked for the friend who usually went with Alyssa on Trivia Night. Erica scrolled through Alyssa's profile and searched for her connections. She finally found Cara and sent her a connection request and a private message, hoping she'd see it and reply.

Chances are they stayed out too late, and Alyssa decided to stay over at her place. It had happened before, but usually Alyssa let her know. It didn't explain why she wasn't home by now. Fridays, Alyssa often got off an hour early or so, and they usually got pizza and streamed a show they both liked to celebrate the end of the work week.

The uneasiness she felt in the pit of her stomach wouldn't let go.

She flipped on the television for a distraction, willing her phone to buzz.

She tried calling Alyssa again, then sent her a text. With no response, she tried to message her on social media.

It had been two hours when her phone finally chimed. It was a message from Cara letting her know she hadn't seen Alyssa yesterday. In fact, Alyssa hadn't come to work. She thought she must be sick.

With shaking fingers, Erica typed in a reply and thanked her. She asked if she did see her, to have her call right away. She was worried about her.

Cara promised she would.

Erica racked her brain for anyone else that might know

where Alyssa would be, but she came up empty. Cara was the only work friend she ever mentioned, and Alyssa wasn't a social butterfly. Despite being almost ten years younger than Erica, she was an old soul who loved to read, watch movies, and go to secondhand stores.

After thinking more about it, she called the hospital where she worked and asked if Alyssa or anyone fitting her description had been admitted. Once she confirmed Alyssa wasn't there, she moved onto the other hospitals in the Knoxville area. She struck out with all of them.

Filled with dread, Erica contemplated calling Alyssa's mother. She hated to worry her for nothing. She and Alyssa's sister lived in Oklahoma. Her dad died a few years ago, and they didn't need any more drama in their lives.

She checked the time on her phone. It was almost eight o'clock. She looked up the phone number for the sheriff's department. The woman who answered the phone said she would have a deputy enroute to speak with Erica.

Erica paced the floor while she waited. The small town where they lived, tucked along Watts Bar Lake, was serviced by Roane County Sheriff's Department.

Less than fifteen minutes later, a knock on her door jarred Erica from her pacing. She checked out the window and saw the sheriff's department truck in her driveway.

A young deputy greeted her with a smile. "Ms. Erica Walker?"

"Yes, please come in."

She stepped aside, and he came into the living area. "I'm Deputy Bennett. Dispatch said your roommate is missing. Can you tell me her full name and the last time you saw her?"

She led him to the dining room table. His leather gun belt squeaked as he took a seat and unzipped the portfolio he carried. Erica rattled off the particulars about Alyssa Morgan and told him she'd already checked the area hospitals, and none of them reported anyone matching Alyssa's description being admitted.

"Are you the owner of the house, or is she?"

"I'm the owner. She pays me rent as a roommate. She just moved in a few months ago, but it's been great. I work at the hospital and pull some crazy shifts, so we don't hang out much, but we usually spend our Friday nights here with pizza and a movie."

He asked about Alyssa's car and license plate number.

Erica forehead creased, and she held up her finger. "She's got a file box in her room. Let me go see if she's got any paperwork in there that will help."

Deputy Bennett nodded. "If not, we can locate it through a search in the motor vehicle database."

Erica hurried to Alyssa's room. As she expected, her files were in perfect order, labeled and current with her registration and insurance information on her old blue Honda. She also found her birth certificate and the paperwork from her new job she was due to start in two weeks. She brought it all to the dining table.

"Here you go. I think it will have everything you need. I even found her cell phone contract, so you'll have the carrier information."

The deputy copied down the relevant information. She also gave him Cara's information from social media. "She could help you contact Alyssa's current employer. Alyssa works at the paper manufacturing warehouse but is due to start at Oak Ridge National Laboratory in just a couple of weeks. She was really excited about it."

He nodded and asked for contact information for her family. Erica scrolled her phone and recited the number of Mrs. Morgan in Oklahoma.

The deputy asked several questions about Alyssa's habits and her schedule. Erica couldn't be sure about the clothes

Alyssa wore when she last saw her, but she reported she typically wore jeans, a shirt with the paper company's logo, and athletic shoes, plus a blue hoodie.

Erica explained that she normally left around five in the morning and drove to the park-n-ride lot by the local supermarket. She took the bus provided by the paper company to Knoxville and back each day, except Fridays, when she got off early. She confirmed Alyssa had no boyfriend and outside of Trivia Night at the local brewpub each week, she was a homebody.

When asked if Alyssa used drugs or was on medications, Erica shook her head. "No, she's not a drug user. Doesn't use any medications I know of. Doesn't smoke. Drinks very little. She's pretty health conscious."

He asked to see her room and gave it a cursory overview. "Does she have a computer or laptop?"

Erica nodded. She pointed at the night table by the bed where a rose-colored laptop rested on a shelf.

"I'll take that and leave a receipt for it."

He surveyed the space again and met Erica's eyes. "Okay, Ms. Walker. I'm going to put out a BOLO on her car, get in touch with her employer, and will contact her mother before we formally file a missing person's report. If Alyssa does get in contact with you, please call me." He slipped a business card from his portfolio. "We'll assign a detective to the case, and he'll be in touch after we file the missing person's report."

Erica took the card and followed the deputy to the door. He stepped outside and turned toward her. "Try not to worry. We'll get right on this. If you think of anything else or hear from her, be sure to call me or the main number, and they'll get in touch with me. I'm working the swing shift for the next five days."

"Thanks, I appreciate that." Part of her didn't want him to leave. She was scared for Alyssa and wasn't sure what her disappearance meant.

He met her eyes. "Are you going to be okay, Ms. Walker? Is there someone I can call for you?"

Erica shook her head as tears filled her eyes. "I'm just really worried about her. This isn't like her at all."

"I'll be in touch if I find out anything, and you'll hear from a detective soon. We take these cases very seriously. Just lock up and try to get some rest tonight." He left her with a reassuring smile, and she flipped the deadbolt as soon as she closed the door.

Erica sighed, resting against the thick wooden door. "Please be okay, Alyssa," she whispered.

2

At midnight, Erica's cell phone rang. With blurry eyes, Erica squinted at the screen. Dread filled her as she saw Mrs. Morgan's name.

With a wary voice, she said, "Hello."

"Erica, it's Carol Morgan, Alyssa's mom." She launched into a series of questions, never taking a breath, telling Erica the police had called her, and she was worried sick about Alyssa. She wasn't answering her calls or texts from her mother either. "Have you heard from her since you talked to the police?"

"No, I'm sorry, I haven't heard anything. Did you talk to a detective?"

"Yes, Detective Mitchell. He's handling the missing person's case." Her sobs came through the phone. "I can't believe this is happening. I don't know what to do, and I'm so far away. I'm checking flights right now but may end up driving."

"You're welcome to stay here if you need to. Just let me know. I was going to call you earlier when I didn't hear from her but thought it best just to call the police and get them involved."

"You did the right thing, dear. I'm just a mess. I'm so sorry to call you so late. I just don't know what to do. I feel so helpless. Alyssa is a good girl. This isn't like her."

"I know. I feel the same way. I'm so sorry."

"I'll let you get some sleep and if I make a flight reservation, I'll let you know. I've got a cousin in Nashville I'm going to call. I'll be in touch."

"Okay, Mrs. Morgan. I'll talk to you soon."

Erica disconnected and pulled the blanket up to her chin, shivering. Her heart ached for the poor woman as a cold finger of fear for Alyssa gripped her.

Saturday morning, Erica stumbled out of bed and made her way to the kitchen where she brewed a pot of coffee. She'd just poured herself a cup when there was a knock on her door.

Looking outside, she saw a vehicle that looked like an old police car, without the lights. Still uneasy, she hollered through the door, "Who is it?"

"Detective Mitchell, ma'am. Roane County Sheriff's Department. I'm here about the missing person you reported last night."

She wrapped the long cardigan she wore over her pajamas tighter around her and opened the door. He smiled. "Morning, Ms. Walker. Sorry to bother you so early."

With a shake of her head, Erica gestured him inside. He was older than the deputy. She noted the gray strands in the dark hair near his temples and guessed him to be in his late forties. "No bother. I've barely slept, worrying about Alyssa. Do you have news?"

He wore a suit and a chain around his neck with his badge. His somber face and kind blue eyes told her things were serious, and he wasn't there to deliver good news. She led the way into the dining area. "I just made coffee. Would you like some?"

He smiled and shook his head. "No, ma'am. I'm fine but thank you."

She retrieved her cup and sat. He took the chair next to hers. "I just wanted to let you know we talked to Alyssa's mother last night. She's tried to get in touch with Alyssa and hasn't had success. She hasn't heard from her since Wednesday evening when they talked on the phone. We talked to Alyssa's manager at the paper plant, and he confirmed she didn't report for work on Thursday morning, and they haven't seen her since her shift ended on Wednesday. He said it was unusual, and Alyssa was a top employee, who was always there for her shift."

Erica gasped. "This is horrible."

He continued, "We talked to the bus driver who drives that route between the parking area and the paper company. He confirmed she wasn't on the bus, and he was familiar with where she usually parked and didn't remember seeing her car."

Erica cocked her head and frowned. "She left here Thursday morning like normal. I only glimpsed her as she headed out the door, but she hollered out goodbye as I was coming into the kitchen that morning."

"We're going through her laptop and getting phone records and checking social media, along with her bank records now." He slipped a business card from his pocket. "I'll leave you my card, and it's got my cell number on it."

"What about her car?" Erica asked.

"We haven't found it. It's not at the park-n-ride lot. We issued the BOLO last night for Tennessee and the surrounding states, so all law enforcement is looking for it and her."

Erica's lips trembled as she reached for her coffee. "Her mom called me late last night. She's worried sick and thinking about coming. I told her she could stay here, and it sounds like she has a cousin in Nashville."

Detective Mitchell nodded. "It's understandable she would want to be here. It's difficult to be so far away and feel out of touch." He paused, then asked her a few more questions related to Alyssa's state of mind over the last week or two.

"I understand why you're asking all of this, but Alyssa was fine. Happy and excited about her new job. She didn't do drugs and has never stayed away for this long without letting me know where she was. She's good about returning calls and texts, and everything about this is wrong. Something bad has happened to her."

The detective nodded. "I understand, and I'm not judging Alyssa. These are just questions we have to ask to make sure we cover every circumstance."

She nodded and sipped her coffee, cradling the warm cup in her hands. "I'm off today but back to work early tomorrow. If something comes up, you can reach me at the hospital." She gave him the number.

He added it to his notes. "I'll add that to our file, thanks." He walked to the door and left her with the promise that he'd be in touch as soon as they knew more.

Erica wished she were due at work today. Sitting at home worrying all day held little appeal. She trudged to the bathroom for a shower.

AFTER SPENDING the day cleaning the already clean house, shopping, and taking a four-hour drive to look for herself around the route Alyssa would have taken had she driven to work, Erica came home to a quiet house.

She felt beyond helpless and couldn't imagine what Erica's mom was dealing with as she sat hundreds of miles away, waiting and worrying.

Erica opened the bag of takeout she had picked up from the café downtown. Despite having only a latte in the morning, she wasn't hungry. As she picked at her food, she flicked on the television.

The local news came on, and she gasped when she saw a video of a building ablaze. The anchor reported that the fire was under investigation. The building was on the edge of town and was an old warehouse that had been converted into apartments on the second floor with warehouse space below. They were awaiting more information from the police and fire investigators but confirmed there was at least one fatality.

After the commercial, the anchor broke the story of Alyssa's disappearance. Tears filled Erica's eyes when her roommate's photo flashed on the screen. The anchor gave a brief summary that a local woman was missing after not showing up at work and, along with her photo, showed a photo of her car and provided the license plate number. She asked viewers with information to reach out to the police.

Erica closed her eyes and hoped someone knew something that would lead to Alyssa being found. She'd looked everywhere she could think of along the way to Knoxville and hadn't seen her car anywhere. She always considered the area she lived in to be small. She always felt like she knew everyone but making the trek to Knoxville left her feeling worse. There were just too many places to look, and she was overwhelmed, expecting danger around every corner.

Alyssa's disappearance made her feel uneasy and wary in the place she'd always considered a haven. She pulled out her cell phone and texted Alyssa again, hoping she might answer.

After checking her phone for what seemed like the thousandth time and seeing no reply, she opted to sleep on the couch, with the television tuned to a classic channel for company and background noise.

Without Alyssa, the silence around her was deafening.

3

Sunday morning, while Coop sipped coffee in Aunt Camille's kitchen and waited for whatever she had in the oven that smelled delicious, his cell phone rang. He smiled when he saw Ben's name. "Morning, Ben."

"Hey, Coop. Sorry to bug you on Sunday. I've got a case for you. There's a missing young woman outside of Knoxville." He went on to explain a good friend of Jen, his wife, had a cousin who lived in Oklahoma, and she was the mother of the missing girl, and the friend reached out to Ben's wife in desperation to try to help her cousin.

Ben sighed. "I put in a call to Detective Mitchell with Roane County. He's in charge of the case. Good guy, but they just got hit with a suspected arson and are stretched thin. Anyway, I told him I've used you as a consultant in the past and highly recommend you. The mother would also hire you, but she's not exactly in great financial shape. I was hoping I could convince the local department to use you."

"That was good of you. What do you know about the case?"

Ben explained it had only been about thirty-six hours since the report was received from the girl's roommate, but

Alyssa had been missing three days now, and time was of the essence. "I told Detective Mitchell I'd pass on his number to you, and he could give you more details. I know it would ease the mom's mind. Her name is Carol Morgan. Lives outside of Tulsa."

Coop's hope of avoiding complicated cases waned as he thought about the poor woman missing her daughter and the fact that it had been three days. He sighed, resigned to do what he could. "I'll call Detective Mitchell right now."

He disconnected as Camille and Charlie came in from outside. They'd been sipping coffee on the patio and enjoying the morning sunshine.

"Morning, Coop. Breakfast will be ready in a few minutes." Camille made her way to the oven to peek at it. With the cut on her hand healed, she was back to her normal busy self.

"I just got a call from Ben, and it sounds like I'm going to be working on a case over near Knoxville. Roane County. Missing young woman."

"Oh, dear," said Camille, her face filled with concern.

"AB and I were trying to keep things lowkey after our last case, but I can't walk away from a missing person." He pointed at his phone. "I need to make a call to the detective in charge of this one, but I suspect I'll be heading out after a quick breakfast."

Charlie slid into his spot at the island counter and proceeded to rub the top of Gus' head. "Don't worry, son. You go make your call, and we'll watch over Gus while you're gone."

Coop wandered back to his wing of the house and sat at his desk, notepad ready. He dialed Detective Mitchell.

He answered on the first ring, "Mitchell."

"This is Cooper Harrington. Chief Mason in Nashville gave me your number and said you might need some help on a missing person case."

"Oh, great. Yes, I got the okay to bring on a consultant and if you can start right away, that would be best. We're already three days out from the last time anyone saw Alyssa."

"I can take off from here within the hour. It will take me a little over two hours to get there."

Mitchell gave him directions and told him to call when he was thirty minutes out, and he'd meet him at his office and have the case file ready, along with the camera footage they'd collected to date.

Coop emerged and made his way to the kitchen, already dreading the drive. After a wedge of Aunt Camille's cheesy egg casserole and a biscuit, he left Gus with his dad and set out for Knoxville.

On the way, he called AB to let her know they had a new case. He gave Detective Mitchell's name as point of contact, so she could organize the billing file.

As he explained more about the case, she sighed. "This doesn't sound like an easy one."

"I know," he said, changing lanes to get out of the way of a speeding driver.

"Well, keep me posted and if you need me to come in today, I'm available. If not, I'll see you early in the morning."

"Thanks, AB. I'll be in touch."

Traffic was light, and he was making good time. Soon, he called and left a voicemail on Detective Mitchell's phone to let him know he was close. Within twenty minutes, he took the exit for the picturesque small town situated thirty-five miles from Knoxville and found the sheriff's department less than a mile from the exit.

He parked in front of the brick building next to a Dollar General and climbed from the driver's seat. Coop stretched his shoulder as he made his way to the entrance. He hadn't given any thought to his shirt and hoped the detective wouldn't be offended by the green one he wore stenciled with YOU KNOW WHAT I LIKE ABOUT PEOPLE? THEIR DOGS. He ran his hand over the short beard he'd decided to keep after letting it grow out during the winter. He'd been put off by the visible gray in it, but AB told him he looked distinguished.

The office was closed on the weekends, but as soon as he reached the smoked glass door, it opened, and a dark-haired man greeted him with a firm handshake and a smile. "Mr. Harrington, I'm Detective Mitchell. Jim."

Coop shook his hand. "Call me Coop, please."

"Come on in, and I'll get you situated. We're just getting ready to send out for lunch. There's a great burger place around the corner that delivers."

"I wouldn't say no to a burger." Coop chuckled as he followed him down the hallway.

A deputy walked by as Jim pointed at the door of the squad room. "Atkins, Coop is our consultant who's going to be working the Alyssa Morgan case."

The young deputy smiled and extended his hand. "I'm ordering lunch. What can I add for you? The cheeseburger basket deal is popular."

"Sounds good." Coop thanked him and pulled out his wallet.

Jim shook his head. "No, this is on me. I appreciate you making the trip over here on such short notice."

He led him to the whiteboard that dominated one wall of the squad room. "We're working on a timeline here. We've been gathering camera footage from around the park-n-ride lot. We're shorthanded with a detective out on medical and just started going through the footage when we got hit with this arson fatality. We've got everyone on it, working overtime. Needless to say, we need your help on that front."

Coop nodded.

Jim pointed at a notation on the whiteboard. "We do have one thing that just came in today. Alyssa's phone pinged, and we've got a location near Lenoir City, about fifteen minutes from here along the interstate. It had no activity since Thursday morning. We've got a search team out now."

"Still no activity on the phone, right?"

Jim nodded. "Yeah, nothing on it since Thursday morning. The carrier provided history information, and the last location was the area of the park-n-ride. Then nothing until this morning."

"So, the theory is someone took her and her car from that lot. She or the person who took her turned off her phone until today?" Coop shook his head. "That's odd."

"Agreed. We're hoping she's there, but at the same time, continuing the investigation. We'll give you a drive with all the footage and provide you with the credentials to get into our secure system so we can share more with you. I've got you a hardcopy of the file, too." He pointed to a folder on the table and an open laptop.

"No sign of her car yet? Nothing on traffic cameras?"

Jim shook his head. "We don't have many highway cameras until you get closer to Knoxville. We've been concentrating on the area around the park-n-ride to see if she ever made it there and looking along the route she would take. We have to rely on businesses or homeowners that may have cameras."

Coop studied the whiteboard. "Nothing to lead you to a domestic dispute, boyfriend, work problem?"

Jim's jaw tensed. "No, nothing. That's where we spent quite a bit of time. Making sure nothing was amiss at her workplace. Checking social media for any secret relationships or disputes. Nothing. She leads a quiet life. She's well liked at work, respected, and has a good reputation. We checked with her soon-to-be supervisor at Oak Ridge. No joy there. The HR department has been in contact getting her setup in their system, but no problems."

Coop flipped open the file. "Nothing to indicate she had any type of mental issues and just left on her own accord?"

Jim frowned. "No, she's stable. No hint of a problem of any kind."

Coop tapped his finger on the cover of the file. "I can tell by your face you think she was taken."

"At this point, I do. Absolutely nothing points to her taking off of her own accord. I have a bad feeling about this one. No activity on her credit or bank cards. No activity on her phone. That doesn't paint a picture of someone who decided to leave town on her own."

Coop sighed. "Okay, I'll study this file, then I want to take a look at the route myself. I'll get my office started on the camera footage, too."

"I'll get our tech guy in here to set you up with remote access to our system. Each time we add something, you'll get an email notification, so you'll know if we get new footage."

As Coop read the statement from the roommate, Atkins came into the room with a bag and a drink cup. "Lunch has arrived. Enjoy."

Coop thanked him and ate as he read through every document in the file. When he finished, like Detective Mitchell, he was filled with dread. Young women like Alyssa didn't just disappear.

WHEN HE CHECKED the credit card report, Coop noticed a purchase of gas the day before Alyssa's disappearance. From the total charge, it would appear she had a full tank. He used the computer to check the fuel capacity of a 1992 Honda Accord. After a calculation, he figured the car would go around four hundred miles before running out of gas. He plotted that radius on a map, and his heart sank. He wasn't holding out much hope that Alyssa would be found fifteen minutes away.

Her phone might be there, but in his gut, he didn't think she would.

The car could have traveled all the way to Ohio, Indiana, even Florida, not to mention all the neighboring states. Coop's heart sank as the enormity of the case hit him.

As he considered the best approach, footsteps rushing in the hallway made him turn his head. Detective Mitchell appeared in the doorway. "Deputy Bennett has something off a camera." He motioned Coop to join him and led the way to a room filled with screens and computers.

With a renewed sense of hope, Coop hurried to follow him.

The deputy at the console, who appeared to have a perpetual smile on his face, pointed up at the screen on the wall. "We've got Alyssa's car arriving at 5:14 and a male subject who looks like he came from the South. Hoodie, jeans, hands in pockets, can't make out his face. This is from the supermarket, and the resolution is poor."

They watched as the man walked across the parking lot and approached the driver's door of Alyssa's car. The camera view was from the other side of the car, so it was impossible to see any details.

Moments later, the subject was inside the car, and the car backed out of the spot and sped away at 5:17, taking the main road back toward the interstate. The deputy shrugged. "That's all we have so far. I'm going to search more footage and see if we can figure out where he came from."

"Good work, Bennett," said Detective Mitchell, patting his shoulder. "That promotion to detective is soon to be yours at this rate. Keep at it. They're a few homeless people who sometimes hang around the underpass nearby. He could have come from there. We'll check it out."

Coop stared at the screen. He was antsy to see the area for himself. After letting Detective Mitchell know he would check out Alyssa's route before heading back to Nashville, Coop left the building. He added the stack of business cards Jim provided him to his portfolio. He could use them in case he encountered someone who needed to confirm his involvement in the case.

Loaded down with the case files and the camera footage on a drive to take back to his office, along with access to the system the detectives used, Coop set out for Alyssa's house she shared with Erica Walker.

It didn't take long to reach the quiet street. He didn't have anything of importance to ask Erica but was curious about the neighborhood. He parked and walked to the front door.

A woman dressed in blue scrubs, with a wary look in her eyes, answered his knock. "Ms. Walker, my name is Cooper Harrington, and I'm a private detective from Nashville. I'm working with Detective Mitchell on Alyssa's case. They brought me in as a consultant."

As he spoke, Erica's stance relaxed. "Come on in. I have to get back to work in a few minutes, but I'm glad they're getting help."

Coop followed her into the dining area. "I just read the file and wanted to get a feel for the route she normally took. I don't have any pressing questions for you, but when I get back to the office, and we start going through things in more detail, I may reach out."

She nodded. "Sure, just call my cell number. If I'm at work, I'll check messages when I can and call you back." Coop noticed tears in her eyes. "I'm really worried, Mr. Harrington."

"Call me Coop." He smiled at the young woman. "Everyone is working to find Alyssa. I assure you, I'll do my best. Anybody new move into the neighborhood lately? Anybody around here give you a bad feeling or pay more attention to Alyssa than normal?"

She shook her head. "No, this is a great neighborhood, and I know everyone on the street. Nobody new, and most everyone is older. It's quiet and nice."

"Okay. If you do think of anyone who crossed Alyssa's path, let me know. Anybody out of her normal routine. Not necessarily someone she knew or spoke with, just someone who she encountered."

"I can't think of anyone." She dropped her head. "It's a bad sign that they haven't found anything. I have the worst feeling about this. It's not like Alyssa at all."

"I'd say try not to worry, but I know it's impossible. One more thing, then I'll get out of your hair. Had Alyssa visited anywhere new? A bar? A store?"

Erica shook her head. "No. She was pretty set in her routines. She was the same old Alyssa. She worked and came home, except for Trivia Night. Excited about her new job but hadn't gone anywhere new or mentioned anyone at all."

Coop nodded, having read the interview report with Cara, Alyssa's friend who went to Trivia Night with her each week. "Okay, I'm going to head out and get a feel for the route she took and check out the area. Call me if you think of anything else."

He left her at the door, her eyes filled with worry.

Coop had the same feeling. He set out for the park-n-ride lot near the supermarket he'd seen in the camera footage. It didn't take long to get there, on the other side of the highway from the sheriff's department. As he passed under the highway, he took note of a gas station, a couple of fast-food joints, a hardware store, and a dental office, along with a bank across the street, where he made the turn into the supermarket.

He drove the short distance to the park-n-ride lot next to the supermarket parking and got out of the Jeep. He walked to where Alyssa had parked, then back to where the man appeared on camera. It wasn't far from the overpass.

He noticed a uniformed officer was already there, approaching a few of the people, no doubt hoping to find the man they'd seen approach Alyssa's car or someone who might know him.

Coop kept walking along the main road that led to the shopping area and followed it for a quarter of a mile, where another street went to the right. He opted to walk down it. There was a lot for sale then a large, fenced property, with a sign for a lumber company. As he got closer, he noticed the gates were locked, and it was no longer in business.

He peered through the chain-link fencing that stopped access to the buildings but took note of the large, paved road that circled the entire property. He walked along it as it wound around to where trucks could deliver and pick up loads with ease. The fencing around the property was high and in good shape, topped with razor wire that would deter most criminals.

The gates were all secured, and he found no breaches in the fencing. It didn't look like it had been taken over by the homeless, which surprised him since it was ringed by dense trees and off the beaten path. With the town being so small, Coop was certain the deputies knew most of the homeless. If the unknown man who approached Alyssa was part of that community, it would make identifying him easy.

Coop completed his circle, finding nothing beyond the defunct lumber company, except the exit road from the freeway. He made his way back down the street to the main road he'd come in on and continued on it, away from the shopping center.

The paved road curved and fed into a residential neighborhood. Where the road curved, a narrow dirt road went back toward the freeway. It ran behind the property Coop had just explored where he found the lumberyard.

He stood at the curve and contemplated the dirt road. It was flanked on both sides by a thick growth of trees. He set out down it and after about two hundred yards on the left, a driveway appeared that led to what looked like an old barn, visible from the road.

It had an uninhabited vibe, with large holes in the roof and sides. He took a photo with his phone and sent it to Detective Mitchell, asking if anyone had checked it out. He eyed the tracks in the dirt driveway. It was hard to tell, but they looked fresh.

He kept walking, and the road narrowed as the trees on each side became denser. Coop saw the top of the lumberyard building to his right and was about to turn around when he spotted what looked like tire tracks that had flattened the tall weeds at the narrowest part of the road.

Careful not to walk on the flattened weeds, he crouched and peered through the trees. Light flashed in his eyes, and he cupped his hand over them. He tilted his head and noticed the glint of sunlight off the windshield of a car parked on the edge of the clearing. He made a pathway through the trees and emerged on the other side of them.

He took in the expanse of the large dirt clearing ringed by trees and focused on the car tucked along the edge. He needed to get a closer look.

4

Coop used his hand to shade his eyes from the sun and took several steps forward to get a better look at the car. It was an old, faded, blue Honda Accord. It looked just like Alyssa's.

He resisted the urge to run toward it with the hope of finding Alyssa. He didn't want to destroy any evidence and opted to call Detective Mitchell.

He answered immediately. "Mitchell."

"Jim, this is Coop. I'm over by the abandoned lumberyard next to the freeway. Behind it actually, on a dirt road. I found a blue Honda Accord in a clearing."

"By that old barn you just sent me?"

"Right. I haven't approached the car. Didn't want to disturb anything."

"Hang tight. I'm on my way."

Coop moved a few feet, hoping to get a better look inside the car, but saw no activity.

The wait was excruciating. As Coop checked his watch again, his phone rang.

"Hey, Jim," he answered.

"We're at the end of the dirt road, walking in. We don't want to disturb any tracks we might be able to get. Be there shortly."

"Got it."

Coop disconnected and only had to wait a few minutes before he heard Detective Mitchell's voice call out from the other side of the trees. Coop dashed back, retracing his steps on the path he'd made and found Detective Mitchell and Deputy Atkins, both toting metal cases and bags.

Coop pointed behind him. "I opted to make my own path and not disturb any evidence."

Detective Mitchell smiled. "Good man. Lead the way. We've got Knox County rolling with their forensic team, but we need to see if Alyssa is in the vehicle."

Coop took them through the branches and overgrowth, and they emerged on the other side of the grove of trees, where Coop pointed across the clearing where the car was positioned along the edge of it, where the trees hid most of it from view.

Detective Mitchell used binoculars and after a quick look, he nodded. "The plates match Alyssa's." They donned gloves, then put Coop to work, carrying two of their cases, and made their way to the car with Detective Mitchell in the lead, looking for tracks and avoiding a direct route. Deputy Askins took photos as they walked, stopping to examine the soil.

When they got close to the vehicle, Coop helped lay out plastic walking blocks so Detective Mitchell could approach the vehicle without leaving his footprints. He looked through the windows and turned with a shake of his head. "No sign of her inside."

He moved to the trunk and used a tool from his bag to pop it open. Another shake of his head. "Nothing here."

Detective Mitchell pointed at Atkins. "Come on and photograph everything, and we'll start processing prints and see what we have. The forensics team should be here soon and will tow the car to the lab for a complete analysis."

"Got it, boss," said Atkins. "I didn't see any good footprints, and it looks like the only tire tracks are from the Honda."

The detective's jaw tightened. "I noticed that, too."

As they set up their gear, Detective Mitchell nodded at Coop. "Excellent find, by the way. We'll look for footage that might show when the car was placed here and hopefully get our guy on camera again."

"That's what I was thinking." Coop pulled up the map on his phone. "I'll take a drive and see if there are any more cameras we might want to check."

To stay out of the crime scene, Coop went back through the trees and walked back to the parking lot and his Jeep. Instead of going back the way he'd come in, he opted to follow the road he walked and take the paved curve that led to the residential area.

From the map, he noticed Highway 70, along the Cinch River provided another access point to the neighborhood. The car had to come from either Interstate 40 or the smaller highway to access the clearing on the dirt road. He traversed the short residential street, not seeing any cameras. As he continued to make the loop that the car may have taken across the Cinch River, he noted a gas station, a church, a bank, and a county park that might have cameras that could pick up a car on the road.

The highway looped back to the street where the park-n-ride was located, and he found a post office and another church that might have cameras. He pulled over and parked and keyed in a message to Detective Mitchell with the possible cameras he could search.

Part of Coop longed to stay and wait for what they found at the scene, but he suspected they might not have any real answers until the lab finished their processing. It was already late in the afternoon, and he opted to take the entrance for Interstate 40 and head back to Nashville.

He spent the two-hour drive thinking of scenarios that would cause Alyssa's car to be left in that clearing. None of them were good.

Gus greeted him at the door and the enticing aroma of roasted meat tickled his nose. He was starving and found Aunt Camille and Charlie in the kitchen, doing dishes.

Charlie looked up from drying a bowl and smiled. "Coop, we've got a plate in the oven with your name on it."

"And I've got a lemon meringue pie for dessert," said Camille.

Coop stood from where he kneeled next to Gus and finished scratching the dog's soft ears. "That sounds fantastic. I'm worn out."

After washing his hands, Coop slid into his chair at the island counter and welcomed the plate of pot roast and veggies. As he ate, he told them about the case and finding the missing woman's car.

"Wow," said Charlie. "That's quite a find. I wonder how long the car has been there? What made you look there?"

Coop shook his head. "I was searching for where the guy may have come from when he appeared on the camera. It just looked like a good hiding spot. I'm not sure how long the car has been there, but it traveled away from where I found it the day Alyssa was abducted. So, between Thursday morning and today."

Charlie frowned. "He must have had a gun or something to make her move and allow him inside."

As Coop scooped up another forkful of potatoes, he nodded. "Yeah, I can't imagine just letting a strange guy in my car."

Camille shivered. "It just makes me sick. I'm worried about that poor young woman."

"Me, too. Now that the car's been found, it's going to make finding her harder. He could have taken her miles away. Hopefully, when they process the vehicle, we can get a better idea from how much gas is left in the tank."

"Her poor mother must be terrified," said Charlie, reaching to pet Gus.

Coop added butter to one of Aunt Camille's biscuits. "Yeah, I can't imagine. I'm hoping the car provides a clue that helps us find her quickly. Every hour that goes by makes the situation more dire."

Monday, Coop and Gus took off early for the office. He only had time for one cup of the rich coffee he brewed before AB arrived. He was emptying the pot into his cup, sneaking a second, when she came through the back door. Not only was she early to dig into the case, but she toted a blue box from an artisan bakery she loved and considered a rare treat.

Gus' nose rose to sniff at the box, and Coop was tempted to do the same.

She smiled at both of them. "I figured this is going to be a tough week, so I stopped by Sunshine Bakery." She set the box on the kitchen table and flipped it open.

Coop plucked one of their sunshine rolls from the box and took it to his office. He bit into the flaky dough smothered in sugar and cinnamon with a hint of orange. AB joined him with a cup of tea and her favorite almond croissant.

He passed the case file from Detective Mitchell to her. "They've got the login information in there so we can sign onto their internal system and get the latest reports and information."

She nodded. "I'll get it set up right away."

He took a few minutes and told her about finding Alyssa's

car late yesterday afternoon. "I'm anxious to get the report back on any evidence in the car but suspect it will take some time to analyze it."

"I'll check out the camera footage and concentrate on those areas you pointed out, especially the bank. They typically have the best cameras."

"I'm going to call Detective Mitchell this morning and see if they have any new updates. We need to coordinate the camera footage review so between us, we can cover more ground and not duplicate efforts."

AB sighed. "We're on a full four days plus since she's been seen. No ransom demands or anything. That scares me."

Coop nodded. "Exactly. Nobody has said it, but I can see it in their eyes. They all fear the worst."

She took the file and headed back to her desk, outfitted with dual screens, which would make viewing the camera footage easier, while Coop plotted a timeline on the whiteboard, then picked up his phone to call Detective Mitchell.

His tired voice answered on the first ring, "Coop."

"Just checking in to see if you have any new updates and wanted to coordinate on reviewing the camera footage."

"Right. They towed the vehicle to the lab in Knoxville. We didn't get any prints but hers from the car. Luckily, the new job took her prints for an extensive background check, so we had them to compare. The guy must have worn gloves."

Coop frowned as he listened. "This is sounding more and more like a meticulously planned abduction. Not a spontaneous crime. I had that feeling when we watched the guy on camera."

"We're thinking the same thing. We did work on that photo of him and figured out he's somewhere between six feet and six-two. I don't think he's from the homeless camp. We talked to all of them and got nothing. Like you said, this was planned."

"Like he's done it before?" Coop asked.

"I'm thinking yes. We're running down any similar cases and checking suspects from those and any prior convicted subjects who are out of prison and in the area."

Coop nodded. "Any clue from the lab on how much gas was left in the tank of her Honda?"

Keys clacking on the keyboard and another phone ringing filled Coop's ear. Moments later, Detective Mitchell said, "Sorry, it's crazy here. Yeah, they determined it had about half a tank left. So, provided he didn't fill up the car again, we're talking about a two-hundred-mile radius, which really means one hundred miles from here, since the car was returned."

Coop added that note to his tablet. "That's helpful. What about the ping on her phone?"

"Nada. The search team came up empty. They're back today but haven't found any sign of her or the phone. The carrier said a ping like that could be an error, but regardless, I'm not holding out much hope on that front. No further activity on the phone, no further pings."

"Could be an error, like they said, or could be designed by the perp to throw us off course. Obviously, he disabled her phone when he took her. Could be he turned it back on long enough to divert attention, keep everyone busy, and send us on a wild goose chase."

"Right. We have to check it out and use resources, but we're pouring most of the effort into the camera footage we can gather. On that front, you'll see a file that we put up to record what specific footage has been reviewed or is being reviewed. That way, you can concentrate on others, just make sure and update the file. We're loading more from those places you suggested yesterday. We were able to obtain the footage from the churches, gas stations, and that other bank. Still working on the post office and the county park."

Coop made a note. "Okay, we'll start on those new ones you just gathered. That way, we won't step on anyone else who's looking at the other footage. We'll concentrate on the Honda and see if we can pinpoint when it was returned to the area."

Another phone ringing and muffled voices in the background came through Coop's phone. "Sounds good, Coop. If we learn anything new, I'll be in touch."

Coop disconnected and added the one-hundred-mile statistic to the whiteboard. He brought up a map and plotted out where the kidnapper could have traveled. It was still overwhelming as it stretched from New Middleton all the way across eastern Tennessee into North Carolina, down into northern Georgia, and up into southern Kentucky.

If, like Coop suspected, this guy had done this before, he'd stick to rural areas and avoid cameras. The Knoxville area had far more highway cameras than Roane County and the rural area surrounding it.

AB came through the door as Coop was pondering. "I've got my computer set up. I'll just get yours done." She took the chair behind his desk, and her fingers flew over the keys.

"Detective Mitchell said they have new camera footage from the route I took yesterday, and we can concentrate on that first. They're working the original footage."

As AB focused on the screen, she nodded. "Almost done here, then I'll dive into it."

Coop turned from the whiteboard and stepped toward his desk. AB pointed at the icon she installed on the desktop that would take him to the electronic case file in Roane County. She clicked it, then brought up the camera footage file.

Coop pointed at it. "I'll start with that new bank I found. You can take the gas station. They're our best options for higher quality cameras."

She vacated his chair, and he slid into it. He glanced at the various files available. "I'm going to start from yesterday afternoon and work backward. You start at Thursday morning and work forward."

"Got it," said AB, as she stepped toward the door and headed back to her desk.

Coop settled in and began the mind-numbing and painstaking task of watching cars go by the bank. The bank was close to the road and had good coverage, with high resolution. Without much traffic in the area, he adjusted the speed, confident he could spot the Honda.

After hours and hours of staring at the screen, with only a short break for lunch, Coop tapped the mouse and slowed down the playback speed. He blinked his eyes a few times and checked the screen. It looked like Alyssa's blue Honda driving by the bank Sunday morning.

Was it wishful thinking, or was it hers?

5

Coop replayed the video footage and while he couldn't make out the driver, he could only see one person in the vehicle. The driver's head was covered with a hoodie, like the man he'd seen approach Alyssa's car at the parking lot.

He hollered for AB, and she came rushing through the door. "I'm going to call Detective Mitchell, but I'm certain this is her car. That splotch on the hood where the paint is gone is distinctive. They can probably enhance it a bit and make out the license plate."

She agreed and hurried back to her desk to check on the footage closer to the area where Coop located the car and the park-n-ride lot.

Coop reached for his phone. As usual, Detective Mitchell answered after the first ring. "Mitchell."

"It's Coop. We've spotted Alyssa's car yesterday morning." He gave him the particulars. "From the direction it's coming, I would guess he took the state highway over the river instead of the interstate. A less direct route, you might say."

"That's great news. We'll get on it and see if we can enhance it and check for more footage."

"My associate is doing that now, too. She's concentrating on the camera coverage near the parking lot, where he would have come from after leaving the car behind it in that clearing. We're curious what he drove after he left her car."

"Exactly," said the detective. "The lab found a few small drops of blood on the passenger seat area. They've matched it to Alyssa, which makes us think she could have been injured. Other than that, we still haven't found anything useful in the vehicle. No other prints. Exterior door handles were wiped clean. The fuel door only has Alyssa's prints and wasn't wiped, so we're confident he didn't fill the car with gas. They're running all the trace evidence, but nothing has popped yet. We'll get everyone working the footage we have around that time and be in touch."

Coop's brow creased. "There's no way this is this guy's first rodeo."

"We agree. It's not looking good."

"We'll call you back if we find anything useful."

"Same here, Coop. Thanks."

AFTER POURING OVER THE FOOTAGE, AB and Coop came up with a list of seven vehicles that came from the road along the side of the supermarket, leading to the clearing where Coop found Alyssa's car. They still needed to check the other cameras that led to the state highway, where he could have bypassed the camera they were studying, but they had to start somewhere and liked the odds of only having to check the seven vehicles they found in that area on a quiet Sunday morning.

Coop sent a message to Detective Mitchell with the timestamps from the camera footage. Next, he and AB went back to the footage from the day of Alyssa's disappearance and looked for any of those seven vehicles that were captured on the same camera prior to Alyssa's arrival at the park-n-ride. They worked backward from the 5:14 mark.

It was slow and tedious work, but at the 4:10 timestamp on Thursday morning, Coop and AB both gasped and pointed at the screen. They watched a truck travel down the side street and disappear where the road curved. It looked like the same truck they found on the footage from Sunday morning after they saw Alyssa's car arrive again.

They went back and forth between the footage of the truck in question on Sunday and compared it to the early Thursday morning footage. With it being so early, it was dark and hard to make out many details, but Coop was confident the truck that arrived in the early morning hours of the day Alyssa disappeared was a Chevy that matched the one that left the same area on Sunday.

The footage wasn't good enough to get a license plate and in the daylight from Sunday, it looked to be a dark blue, black, or gray. Coop pointed at the two screens. "That sure looks like the same truck. At least the same model."

AB nodded. "I agree. I'll flag it, send it to Detective Mitchell, and update the file so they can work on enhancing both of these and comparing them."

Coop nodded. "I'm sure they've got access to better software that might help determine if they're in fact the same vehicle."

"If they could get a license plate, it would be even better."

Coop grimaced. "I wouldn't count on it. That angle doesn't look good, and it's too dark in the Thursday footage. It looks like he turned to go back to the interstate on Sunday though. If he went toward Knoxville, we might find him on a traffic camera."

AB nodded. "If he went west, we're out of luck. Not many

cameras on that stretch of the road until you get closer to Nashville."

Coop sighed and glanced at the clock. It was after five. "Let's call it a day, AB. We'll know more tomorrow after Mitchell and his team work on what we've found. If it turns out those two vehicles aren't a match, we'll keep checking the footage."

She nodded and tapped her pen on the calendar on her desk. "By tomorrow, it will be five days. I can't help thinking about what Alyssa is going through and her poor mother."

The hair rose on Coop's arm as his stomach knotted. "It's not something you need to dwell on, AB." Coop reached down to pet Gus, who was wagging his tail as he stared at the front door.

Moments later, Ben appeared at the door. A thin woman stood next to him and followed him inside the office.

"Hey, Ben. What brings you by?" Gus slipped from Coop and hurried to greet the visitors.

"Hey, Coop. This is Mrs. Morgan from Oklahoma. Alyssa's mom. She wanted to come by and meet you."

The woman, with dark purple circles under her tired eyes, gave them a weak smile as she extended her hand. "Call me Carol, please. Chief Mason tells me you're helping the detectives on Alyssa's case. I just wanted to come by and personally thank you."

Coop shook his head. "No need to thank us or worry about us. We just want to find Alyssa."

Tears flowed from Carol's eyes. "I was going to stay with my cousin here, but I think I'm going to take Erica up on her offer and spend some time at her house. I want to see Alyssa's room and her things."

Ben nodded. "Carol is going to head over there tomorrow to meet with Detective Mitchell."

Coop met Carol's eyes. "He's very determined, working

around the clock to find Alyssa. We just got off the phone with him a few minutes ago."

AB offered Carol a box of tissues. "Thank you. He's been very good about keeping me apprised. He told me you found Alyssa's car. I hope that helps them find my little girl. I can't lose her."

Coop's throat went dry. Carol's agony made his heart hurt. He reached out his hand and took hers. "We're so sorry you're going through this heartache. I know there's nothing we can say that will help but know we're all doing our very best to find your daughter."

Ben put his hand on Carol's shoulder. "I told her you and AB would be focused on this like lasers."

"I just wanted to meet you and thank you and let you know Alyssa has a family who loves her very much, and we need her home. She's a good girl and was so excited about her new job and her new life." Her voice broke as she sobbed. "I remember a quote I read—*her absence is like the sky spread over everything*. I didn't get it until now, but that's exactly what Alyssa's absence feels like."

Coop glanced over at AB and noticed tears on her cheeks. "We won't rest until we find her, Mrs. Morgan. If you find anything that might help, reach out to me." Coop handed her his card.

She took it and leaned closer to Coop, giving him a hug. With tears still streaming from her eyes, she nodded. "Thank you, Mr. Harrington. I truly appreciate your help. I just don't know what to do and feel utterly helpless. Erica suggested we organize some volunteers to search for her. At least that will make me feel like I'm doing something." She reached into her handbag and pulled out a bright yellow flyer. "We're going to pass these out and get them posted."

Ben cleared his throat. "We're going to coordinate that with Detective Mitchell, so we aren't duplicating efforts."

Coop took the flyer and nodded. It had a photo of Alyssa smiling, along with her car, and a photo of the park-n-ride lot with the particulars of where she was last seen. "This looks good, and it might help jog someone's memory or prompt someone to come forward that remembers something."

Carol sniffed. "I sure hope so. That's all I have right now. Hope."

The shattered woman before him, hanging onto a thin thread of hope broke Coop's heart. "If you need some help getting those flyers handed out around Nashville, let us know. We'll call some friends."

With tears in her eyes, Carol smiled at him. "Thanks," she whispered. She followed Ben to the door, and he nodded at Coop and AB before he closed it behind him.

The look shared between the three old friends communicated all they needed to say.

∼

AFTER DINNER and telling Aunt Camille and his dad about Alyssa's case and meeting her mother, Coop and Gus retired to his wing of the house. He couldn't quit thinking about Carol Morgan's haunted eyes and the hunch of her shoulders.

Exhausted and drained, Coop managed to sleep for a few hours but was up in the wee hours and made his way to his desk. He logged into the police file from Roane County and checked the latest activity.

They had enhanced the photo of the truck and confirmed both trucks he and AB found on the footage were the same. They had identified the truck as a 2020-2022 Chevy Silverado High Country. The color was hard to distinguish, but it was either gray or blue. They couldn't get a license plate from the footage. They were going public with pleas for help in identifying the truck and sent it to all the news outlets for publication. Coop checked the time and realized it would have run on the late news channels just a few hours ago.

As Coop read the report, he wondered how many of those trucks were registered in Tennessee. His heart lurched when he saw the number cited in the report. Thousands of trucks matched the criteria, and that was assuming the truck was registered in Tennessee.

Tips that came in from the public would be documented and evaluated, and teams would be dispatched to inspect credible tips. There was a new log where all the tips were recorded and researched. There were already dozens of entries. So far, none of them matched the specific model with the trim level of the truck.

The beauty of appealing for help would be that everyone would be looking, but that was also the huge downside. Many people didn't know the difference between makes of vehicles or models, for that matter. They would be dealing with hundreds, if not thousands of reports that would be total timewasters.

Every minute that ticked by decreased Alyssa's chance of survival. The publicity was good in many respects, but it could also pressure the kidnapper and lead to him taking steps to eliminate Alyssa. Coop suspected Detective Mitchell and those in charge had the same feeling he did.

He wasn't convinced Alyssa was still alive.

6

Coop managed to get a couple more hours of sleep before he rolled out of bed and made his way to the kitchen to pour himself a large cup of coffee.

He retrieved the morning paper and settled in at the island counter. His eyes widened as he unfolded it. Alyssa's story and plea for help had made the top story in *The Tennessean*. They printed the salient points he'd read in Detective Mitchell's report last night.

Mitchell was quoted in the article, thanking the public for their diligence in helping with the search for Alyssa, and he urged them to contact the tip line if they recognized the truck, specifying the make and model. After reminding the public of the timeline of Alyssa's disappearance and last known location, he also thanked the local search and rescue volunteers from neighboring counties who were manning the tip lines and helping police with the investigation.

While Gus ate his breakfast, Coop added a bit more coffee to warm up his cup and perused the paper. His mind focused on Alyssa, he couldn't concentrate on anything and after swallowing the last of his coffee, Coop loaded Gus into the Jeep, and they headed to the office.

As they walked to the back door, AB's VW pulled into the parking lot. Gus wouldn't budge and waited for her at the door.

Coop held it open for her. "You're early today, AB."

"Yeah, I couldn't quit thinking about poor Mrs. Morgan and Alyssa."

"Same here."

While AB worked on getting a pot of decaf brewing, Coop settled in behind his desk and logged onto the case file at Roane County. The tip file had grown by hundreds overnight.

Calls were logged as far away as North Carolina and Georgia, not to mention all across Tennessee. As Coop scrolled through the list, he noticed many of the tips had been closed due to the make and model or color not matching the vehicle in question. The list was organized by county but could be sorted by any field. As he studied the open tips, his cell phone rang.

Detective Mitchell's name appeared on the screen, and Coop tapped the green button. "Morning. I was just checking the tip log."

Detective Mitchell sighed. "Yeah, that's why I'm calling. As expected, it's overwhelming. I was hoping you could help us investigate the possibles in the smaller counties east of Nashville. We've got lots of help in the metro areas of Nashville and Knoxville, running down leads, but the more rural areas could use some assistance."

"Sure thing."

Detective Mitchell outlined their system, which Coop surmised from viewing the log. A team reviewed each tip and checked the vehicles, using computer systems and manpower for visual examinations when necessary.

As he explained more, Detective Mitchell let Coop know they withheld two critical pieces of information about the truck from the public. "We know we're taking a chance of spooking the guy by putting out the public appeal, but we're running out of time and need to find Alyssa. When the tech team analyzed the footage you found, they noticed two unique things about the truck. It had the optional extra-small Chevy bowtie added to the front driver's side of the grill and some kind of additional fog lights in the grill. Those two items make it fairly distinct, which will help us eliminate many of the vehicles with a quick visual inspection."

Coop nodded as he wrote notes on the pad near his computer. "Got it."

Detective Mitchell cleared his throat. "We can't get a clear read on the license plate, not even a partial. The best we can do is confirm it appears to be a Tennessee plate with the standard blue background and the white county sticker across the bottom. We can't make out the county either."

He continued and asked Coop to handle Cumberland, Smith, White, and Dekalb counties. "We're trying to keep the list updated in real time, so just call into our incident command center to report on any tips we can close. If you find something promising, don't approach and call me directly."

"Understood," said Coop as he added the command center phone number to his cell. "I'll head out in just a few minutes."

He asked AB to print out the list by county and dug out some bottles of water and iced tea from the fridge to take in the Jeep. He also couldn't resist the leftover cookies on the counter and added them to his provisions. After Coop made sure he had a pair of binoculars and extra treats for Gus in the bag he kept in the back of the Jeep, he collected the list from AB and promised to stay in touch with her throughout the day.

Gus hopped into the passenger seat, and the two of them set out for the counties to the east of Nashville. After a quick stop to add fuel to the Jeep and a breakfast sandwich for the road, they made their way to Gordonsville in Smith County.

As they sped along I-40, Gus looked out the window. The

dog loved nothing more than a road trip. Within an hour, they arrived, and Coop set out to explore the addresses on the list. After checking the vehicles he could find in Gordonsville and calling in to report they didn't match the suspect, he headed up to Carthage.

Striking out in Carthage and the surrounding area, Coop and Gus got back on the interstate and took the exit for Smithville. It took him past noon to check the vehicles on the list for Dekalb County.

Back on the road, Coop set out to find a bite for lunch near Cookeville, before he would begin the search in White County. After a burger at a place with a dog friendly patio, plus a plain patty for Gus, they continued their quest.

Coop got excited when he spotted a blue truck in a driveway on his list. It looked to be a match until he made a U-turn and parked to get a better look at the front of it. No extra emblem and no extra fog lights.

He kept at it for the next couple of hours and pulled over at a park to call the command center and remove some more vehicles from the list. He took Gus for a walk, gave him a big drink of water, and sat on a bench to call AB and report their progress, or lack thereof. She let him know the list was continuing to grow.

"This is a bit like whack-a-mole," said Coop. "I've probably eliminated close to fifty vehicles today, but I have a feeling by the time I get back, I'll have at least that many more."

"Be glad they didn't send you to Knox County." She chuckled and added, "Aunt Camille stopped by with a fresh batch of cookies for us. I told her you and Gus were on a road trip."

"I've got one more section, but Cumberland is the most populated county on my list. I don't think I'll be back in time for dinner."

With a sense of despair, he turned back to the interstate and set out for Crossville and the largest number of vehicles on his list. As he and Gus drove through the neighborhoods close to town, he checked off several trucks that were close but didn't match the unique aspects Detective Miller held back from the press.

He called AB to report so she could update the log in real time before she left for the day.

As five o'clock approached, the traffic increased, and Coop opted to head out of town, into the more rural areas of the county and tackle the tips on his list. The rural areas took longer, with less visible driveways, and required Coop to pull over several times and use binoculars to get a good look at the vehicles in question.

They drove by Cumberland Mountain State Park, which looked to be a place Gus would enjoy exploring, and turned onto a road with a tip to check. He glanced over at his partner in the passenger seat, who was focused on the view out the window. "I promise we'll come back and find a park for you." Coop kept his eye on the mailboxes as he inched along the country road.

He spotted the number he was looking for and pulled to the side of the road. The house in question sat back on a large lot that looked to be close to an acre. He noticed a white sedan parked in front of the garage door at the end of the house. There was also a white truck with a company logo on the door parked near the house. The plain tan house had a detached building next to it that Coop suspected was a workshop or garage.

He edged the Jeep forward and spotted the Chevy truck parked next to it. To get a view of the front of the truck, he had to drive further down the road. He pulled over under the branches of a large tree and picked up the binoculars to get a better look.

The truck matched the pewter color the techs suspected

and as he focused on the grill, he spotted the small gold bowtie Detective Mitchell mentioned. As he moved the binoculars further down, he saw the additional fog lights in the grill.

His pulse quickened, and he hurried to bring the license plate into view. He scribbled it on the notepad he kept on the dash. While he was at it, he also wrote down the license plate of the white sedan. Not wanting to spook the owner, he started the Jeep and drove further down the road before making a U-turn and heading back toward the state park.

He pulled into the lot of a self-storage place and tapped the button on his phone.

"Miller," answered the detective.

"It's Coop. I have something outside of Crossville in Cumberland County. Truck matches, including the fog lights and the small decorative bowtie." Coop read off the license plate and gave him the reference number from the tip sheet and the street address." He also gave him the license plate from the sedan.

"Excellent," said Detective Miller, with a hint of excitement in his voice. "I'll contact Cumberland County, and we'll get to work on this. We've got another vehicle that also matches that we're checking on in Knox County right now."

"Hopefully, one of them is our guy."

"I'll call you later and let you know where we are."

"I've still got a few vehicles left on this list for Cumberland County. I'll keep searching, then head home in an hour or so."

"Sounds good. Thanks again, Coop. I'll be in touch."

Coop disconnected and set out for the next address on the tip log. Within forty-five minutes, he and Gus eliminated the others on the list and made their way back toward Crossville and the interstate that would take them home. He contacted the command center and updated them on his progress before he got on the highway.

As he left Crossville, he called Aunt Camille from the road

to let her know he was less than two hours from home. She promised to have dinner waiting for him and Gus and asked him to call when he was close.

As he drove, Coop kept his eyes peeled for any trucks that matched the description of the suspect, but at highway speed, it was hard to spot the small nuances he was searching for on the front of each truck and equally hard to tell the exact trim package of the Chevys he saw.

It was a futile activity but kept his mind off his growling stomach. His loyal friend in the passenger seat kept his eyes focused on the road and never complained about the lateness of his dinner. When Gus was on the job, nothing disturbed him.

Close to eight o'clock, Coop pulled into the driveway and tucked the Jeep in the garage. He and Gus found Aunt Camille and Charlie at the dining room table. She had fried chicken with all the fixings on the table.

"Wow, this looks great, and I'm starving. Thanks for waiting for us."

Charlie grinned. "We had some cheese and crackers to tide us over."

Gus stopped for a quick pet but made a beeline for his dinner bowl waiting in the kitchen. By the time Coop washed his hands, Gus had gulped down his food and followed him to the dining room, where he plopped onto the floor next to Charlie.

As Coop loaded his plate with mashed potatoes and gravy, his dad asked if he'd had any luck. Coop nodded. "I found a truck that matched everything. I haven't heard back yet and know they were also checking another match in Knox County."

Aunt Camille shuddered. "I hope to heaven they find that poor girl."

Coop didn't divulge his feeling of dread when it came to finding Alyssa alive. Too much time had passed to give him much hope. He didn't need to burden his sweet aunt with more worry. Instead, he reached for another of Aunt Camille's rolls and kept chewing.

Coop carried the last of the dishes into the kitchen, where his dad was at the sink, rinsing and loading the dishwasher, when Coop's cell phone rang.

He glanced between it and the apple pie Aunt Camille was slicing and held up a finger when he saw Detective Mitchell's name. "I have to take this."

7

Coop tapped the button as he wandered to his wing of the house. "Detective, I hope you have some good news."

"The truck in Knox County turned out to belong to a woman. She had possession of the truck during the time in question. We're still checking, but she doesn't have a husband or boyfriend who drives the truck. We're digging into her relatives and contacts. We'll continue to keep an eye on her movements and investigate."

"What about the one in Cumberland County?"

"Much more promising. It's registered to a guy named Royce Stanton, forty-five years old. He goes by Roy. Lives there outside of Crossville where you found the truck. The house is a rental he shares with his girlfriend. A Christine Hayes. I've added what we know to the file, so feel free to dig around and see what you can find on him. He works for a large construction company with their main office in Knoxville. He's a foreman."

Background noise came through the speaker, then was

muffled. Detective Miller continued, "We're in the process of getting a warrant for his phone. Planning to watch him and look into his movements prior to Thursday and since."

"Sounds good. We'll start an in-depth look at the suspect and get back to you soon."

"We're considering an in-person briefing tomorrow with everyone on the case. I'll keep you posted on timing."

Coop disconnected and made his way back toward the dining room. The exhaustion he'd felt after his long day was replaced with a surge of adrenaline and the thought of an actual suspect in the case. One with a name.

He explained the new development to Aunt Camille and his dad and after wolfing down his pie, he excused himself and hurried back to his home office and his computer.

He checked out the police log on the case and jotted down the particulars related to Royce Stanton. The forty-five-year-old worked as a foreman for Arian Group, part of a larger global company involved in all aspects of construction.

Coop stared at Royce's driver's license photo. He had very short, gray hair, with a high forehead. Despite very little hair on his head, he sported a full goatee with the hair on his chin long and dark but streaked with gray. His height and build matched that of the man on foot approaching Alyssa's car on Thursday morning.

As Coop worked, he noticed Gus nose his way through the door he left cracked for him. Soon, he was snuggled into the oversized chair near to Coop's desk and moments later, Aunt Camille delivered a tray with a pot of decaf and a plate of cookies. She left Coop with a smile and made him promise to get some sleep before morning.

Coop logged onto the service he and AB used at the office to conduct their background investigations. In no time, he compiled a history of Royce related to his employment, finances, past residences, and most importantly, his criminal activity.

As Coop perused the report, his eyes widened. Royce's first brush with the law was when he was only twelve in his home state of Georgia. He was sentenced to community service for shoplifting and for hunting out of season. As he got older, he was sentenced to a youth correctional center when he was only fifteen for brandishing a weapon and threatening another teen with it.

With a low whistle, Coop glanced over at Gus. "This guy is a total loser. I think he's our man." Gus' ears perked at the lilt in Coop's voice, but he went back to sleep.

Coop poured another cup of decaf and kept reading. At eighteen, things escalated. Royce was sentenced to fifteen years in prison for the part he played in the murder of a nineteen-year-old man, who was lured to Royce's family property, where the victim's girlfriend shot and killed him. Royce then disposed of the body by dumping it in a remote area off a rural highway, where he buried it. Along with the charges related to that, he was also charged with committing several armed robberies just days before the murder.

Since being released from prison, Royce worked a variety of construction and mining jobs and moved around often, having lived in Georgia, North Dakota, Nevada, Idaho, and now Tennessee.

He'd been living in Tennessee for the past three years, having worked for a mining company that operated several zinc mines in Tennessee. They closed the mines last year, and he got the job with Arian Group. Despite his early criminal history, his record since his release from prison twelve years ago was clean. He'd held a supervisor position with the zinc mining company and was hired as a foreman for Arian Group.

Coop frowned as he looked through the report. He emailed

a copy of it to AB, so she'd have it in the morning. If Detective Mitchell called a briefing tomorrow, Coop was determined to be there, no matter what time it was.

In his gut, he knew this was the guy who took Alyssa.

Men like Royce, with an early record of criminal activity, including weapons and involvement in murder, didn't usually return from prison and lead a reformed life. From Coop's experience, many young felons learned how to be better criminals while in prison and emerged even more hardened. With Royce spending his youth inside with criminals far more experienced than he, it wasn't a stretch to think he'd learned a few tricks while in prison.

Thinking about him and what he might have done to Alyssa made Coop shudder. The more he read about Royce's history, what little hope he had left for Alyssa faded. Royce was violent at a very young age and for an eighteen-year-old to participate in a murder and orchestrate dumping a body was a bad sign.

A terrifying sign.

As Coop made a list of the places Royce had lived over the past twelve years, he searched online for any unsolved cases that involved a kidnapping or murder. The methodology the kidnapper used in Alyssa's case wasn't that of someone committing such a crime for the first time. This guy was organized and experienced. Coop was convinced he'd done this before.

Coop also ran a report on the girlfriend. Christine had two teenage daughters who lived with her and one older son who did not. She worked as a housekeeper with her own business and from what he saw online, she had good reviews and ratings.

The white sedan he saw at the house was hers.

It was after midnight when Coop looked up from his research. He finished off the cookies and sipped from his lukewarm cup of decaf. With his mind racing, he wasn't ready to sleep yet.

Two hours later, his eyes were blurry from too much screen-time. He'd been searching for articles about kidnappings and murders near where Royce worked across the country. He found several possibilities, but not enough details to determine anything significant. He added what he'd discovered to the police file with a note to Detective Mitchell, asking him to get in touch with the jurisdictions in those states and pave the way so Coop could contact them and get specific information related to their open cold cases.

Royce had stayed in Georgia after his release, and there were several women missing from the area. Some had been found dead, and others were still missing. Coop wondered if Royce had been on law enforcement's radar for any of them.

Sadly, there were missing women and murdered women littered across all the states Royce had lived in, but that meant nothing unless there was something to tie Royce to any of the crimes. All Coop had at the moment was a gut feeling and coincidences.

Alyssa was the priority.

If Royce took her, they needed him to locate her. Detective Mitchell and everyone working on the case were focused on finding Alyssa, and Coop understood the desire to observe Royce with the hope he would lead them to her.

Coop wasn't sure he would.

This guy was too careful and organized. He'd wiped the car, hid it in a spot that was difficult to find and not visible from the road, and left no trace of himself, except for the video images they'd been able to piece together.

Time wasn't on their side.

∼

AFTER A FEW HOURS OF SLEEP, Coop woke and hurried to the office. He set the coffee to brew and checked for overnight developments on the case. As he filtered through the reports, which summarized the covert surveillance on Royce Stanton, the aroma of fully caffeinated coffee tickled his nose.

He hurried to the kitchen and filled his oversized cup. The first sip made him close his eyes. It was heavenly.

After a few more swallows and a quick refill, he carried it to his desk and got back to the file.

Last night, the surveillance team observed Royce remove his company truck from the detached garage at the rental house and put his Chevy inside. He and his girlfriend made a trip to town and picked up food. Other than that, neither had left the residence.

As he read the file, a new entry appeared with a report that Royce was on the move in his personal truck with the girlfriend, and the surveillance team followed them to a local tire shop in Crossville.

By the time AB arrived, the log was updated again and showed one team following Royce, who was back on I-40, headed in the direction of Knoxville. Moments later, another entry appeared from a different team who had interviewed the staff at the tire shop. They discovered Royce was looking for tires for his Chevy and needed them today.

The store in Crossville didn't have them in stock, but one of the stores in Knoxville did, and Royce was determined to get them and asked that they hold them for him.

"Interesting," muttered Coop.

While Coop read, his computer chimed with an email notification. Coop clicked over to check and saw a message from Deputy Bennett. He let Coop know he was assigned to coordinate checking on other cases in the areas where Royce Stanton lived prior to moving to Tennessee. He suggested they split the load and provided the contact information for detectives in

Idaho and Nevada and let Coop know he'd already reached out to share Coop's involvement so he would be free to inquire. He also let Coop know Detective Mitchell called a two o'clock briefing.

Coop replied and confirmed that he and AB would dig into researching the Idaho and Nevada jurisdictions and promised to see him at the briefing.

AB came through the door with a steaming cup of decaf for him and a mug of hot tea for herself. "I saw the latest developments from the case file and the background report. From reading that, I'd say this guy looks like a strong suspect."

Coop nodded and pointed at the screen. "We have the contact information for Nevada and Idaho now. I'll get started on that, then have you continue. I want to be there for the briefing this afternoon."

"Sure thing," said AB. "I've got a few quick things to handle for a couple of our corporate clients this morning, then I'll dedicate the rest of my day to the cold case research."

Coop started with Nevada, since he'd grown up there and knew the area. He checked the clock. With Nevada being two hours behind Nashville, it was a little early, but Coop tapped in the number for a Detective Sanford in Elko, Nevada.

He expected to have to leave a message, so he was surprised when a deep voice answered. "Sanford," was the only greeting.

"Detective Sanford, I'm Cooper Harrington calling from Nashville at the request of Deputy Bennett and Detective Mitchell who are working on a missing person case."

"Right, I got a call and an email from them late yesterday. What can I do for you?"

"We're looking into jurisdictions where Royce Stanton lived. He's a suspect in the current case, and we have a feeling he's been involved in similar crimes before. I'm hoping you might be able to look at your cold cases and see if he was ever a suspect. He lived in your area from 2019 to 2021 and worked at a local mine."

Coop gave the detective the particulars on Royce and listened as keyboard keys clicked in the background.

After a few minutes, Sanford said, "Hmm. We've got two missing women that were reported in 2020 and 2021. One was in her twenties, who called her parents and said she was hitchhiking in the area and headed home. She stated she was in Elko at that time but was never heard from or seen again. She's never been found. We have next to nothing in the case file. Nobody knew her. She stayed at a cheap motel the night before. Nobody remembers seeing her with anyone. We suspect she was taken on the road."

More clicking, then Sanford spoke again, "The other one was a young woman who went for a hike, and her car was found abandoned on the forest road near the trailhead. Sarah Johnson was her name, and she'd only been in the area for a year or so. Worked at a convenience store and did quite a bit of hiking. Nothing found in her car, and nobody saw her or anything suspicious."

After a short pause, he continued, "Stanton's name is listed as someone who frequented the convenience store and gas station where Sarah worked, but so did dozens of other people. He was interviewed, but nothing came of it."

Coop scribbled on his notepad. "Can you send me that interview and what you have on him from that period. Wife or girlfriend? Coworkers?"

"I'll send you that and the entire case file we have on Sarah." Sanford sighed. "This is a case that has haunted the department for years."

"It's a longshot, but it might help us. You can send it to Deputy Bennett, and I'll get it from him. We're using their secure system for sharing files."

"I'll get it done right away. If you connect any dots, please let me know."

Coop thanked him and disconnected. As he glanced at his notes, a chill went through him.

Missing young women.

Cases from a decade ago and no bodies ever recovered.

He closed his eyes and hoped Alyssa wouldn't be another one of the unsolved cold cases.

8

Coop spoke with Detective Josephs in Coeur d'Alene, Idaho. Like the detective in Nevada, he ran a search on their system and unearthed two cases from the time Stanton lived in the area, between 2016 and 2019.

Both were young women, one twenty-five and one twenty-nine. The eldest of the two went missing from a jogging trail. Her car was found with all her belongings, and she was never seen again.

The younger victim went missing, and her vehicle was found abandoned three days later. All of her things were locked inside of it, but there was no sign of her. She had never been found.

The eerie similarity between these cases and Alyssa's piqued Coop's interest. By the time he got off the call with Detective Josephs, who promised to send the case files and anything they had on Stanton, the files from Nevada were in the system.

He was immersed in reading the cases when AB came through the door, carrying a takeout bag from the deli. She raised her brows at him. "Thought you better eat early and hit the road to get to the briefing."

Coop checked his watch. "Thanks, AB. I lost track of time."

They opted to eat in the kitchen and while Coop ate the pulled pork sandwich, he told AB more about similar cases and Stanton's time in Nevada. "He worked for a mining company in the Elko area. Same kind of work in Coeur d'Alene. Could you contact his past supervisors in both places and see what you can learn about him during his tenure?"

AB nodded. "I'll get right on it."

"Same with any ex-girlfriends. It doesn't look like he was ever married. No kids."

She nodded as she wiped her fingers on a napkin. "I'll dedicate the rest of the day to it."

Coop didn't bother changing his shirt. The detectives in Roane County had already seen him in his usual attire and knew what they were getting when they hired him. He did brush a few crumbs from the blue t-shirt emblazoned with YOU COULDN'T HANDLE ME EVEN IF I CAME WITH INSTRUCTIONS on his way out the door while he petted Gus and assured him AB would keep him company.

He stopped by the house to let his dad and aunt know he'd be later than usual. Aunt Camille assured him dinner would be waiting and handed him a tin of her freshly baked chocolate chunk pecan cookies for his road trip. After a quick stop for gas and a large coffee, he hit the interstate.

The drive was long but uneventful. The old cases from Nevada and Idaho occupied his mind as he made his way to Roane County. For those women to disappear and never be found, and for the police to have little in the way of evidence, the perpetrator was a planner. Stanton's crime that landed him in prison at eighteen involved disposing of a body.

Burying a body.

As Coop climbed from the Jeep, he flicked the cookie

crumbs from his shirt, grabbed his notebook, and collected his empty cup to toss in the garbage can near the door of the sheriff's office.

The receptionist smiled at him, and he introduced himself and let her know he was expected by Detective Mitchell.

She nodded and reached for a lanyard with a badge attached to it. "This is for you, Mr. Harrington." She buzzed him through the door and pointed to the hallway. They're all in the squad room."

Coop hung the lanyard around his neck. "Great, thanks. I remember where that is."

He stepped through the door of the large room and found several deputies gathered around the large table, open boxes of donuts in the middle of it, and the aroma of freshly brewed coffee coming from the large urn situated on the counter.

He helped himself to a cup and settled into a chair next to Deputy Bennett. The man turned and greeted Coop with a firm handshake and his telltale smile. "Hey, Mr. Harrington. Great to see you again. Glad you could make the trip."

"Call me Coop, please. When the briefing is done, could we compare notes on the cold cases? I spoke with Nevada and Idaho this morning."

He nodded. "Sounds great. I've got some preliminary information from North Dakota and Georgia."

While they chatted, the room filled with other men and women, all in quiet discussions. The low hum of conversation ceased the moment Detective Mitchell came through the door with the man Coop recognized from the news as Sheriff Lawson.

The two of them stood at the front of the room near the large screen mounted on the wall. Sheriff Lawson thanked everyone for coming and acknowledged the hard work and dedication of all the departments involved. After his short introduction, he turned the meeting over to Detective Mitchell.

Jim nodded at a technician in the back of the room who was in front of a laptop. The screen came to life, and Mitchell walked through the current status of the case. "The most noteworthy new development was found early this morning. This is footage from the bank camera near where Alyssa was abducted."

The screen filled with a clear image of Royce Stanton, dressed in jeans and a hoodie, but the hood was off his head, and his entire face was visible. He was walking toward the parking lot where Alyssa had parked the morning she disappeared.

Detective Mitchell pointed at the screen. "This was taken the afternoon before Alyssa was abducted. Our theory is Stanton was exploring the area, planning the kidnapping."

Coop's coffee soured in his throat.

"We've had Stanton under surveillance since our colleague, Cooper Harrington, found him during his tedious search of the tips that were called into the office. We followed him to the tire shop in Knoxville where he had his truck tires replaced, and we collected the old tires and have them at the crime lab now, but they match the castings we took from that driveway leading to the old barn next to where Alyssa's car was found."

Coop listened as Detective Mitchell explained that Stanton and his girlfriend, who had accompanied him to the tire shop, drove back to the house in Cumberland County, where he parked his truck with the new tires in the detached shop, then drove his white work truck to a job site.

Detective Mitchell pointed at a woman with short, dark hair, sitting along the side of the room. "Detective Anne Rocklin, who is on loan to us from Knox County, has been doing a deep dive into Stanton and his movements in the week leading up to the abduction until he came under our round-the-clock surveillance."

She stood and gave a concise summary as she explained the

steps she took to track Stanton's physical and digital footprints. Coop homed in on the fact that Stanton's personal cell phone never left his home from Thursday to Sunday afternoon. He had a work cell phone, and that phone was off during that time.

Detective Rocklin continued and reported that she confirmed Stanton was on leave Thursday and Friday, off on the weekend, and had called in to say he would be late on Monday due to a tire problem.

Detective Mitchell interrupted to state that the tires Stanton replaced had no irregularities and weren't worn to the point of needing to be replaced.

Detective Rocklin continued and highlighted a few visits Stanton made to the lot where Alyssa was taken from and to nearby park-n-ride lots in the weeks prior to the abduction. "Our working theory is that he was stalking these areas for victims but chose this location and Alyssa. At this point, we haven't found any connection between Alyssa and Stanton. There's no overlap in their phone histories, workplaces, or social circles."

A collective sigh and a few choice words came from those around the table.

Coop's thoughts drifted to Alyssa and how she was in the clutches of someone who had meticulously planned her kidnapping. He could only imagine her fear. The more he thought, the more the sliver of hope he'd held onto over the last day waned.

Detective Mitchell thanked Anne for her work. He studied the faces in the room and cleared his throat. "We've been talking with the district attorney and will be arresting Royce Stanton this afternoon at his office in Knoxville. He's in a mandatory meeting there now, and we've got a team in place to apprehend him there. I'll be taking off in a few minutes to meet them and watch for myself how he reacts. We'll also be impounding his personal truck and his company truck. As soon as he's in custody, we'll be working with Cumberland County to interview the girlfriend."

He took a sip from his bottle of water. "Things are going to move quickly, and my main objective is to find Alyssa. We're hoping Stanton will be forthcoming with that information. Regardless, we'll continue our search."

He checked his watch. "If you have further questions, Deputy Bennett and Detective Rocklin will remain here and can field those for you. There'll be a press release and briefing later tonight for the evening news."

He thanked everyone again and urged them to continue their work to find Alyssa.

Several of the people in the room cleared out, with a few following Detective Mitchell and others returning to their offices or workplaces.

Detective Rocklin took the chair on the other side of Deputy Bennett and while he was talking with another officer, she retrieved a cup of coffee, then introduced herself.

Coop shook her hand. "I'm Cooper Harrington, a private detective contracted to help with the case. Everybody calls me Coop."

"Nice to meet you; please call me Anne. I've heard your name spoken with admiration around here. Great job on finding Alyssa's car and our suspect."

"Just doing my job. Plus, I really want to find Alyssa. My heart aches for her family."

Anne's lips thinned as she looked down at her cup. "This guy is organized. I'm not sure this will end well." Her eyes swelled with tears. "I've got a daughter, and this really hits home for me."

Coop waited for her to take a swallow from her cup. "I've been working with Deputy Bennett, and we're checking into similar cases in the states where Stanton lived before coming here. He always worked for construction and mining companies. In Nevada, that means lots of remote areas. Off the beaten path, so to say."

She nodded and took another sip of coffee.

Coop continued, "I've got my associate digging into Stanton's past, talking to his prior supervisors, girlfriends, whatever she can find, but when you mentioned his digital footprints, it got me thinking. Like his past work, I would think Stanton's current job takes him to isolated areas. If he's the meticulous planner he seems to be, I wonder if he visited the place he took Alyssa in the days or weeks leading up to the abduction. He left his phone at home over those crucial days, but could his history lead us to where he prepped and ultimately took her?"

Anne opened her laptop and smiled at Coop. "I was thinking the same thing. I'm expecting a list of the jobsites where he worked over the last thirty days. Let me see if it's here. We're building a history using his phone too, but it takes a little time, so we'll have that as soon as we can. I'm also hoping we can check the GPS in his truck once we impound it."

She scanned the screen and nodded. "Yes, I have the list. I'll upload it to the system but can print a copy right now." Her hands flew over the keyboard and moments later, a printer on the counter whirred to life.

Coop retrieved the pages and brought them back to the table. He scanned the list, which contained a large number of locations that stretched across the state from east of Knoxville to Nashville.

Anne looked at the list and frowned. "It's a starting point. We can cross-reference these dates and locations with his cell phone history and build a pattern of life. We'll also look for any extra trips to these locations that don't match the company records."

Deputy Bennett finished his discussion with the other officers and turned his attention to Anne and Coop. As he read over the list, his cell phone buzzed. After a brief conversation, he slipped his phone back in his pocket.

He raised his brows and nodded. "They've got our suspect in custody. Mitchell said despite being taken down in the parking lot, Stanton was calm and didn't even ask why they were arresting him. They're enroute now and will book him, then we'll start the interrogation. We've got a small team already in Cumberland County who are handling the warrant at the house and impounding the vehicle. They'll be interviewing the girlfriend."

Coop glanced at his watch.

Bennett drummed his fingers on the table and met Coop's eyes. "We'll upload the interviews, so you won't miss anything."

Coop nodded. "Yeah, I need to get back. We're still working on the Idaho and Nevada cases. There are two in each state during the time Stanton lived there that look like possible matches. Neither of the women have been recovered."

Bennett patted a thick file folder next to him. "I'd say the same about North Dakota and Georgia. I've got four possibles in Georgia and one in North Dakota. Similar circumstances with young women disappearing from public places, no ransom demands, no bodies ever recovered. We're going through the more recent cases in Tennessee. Sadly, there are dozens of missing women in the past three years, so it's slow going."

Bennett slid the folder closer and sighed. "The problem with all of these old cases so far is no evidence. No prints, nothing to tie to a suspect. Our priority now is Alyssa and getting information from Stanton."

Coop nodded. "Yes, we need to find her. With him getting new tires, it leads me to believe he didn't plan to return to the place where he has Alyssa. That only increases my fear she's been killed."

The two detectives' somber looks confirmed their agreement with Coop.

He slipped the copy of Stanton's job history into his notebook and stood. "I'm going to head back. I'll be in touch if we find anything in his past that might help."

Bennett shook Coop's hand and thanked him for coming, and he and Detective Rocklin promised to keep in touch with any updates from the interviews.

As Bennett walked him to the front door, he darted into the breakroom and grabbed two bottles of iced tea from a large cooler. "Take these for the road. It's a long drive."

Coop smiled and thanked him. His slid behind the wheel of the Jeep, his heart heavy but anxious to see what Stanton might reveal when they finally got him in an interview room.

9

As he neared home, Coop put in a call to AB, who was still at the office working late. "Hey, AB, I'm about thirty minutes out, just checking in."

"I've made a little progress, but nowhere near what I'd hoped. Aunt Camille just called to see if I'd heard from you. She asked me to come for dinner. Gus and I are about to leave."

"Turn on the news and watch it. They arrested Royce Stanton this afternoon in Knoxville. It will be all over the local networks, I'm sure. They were transporting him back to Roane County for processing when I left. I expect the detectives will have the interviews with him and his girlfriend available in the system tonight. I'm hoping they learn something from him that leads us to Alyssa."

"Me, too. So far, the picture I'm getting paints Stanton as a quiet guy at work. He wasn't one to socialize and handled his responsibilities at work well. When I asked what he did on his time off, everyone said he liked the outdoors. Camping, hunting, fishing. His supervisors did say he was organized and detailed, which fits what we're thinking. I get the impression he was a loner. They mentioned girlfriends, but nobody remembered their names or anything about them."

"Hunting, fishing, camping, huh? Those skills would serve him well if he were into abducting young women. I would think he would take them to a place he wouldn't frequent again. Not like his favorite camping spot."

"Makes sense. I'll bring my file and see you at the house. I'll have Camille record the news so you can rewatch it."

"See you in a few." Coop disconnected, eager to get home and see what the detectives had learned.

Coop drove down his aunt's driveway and parked. When he opened the door, he smiled at Gus' friendly face and wagging tail waiting for him. He bent and petted his furry companion, stopped by the bathroom to wash his hands, and followed the scent of dinner to the kitchen.

His dad, Aunt Camille, and AB were all busy with serving dishes. The comforting aroma of pulled pork made Coop's stomach growl. He plucked a warm roll from the platter and tore off half of it.

Aunt Camille looked up from a heaping dish of macaroni and cheese and smiled. "Ah, Coop, we just watched the news and are almost ready."

"It looks delicious. I'm starving!" He carried the platter of pulled pork and poured them all iced teas before taking his seat.

As Coop scooped macaroni and cheese onto his plate, he glanced over at AB and raised his brows. "So, what did you learn from the news?"

AB shook her head. "Not much. They just said they arrested Stanton, a resident of Crossville, for kidnapping Alyssa. They didn't take any of the questions the reporters were barking at them."

With a shake of her head, Aunt Camille met Coop's eyes. "They said they're still searching for Alyssa and urged people to continue to report, showing a photo of his truck. They asked anyone who had seen him or the truck to contact them."

As they ate, Coop filled AB in on what he learned from the briefing. He highlighted the similar cases Bennett had discovered in Georgia and North Dakota.

After they stuffed themselves, Charlie and Aunt Camille volunteered to clean up so AB and Coop could work on the case in his home office. Gus opted to stick around the kitchen. He never missed an opportunity to grab a nibble or two and considered it his job to prewash the dishes after Charlie stacked them in the dishwasher.

Coop gave AB his office chair and moved one of the leather chairs around so he could view the computer screen with her. By the time he was situated, AB had the secure system up and the interview files ready.

He pointed at Stanton's file, and AB tapped the mouse button. A typical interview room filled the screen and within minutes, the man Coop recognized as Stanton, but with a now-trimmed goatee and much less facial hair, was ushered to the table, handcuffed.

Detective Mitchell and another detective Coop didn't know sat across the table and began their questioning. They read Stanton his rights again, and he declined a lawyer. Over the course of the next hour, they asked him about his movements on Thursday, and he said he was camping. Stanton said he took a tent and stayed near Jackson Island.

That area was only about thirty miles from his home. He had no receipts for gas or food and said he didn't stop anywhere, just enjoyed the peaceful seclusion on his own.

Stanton denied knowing Alyssa or kidnapping her. He refused to answer most of their questions and insisted they made a mistake; he had nothing to do with Alyssa's disappearance. He remained calm and said very little unless asked a specific question.

There was a note in the file that technicians were looking for any camera footage along the route to Jackson Island but weren't hopeful, as it was a rural area.

They had a warrant for DNA and collected a cheek swab from Stanton.

Coop pointed at the screen. "He's a cool customer. Lying through his teeth but doesn't show any of the usual physical indications that are hallmarks. He thinks he's smarter than us."

AB clicked the file for the girlfriend's interview. The screen filled with a different interview room. After a few moments, a detective ushered in a woman with long, dark hair, dressed in shorts and a t-shirt.

The two detectives from Cumberland County, a man and a woman, were very gentle with Christine, who was visibly shaken. They asked about her history with Royce.

With a shaky voice, she explained she met Royce a year ago online via a dating app. She admitted she was aware he had been in prison but brushed it off as something he was punished for that he didn't do. His version of the story was he was in the wrong place at the wrong time and took the brunt of the blame. She seemed to believe him.

They probed more about Royce's whereabouts from Thursday through Sunday. Christine divulged that she and her two daughters were out of town. They'd taken a family trip that was planned several weeks ago to visit her son in Huntsville. It was his birthday, and they drove home on Sunday.

She thought Roy, as she called him, was going with them, but he let her know Wednesday night that he wasn't and was going camping.

The female detective asked, "Is that unusual? Does Roy go camping by himself often?"

Christine shrugged. "Sometimes." Her forehead creased, and she shook her head. "This trip was a real surprise to me though. We had this planned for quite some time, and I was disappointed that he wouldn't go. He offered to let us go camping with him, but we had this trip for my son's birthday planned." She frowned. "It didn't make sense that he would decide to go camping. We had an argument about it."

She went on to explain that she and the daughters left the house Thursday morning after Roy, who took off early for his camping trip. When asked, she provided her son's name, address, and phone number and assured them he could verify her visit.

They continued to push for more information, and she remembered getting gas on Sunday before they drove home and said she had a receipt for that. She also gave permission for them to interview her daughters.

Tears streamed down her face when they showed her Alyssa's photo and one of her vehicle. "This has to be a mistake." She confirmed she didn't know Alyssa and had never seen her or the vehicle.

She reached for a tissue from the box on the table next to her. "When I saw that photo of the truck on the news, I even told Roy that it looked like his truck. Sort of joking about it."

The male detective stopped writing notes. "How did he react to that?"

Christine wiped her nose. "He was a little cranky about it. Told me it wasn't his truck, and it looked blue to him."

The detective continued, "Do you know if he came home at any time during the time you were away at your son's? He was only a couple of hours from home."

She shook her head. "I don't know."

"Did he act differently on Sunday? Did you notice anything odd about him?"

She shrugged. "Not really." Her eyes widened, and she added, "He did cut his beard. It was longer, and I noticed when we got home that it was trimmed and didn't hang past his chin anymore."

The female detective made a note and asked, "Did you ask him about it?"

Christine nodded. "He just said it was time with the weather warming up."

The detective continued, "You accompanied him to the tire store. Was that a planned purchase for the truck?"

She shook her head. "No, he just said he needed to replace them because they were worn and riding funny. He's a perfectionist."

He made a note on his pad. "He was scheduled to be back at work but called in to say he'd be late because of the tires. Did he indicate why he was in such a hurry for the tires?"

Christine tilted her head and frowned. "No. I even asked him when we were at the first shop why he couldn't just let them order them in, and I could bring the truck in the next day or two when they arrived."

"What did he say to that idea?"

She arched her brows. "He snapped at me and told me not to worry about it. He wanted to handle it himself."

The female detective took over. "Going back to when you first met Roy, did you go camping together or did he take you to any special places he liked to go?"

"He liked getting away from people and finding spots where we could be alone. I remember the first time we went out, he drove us somewhere off the highway. It was a quiet spot, and we just sat on an old log and talked. I'm not sure exactly where it was."

The other detective interrupted and asked which direction they drove.

Christine thought for a few moments. "It was toward Nashville, but he turned off way before we reached the outskirts. There was some little town, but I can't remember the name of it. His work took him all over, so he knows all the backroads." She paused and added, "I remember there was a creek we drove over."

The female detective asked a few more questions, and that's when Christine sighed. "It was a little creepy, that first date. We were sitting there talking, and it was getting darker. He joked and said if he wanted to kill me, he could, and he could bury me out there, and nobody would ever find me."

Coop and AB both gasped, and AB paused the video.

AB shook her head. "Really? You're on a first date with a guy, he tells you he could kill you and bury you in the middle of nowhere, and you decide to continue dating him and move in with him? I thought some of my first dates were bad."

Coop sighed. "Unbelievable. I would get as far away from him as possible, but it reinforces my hunch that this guy is a predator. He preys on women, and Christine is mighty lucky he didn't choose her that night."

AB shivered. "All that, and she still thinks he's innocent."

The door Coop left cracked swung open, and Gus followed Aunt Camille, who was toting a tray of tea and cookies. She set it on the edge of the desk. "I thought you two could use some sustenance. Charlie already turned in, and I'm on my way to bed now."

Coop and AB thanked her and after Gus extracted a few pets from them, he climbed onto his leather chair and shut his eyes.

While AB and Coop sipped their tea and nibbled on cookies, they watched the rest of Christine's interview. The detectives pressed her about that first encounter and asked more about Roy's demeanor.

As Christine spoke, she began to cry. "It did sort of freak me out, but I thought he was joking. Looking back, I think I was dumbfounded and didn't react much. I was anxious to get back home though. It was a little scary."

When asked if he'd ever said anything like that to her again or made any type of threats, she shook her head. "No, never." She also confirmed they never visited that same spot again.

The female detective changed the topic and asked how Christine and Roy spent their free time together. The conversation turned more chatty and less heavy, and Christine talked about going fishing or spending the weekends outdoors or around a campfire.

She paused and added, "Oh, Roy liked to listen to true crime podcasts about murders and read books. He was fascinated with serial killers. His favorite was a serial killer in Alaska. He was a baker but murdered dozens of women. Roy thought he was the best."

Coop and AB both stopped chewing and looked at each other. AB sat back in her chair. "You've got to be kidding me. Is this lady for real?"

With a shake of his head, Coop sighed. "She lives with a guy who talks about how easy it would be to kill her and bury her in the middle of nowhere and who likes to spend his free time reading about serial killers and listening to podcasts about serial killers, but she saw no red flags when it came to Roy and believes he's innocent."

"It's unbelievable. Could it be Stockholm Syndrome?"

Coop shrugged. "Could be. I don't know. She seems very devoted to him despite her shocking revelations."

They continued to watch, and Christine volunteered that she often listened to podcasts with Roy but grew tired of them.

He, on the other hand, couldn't get enough of them and often listened to them over and over.

Coop got the impression Roy was obsessed with the Alaskan serial killer. While they listened, he searched online and discovered more about the man who had preyed upon and murdered women for eleven years in the 1970s and 80s near Anchorage, Alaska. He primarily targeted prostitutes and was known to take his victims in the plane he piloted and hunt them down and bury them in the wilderness.

Like Roy, he was an avid hunter and outdoorsman.

As Coop continued to read about Roy's hero, a chill went through him.

Christine's voice came from the speakers. "Roy was borderline obsessed with this killer from Alaska. Bob was his name. He finally got caught when one of his victims escaped. Roy admired the way the guy planned everything out in advance and thought he was so smart for burying the bodies far from where he lived. He made sure there was no connection to him, and Roy always said that was genius."

10

With wide eyes, Coop and AB stared at each other as soon as Christine's segment ended. AB grimaced. "Listening to her normalize his habits makes my skin crawl."

Coop nodded. "Everything she said makes Stanton look even more guilty. None of what she said makes me feel any better about Alyssa's current state."

As AB reached for her tea, her eyes welled. She took a sip and whispered, "It makes me sick thinking about her and her poor mother."

Coop pointed at his watch. "Let's call it a night and in the morning, we can focus on places Stanton visited that he would deem a good hiding spot. We need to find her."

"Sounds like a plan. I'm beat," said AB, rising from her chair.

Coop walked her to the front door and waved as she pulled away from the house. He padded back to his suite and got ready for bed and the sleep he needed but suspected would be elusive.

THURSDAY MORNING, Coop got up later than usual. After AB left last night, he downloaded the book Christine told the detectives Stanton read about the serial killer in Alaska. He was married and had two children, which was hard to believe. Coop skimmed through it for hours, learning that the killer often transported his victims in his own plane and many times made a sport of hunting them in the forest. After he killed the women, he buried them far from his home, ensuring they would never be found and if by chance they were, he would have no connection to them.

After he finished reading, he tossed and turned until the wee hours. Reading about victims Coop never knew was bad enough, but thoughts and images of Alyssa occupied his mind for several hours as he contemplated her fate and what Stanton had done to her.

After a hot shower, Coop slipped into a clean black t-shirt, lettered with I'M NOT BOSSY. I JUST KNOW WHAT YOU SHOULD BE DOING. He went in search of coffee and joined his dad for scrambled eggs and toast before he loaded Gus into the Jeep and headed for the office.

Coop first stopped in the kitchen and poured himself a cup of the freshly brewed decaf from the carafe. AB was already at her desk, petting Gus, who leaned against her legs, his tongue poking out of his mouth as she stroked his neck. She looked up when the floor squeaked from Coop's steps. "Morning, Coop."

She pointed at one of the monitors on her desk. "I was just getting caught up with the overnight activity on the case. They tried to interview Stanton again, but he's not saying anything. Just that same smug look on his face."

Coop sighed and plopped onto the couch. "That's because he thinks we'll never find her. Like he told his girlfriend on their first date. He's learned how to perfect his crimes. He studied that serial killer who killed for over a decade, and I think Stanton killed those women in Idaho and Nevada and the ones Bennett found in Georgia and North Dakota. He's experienced and convinced he's smarter than everyone."

AB nodded. "They're sending officers to check all the areas where Stanton worked. Arian Group provided that list Anne told us about, and Mitchell wants all those locations checked thoroughly."

Coop studied his mug. "Makes sense. He had this planned, so he would have everything set in advance. I'm not convinced Stanton would take her anywhere there was a chance of someone finding her though. It won't be a site where they're actively working."

Coop stood and wandered to his office. He rifled through the working file he had on Stanton and nodded when he found the document he sought. He carried it out to AB's desk and pointed at it. "See if you can find someone to talk to from Tennessee Valley Zinc and get a similar list from them. See if we can find out places he worked there."

AB eyed the document and tapped a few keys on her keyboard. "I'll see what I can do. They closed down their Middle Tennessee operations but are still active in the eastern part of the state. I should be able to find someone."

He set the file on her desk. "I'm going to call Roane County to see if they have a better location for Stanton and the girlfriend's first date. I think it would be a good idea to look there or at least see when he visited it last."

Coop put in a call to Detective Mitchell, who answered after a few rings. "Coop, what have you got for me?"

"Not much but an idea that might help. I know cell phone providers keep location records for their customers for years. I'd like to search the location of his first date with Christine. He already indicated it was a place he would choose, and she said in her interview they never went there again."

"That's good, Coop. I like it. Let me get on the provider and see what we can dig up while we pinpoint the date with the girlfriend. I'll let you know when we have anything."

Coop tapped his pen on his notepad. "We're looking at his previous employer to see if we can find out where he worked for them. I know you're checking his current jobsites, but I think he would take Alyssa somewhere nobody would look for her. That's not going to be a working site."

"Right. We have to check them, but I agree with you. It's somewhere with no chance of traffic. I'll get the location records for as far back as they have them."

Coop disconnected and studied his monitor with the map of Tennessee displayed. He went back to the hundred-mile radius based on the amount of gas in Alyssa's car.

The red circle stretched along the interstate from Gordonsville in the west to Greenville in the east, covering most of middle and eastern Tennessee. The area wasn't small, but it was a start. Once they had a list of sites he worked and where he took Christine, they could plot those points and investigate anything within the radius.

With the exception of Knoxville, the red circle contained mostly rural counties and communities, all with plenty of remote places. Coop sighed and took another sip from his cup.

As he contemplated the huge task before them, AB came through the door, smiling.

"I talked to a guy at Tennessee Valley Zinc, Joe. He's at their Clarksville office and handles everything related to the now-defunct site in Gordonsville. He remembered Stanton and found his old job log in the system. He's sending it over now. He said one of Stanton's main jobs was closing down the mine site outside of Gordonsville. It's abandoned as the skeleton staff there finished up their work months ago, so nobody is on site."

Coop's brows rose. "That could be where he took her."

AB nodded. "Right. Joe confirmed the other mines further east are still operational, but they shut down the one in Gordonsville. If we're thinking about his past work, that location makes the most sense, with it being abandoned. Joe said it's a large area, and there's still some equipment there."

Coop whistled. "Maybe this is the break we've been waiting for." He glanced over at Gus, snoozing on the leather chair in the corner. "I'm going to call Anne to see if she can search Stanton's recent cell phone location history and put him in that area."

After a few minutes on the phone with Anne, Coop grinned and disconnected. He hurried to AB's desk. "Anne came through. The mining company has two cell towers on their property, and Stanton's phone was there twice in the two weeks prior to Alyssa's abduction. She's going to alert Detective Mitchell, and I'm going to head to Gordonsville. Can you see if Joe can meet us there and get us in?"

AB nodded, already walking toward her desk.

A few minutes later, Coop's cell phone rang. Detective Mitchell was excited at the solid lead and let Coop know he was already on the road. Officers from Smith County would meet him at the mine.

With the surge of adrenaline that came on the heels of the chance of finding Alyssa, Coop loaded up Gus, and they set out for the hour drive east of Nashville. In his rush to get on the road, he'd forgotten to bring water and opted to stop by his favorite drive-thru kiosk, Espresso Lane. Audrey, the young woman who Coop recognized, packed up bottles of cold water for him and Gus and delivered his drink order with a warm smile and a handful of dog cookies. "Y'all have a good day."

Coop thanked her and settled in with his large sweet tea, and Gus munched on the extra cookies Audrey gave him, and the two made their way to the interstate.

Twenty minutes into the drive, AB called to let Coop know Joe was enroute. He was working from home near Nashville and would be right behind Coop. A few minutes later, Mitchell called and let him know Smith County was on scene waiting for Joe to open the gate for them. He was still about forty minutes out.

Coop took the exit for Gordonsville and followed the directions on his GPS to the site of the mine, a few miles from the interstate, down a quiet road. He took another turn and saw the sign for Tennessee Valley Zinc and the patrol cars from Smith County in front of the tall fence that ringed the mining operation. Coop pulled the Jeep next to them and took in the vastness of the property and the near absolute quiet surrounding it.

The only sound was the flex of the metal sign attached to the fence when the breeze hit it just right. He left Gus with the windows rolled down and filled his water bowl.

Coop walked over and introduced himself to the officers from Smith County, who both smiled and shook his hand. The one with the stripes on his shoulder, Lieutenant Stewart, pointed at the gate. "Detective Mitchell from Roane said you'd be coming, and Joe from the mine would be here soon to open the gate for us. Mitchell wanted us to wait until he got here with the warrant anyway. He said you think the kidnapped girl could be in here somewhere."

Coop nodded. "It's a working theory. The suspect worked here and was involved in shutting it down before he moved on to work for another company. Seems like this place is off the beaten path, and nobody is around." Coop waved his hands at the huge space surrounding the property.

Stewart nodded. "Yep, nothing much out here now that they've shut down operations. They were a big employer around here for years. People were sad to see it go. Drove lots of people out of our county to relocate to their other sites."

Coop eyed the heavy fencing that ran for what he guessed

was at least a half mile in both directions from where they stood. "Do you get many calls for vandalism or mischief out here since it's been abandoned?"

Both officers shook their heads. Stewart spoke first, "No, it's secure and well maintained at the moment. We've got less than fifteen hundred people who live here. It's quiet. Everybody knows everybody. No crime to speak of. Most of the population is further up the road in Carthage."

He pointed at Coop's Jeep where Gus stuck his head out of the passenger window. "We've got a golden too. They're the best dogs."

Coop chuckled. "Gus agrees. He's my partner and loves road trips. I figure we won't be here long, but I have a strong gut feeling this is the place. I just want to find Alyssa and if she's not here, I'll move on to other possibilities."

The two officers followed Coop over to the Jeep, and they lavished Gus with some chin scratches and petting until Detective Mitchell and Joe arrived within a few minutes of each other.

An older man with gray hair emerged from the white company truck. He held a large keyring in his hand and a bundle of rolled blueprints was tucked under his arm. Joe introduced himself and shook everyone's hand before pointing at the gate. "Shall I open it?"

Deputy Bennett was with Detective Mitchell, and he provided a copy of the warrant to Joe and Lieutenant Stewart. All the officers slipped on gloves while Joe gave the warrant a cursory look as he found the key on his ring and handed it to Lieutenant Stewart.

He inserted the key in the lock of a heavy-duty man gate that led to a small concrete and metal guardhouse. As they walked toward it, Joe mumbled that they didn't even need the warrant. "If there's a chance that young woman is in here, we want to do all we can to help."

Detective Mitchell thanked him and explained they needed it for the criminal case. Joe pointed at another key, and Lieutenant Stewart opened the guardhouse. He and Joe stepped inside and moments later the huge gate began to slide open.

With a finger pointed at the guardhouse, Detective Mitchell caught Joe's eye. "Would Stanton have access to the guardhouse to open the gate as well as the man gate?"

Joe nodded. "Yes, sir. Mr. Harrington's assistant asked me to check that. I took a look at the key log and noticed we never collected Roy's keys when he left. He was still doing some work for us to wrap up the closure when he landed the new job. It was just an oversight since he stayed on for a couple of months to help." He shook his head. "If it turns out he did this..."

Deputy Bennett and the two officers from Smith County were already focused on the ground on either side of the gate, searching for fresh tire tracks in the gravel. Bennett looked up and met Mitchell's eye and shook his head. The three of them continued on foot, inspecting the ground as they walked toward the main building and paved lot where employees would have parked.

Beyond that paved area, the rest of the complex was serviced by a series of dirt roads that led to more than a dozen different buildings, along with huge shafts that stood above the ground and large conveyer systems that hung in the air and connected to various processing points.

Coop turned and looked at Detective Mitchell. "This place is enormous."

Mitchell nodded. "We've got more people on the way to help us search. They should be here within an hour or two. The buildings alone will take hours, not to mention the outdoor areas."

Bennett's voice hollered from several yards away where he was bent over the powdery dirt road. "Got something here. Tracks look consistent with the Honda."

Mitchell gestured to the gate. "Joe, if you can wait out here, we're going to follow the tracks the deputy found on foot, so we don't disturb evidence. Then we'll need your help once the rest of the team arrives to search the buildings and the entire property."

Coop pointed at the blueprints. "Joe and I can go over the maps while you and your team follow the tracks. We'll see if we can come up with any theories on where Stanton might've taken Alyssa."

Coop and Joe walked back to the main gate and spread the blueprints across the hood of Joe's work truck. He pointed out the various buildings and their usage. Coop wasn't convinced Stanton would have left a victim in a building where someone might discover her at some point.

He kept thinking back to Christine using the word bury. At eighteen, Stanton had buried a victim. Coop suspected that was his method of choice and how he'd managed to keep his prior victims from being discovered. He'd also studied his idol in Alaska who had employed the same method.

Coop let Joe explain the layout and learned the underground mine operated about seven hundred feet below the surface. Joe pointed out the giant hoists that transported both materials and people underground. "It's like a whole city under there. Huge tunnels filled with tons of equipment move around the site and take the ore that's drilled and move it along train tracks to be crushed and milled. It's brought to the surface for processing, then they separate the zinc and leave behind the lime and gravel."

He pointed at the map to an area on the other side of the property. "Those byproducts were stockpiled here, then sold."

As Coop studied the map, his heart sank. There were so many places to search. He pointed at the cooling ponds. "Is there still water in these?"

Joe nodded. "Yes. The water is continually pumped from

below to keep the tunnels clear. Our company is trying to sell this mine to another company, so it's in their interest to keep it up and ready to operate to get the most money for it. It's in a decommissioned state but a turnkey operation."

Coop pointed at a few areas on the map and asked Joe about the feasibility of digging in the earth. Joe frowned and studied the map.

After a few moments, he swallowed hard and placed his finger on an area on the other side of the property near what used to be a truck entrance used for transporting the materials in and out of the mine.

"Here's where we still keep a few pieces of equipment. There's a small backhoe there."

Coop pulled his cell phone from his pocket and hit the button for Mitchell. "Detective, Joe says they keep a small backhoe on the property. You might want to check it for fresh tracks and see if it was used recently. That might lead us to a location." He explained where it was located.

"We're still trying to follow the tracks that match the Honda. We're headed in that direction. I'll call you as soon as we get to the equipment and see what we can see."

Coop disconnected and met Joe's eyes. "They're making their way there now. We should know something soon."

Joe pointed at his truck. "I've got a cooler in there with some cold drinks. Can I get you something?"

Coop smiled at him. "Sure. Sounds good."

Coop walked to his Jeep and let Gus take a break. Joe hurried to the passenger side of his truck and returned with two cold bottles of sweet tea. Coop popped the lid and took a long swallow. "That hits the spot, thanks."

Joe patted the paunch that hung over the waist of his jeans. "Wife keeps telling me I need to cut back on the sweet tea, but this ol' Southern boy can't do it."

"I hear ya," said Coop. "I'm supposed to do the same and need to limit my caffeine. Getting old isn't fun."

After Joe petted Gus and told him how handsome he was, Coop put Gus back in the passenger seat. The two men leaned against the fender of the Jeep, their eyes focused on the massive mine as they held their breath and waited for word from the detectives.

11

After what felt like hours, but in reality, it was only thirty minutes, Coop's cell rang. He didn't bother to say hello when he saw the name on the screen. "Do you have anything, Detective Mitchell?"

"We found the backhoe and recent tracks. There's what looks to be fresh dirt. I've called forensics, and Smith County detectives are enroute. I'm sure we're looking at a burial site."

Coop sighed and closed his eyes. Before he could say anything, Mitchell asked him to quiz Joe on the movement of the equipment and the last time it had been used. He let Coop know Bennett was on his way back to the vehicle to get more equipment.

With a heavy heart, Coop disconnected and turned toward Joe. "Sounds like they found tracks from the backhoe and what looks like a mound of fresh dirt. When is the last time that equipment was used here?"

Joe frowned. "It would have been months ago. We haven't had anybody working here since February or so." His shoulder sagged. "Do they think he buried her?"

"It sounds like a possibility. They've got more detectives

coming and a forensic unit." Coop retrieved his notebook from the Jeep. "Where are the keys for the backhoe kept?"

Joe pointed at the map. "There's a little shed here that's locked, and the equipment keys are inside a box in there."

Coop scribbled a note. "Stanton would have keys to that shed as well as the gate here and the security shack?"

Joe nodded slowly. "Yes."

Coop texted Mitchell to let him know where the keys were kept and that Joe confirmed Stanton also had keys to it.

Coop looked up to see Deputy Bennett and the deputy from Smith County walking toward them. When they reached the fence line, Joe offered them a cold drink. They accepted, and Bennett downed an entire bottle of sweet tea in one large gulp. He pointed at his patrol vehicle. "We want to get castings of the tire tracks to go with all the photos. We need to collect some supplies and take a couple of shovels back with us."

Joe pointed at his work truck. "There's a man gate on the back side of the property. You could move your vehicles back there and have easier access to them. No way to drive through back there unless we take out a section of the fence. When we decommissioned this place, we opted to take out all the access points to make it more secure, so there's just this main gate now. I've got a shovel in the back of my truck, too. You're welcome to it."

Bennett nodded. "That sounds good. Let me get in touch with Detective Mitchell and let him know. We want to print the lock on the gate and the shed, along with the backhoe just in case we luck out and can get anything usable. Might as well process the lock on that back gate too before anybody else touches it."

After a short conversation between Bennett and Mitchell, he left the deputy to fingerprint the locks and security shack, while Joe led the way around the back of the property with

Bennett and Coop following. Before they unlocked the gate, Bennett fingerprinted it, then collected the shovels.

From the fence line, Coop saw them working to remove dirt from the mound. After gently digging and placing the dirt they removed on a clean tarp, Mitchell bent down and examined the area.

A few minutes later, the detective lumbered toward the gate. "We've got a body. I'm going to wait for forensics before we go further. They're only a few minutes away." He turned toward Joe and added, "We'll be here for hours. Well into the evening. We'll get your information, and you can leave until we're done."

Joe nodded. "Yeah, I need to let the boss know what's going on."

Mitchell frowned. "We need to keep this quiet for the time being. I understand you need to report to your boss, but we need you to be discreet. We don't want this getting out before we can identify the remains and let the next of kin know. We also don't want to jeopardize our case or cause a media frenzy here at the scene."

Joe nodded. "Understood. My boss is the big boss, and he's the only one I need to tell. I'll keep it to myself outside of that."

Mitchell shook Joe's hand. "I'll let Bennett collect your information, and he'll be your point of contact. He'll give you a call when we need you back here to secure everything. Smith County may end up leaving a unit overnight."

Joe, his shoulders slumped and the wrinkles in his forehead deeper, looked over at Coop. "Nice to meet you, Mr. Harrington. You and your dog. You take care."

"Same to you, Joe. Thanks for coming out and helping."

Bennett arrived and ushered Joe over to his vehicle where he took out his portfolio and pen.

Mitchell stepped closer to Coop and lowered his voice. "I'll call you when we have an ID. I'm certain it's Alyssa. We also found the remnants of a recent fire. Looks like burnt clothes and a purse. We'll know more when the coroner and forensics take a look." He sighed as he looked back at the crime scene. "Despite the outcome, this was excellent work, Coop. I appreciate your tenacity. I'll be in touch soon."

Coop shook his head. "I'm just sorry it ended like this. I really wanted to find her alive."

"You and everybody else. We're going to process this evidence very carefully, then have another run at Stanton and get the DA to file some new charges. Like you said before, he never thought we'd find her."

"I'm also certain there are others like Alyssa buried in places nobody has found yet." Coop glanced over at the mound of dirt. "Her poor mother."

Mitchell's shoulders sagged. "Yeah, I'm not looking forward to having to tell her the news." He pointed at the roadway where several vehicles and vans made their way. "Looks like the cavalry has arrived."

Coop extended his hand. "I'll leave you to it."

He climbed into the Jeep, where Gus was overjoyed to welcome him. Coop gave Gus another opportunity to slurp up some water from his bowl before he dumped the remainder out the window and headed back toward the interstate.

As he made his way along the quiet road, Coop's throat tightened. He couldn't help but think of Alyssa and all she'd gone through when she traveled along the same path. The fear he suspected she'd endured, not to mention whatever else was done to her before she was killed, made his stomach knot.

He poked the button on his cell phone for the office and let AB know he was on his way back home. He didn't want to discuss details on the phone and promised he'd fill her in when he got there.

It was past the dinner hour when he pulled into the parking lot of his office. His breakfast had worn off long ago, but seeing that crime scene had made his appetite disappear. Gus, however, expected his dinner and when Coop came through the back door, he filled the dog's bowl and left him to eat in peace while he wandered out to AB's desk.

She turned in her chair and raised her brows. "So?"

He slumped onto the couch and shook his head. "They found a body buried on the mine property. Mitchell is going to call when they have an ID, but he's sure it's Alyssa."

AB gasped as tears filled her eyes. "I was holding out hope we'd find her alive."

Coop sighed and rested his head against the back of the couch. "That's why Stanton was so smug. He thought she'd never be found. The place is deserted. No staff. They're trying to sell it, but there's no activity. It's quiet and way out of the way. Nothing around it but trees. Without a body, he's convinced he'll never have to face the consequences."

AB plucked a tissue from the box on her desk. "I'm shocked he wasn't more surprised and resistant when they arrested him."

Coop reached out to pet Gus, who sat next to him, leaning on him. "I think he's very measured and practiced. I don't think he ever contemplated that we'd identify his truck. He was careful, but I think his plan is to deny everything and say nothing that might help. He likes to be in control; it's his way of controlling what's happening now. Once they charge him with murder, things will get interesting."

"It makes me sick," said AB. "Her mother is going to be inconsolable."

"I know. I can't even think about her." He sighed. "Speaking of that, I better call Ben and prepare him."

"I was going to grab something to eat on my way home. Want to come?"

"I'll take a raincheck, AB. I don't think I can eat right now. I feel horrible."

AB collected her things and bent over to give Gus a pat on

the head. She squeezed Coop's shoulder. "Sorry, Coop. You did your best."

He put his hand over hers. "*We* did our best. Sadly, I think her fate was sealed the moment Stanton took her."

"See you in the morning." AB's soft footsteps faded away as she walked out the back door.

Gus crawled up onto the couch and snuggled next to Coop, his head in his master's lap. While Coop petted him, he put in a call to Ben. After he gave him a rough idea of what might be coming, he disconnected and closed his eyes.

He was exhausted and drained.

AN HOUR LATER, the office phone ringing on AB's desk jolted Coop from his impromptu nap. He hurried and plucked it from the cradle. "Harrington and Associates."

As soon as he heard the robotic voice asking him to accept a collect call, he was sorry he answered. He accepted the charges and waited for his mother's voice.

Moments later, it came screeching at him through the handset. "Cooper, I'm out of money at the commissary and have been waiting all day for it to come through. I suppose you thought you could just forget about me up here in the middle of nowhere. I need my cigarettes."

He grimaced as he listened to her tirade. In the busyness of the past few days, he'd forgotten to deposit money into her account. "I got tied up with a case and forgot. I'll do it right now."

"I can't believe you treat me like this, Cooper. I'm suffering up here all alone in the boondocks, and you don't even care. You're such a disappointment."

Coop's head throbbed, and he suspected his blood pressure numbers were off the charts. He didn't take the bait, instead practiced counting to ten while she continued her barrage of insults.

If she only knew what he'd been doing these last few days or how hard he had to work to keep from bawling on the drive home from the burial site. She had no idea who he was or what he did, and he was sure she never would.

When she took a breath, he said, "I need to go, but I'll process the funds right now. You should have access in a few minutes. Have a good night, Mom."

Before she could spew any more venom at him, he hung up the phone and walked into his office where he kept the inmate account information and processed the weekly deposit to fill his mother's coffers.

With that done, he doused the lights and led Gus out the back door, and they set out for home.

As much as he hoped to hear from Detective Mitchell tonight, he suspected he wouldn't know much until tomorrow morning. Alyssa weighed on his mind as he steered the Jeep to Aunt Camille's drive and parked.

He and Gus found Camille and Charlie in the small sitting room she favored, watching television. Gus made a beeline for the couch and snuggled between the two of them.

Camille turned and smiled at Coop. "I left you a chicken salad sandwich on one of those yummy croissants from the bakery. Mrs. Henderson made potato salad, and there's a slab of chocolate cream pie in the fridge for you."

Her kindness and seeing the two people who meant so much to him made Coop's throat tighten. It had been a long day and after the call from his mother, it seemed even longer. Coming home to a house filled with people who loved him and took care of him filled his heart with warmth.

Coop didn't trust his voice and waved a hand of thanks instead as he wandered to the kitchen. After a glass of sweet tea and a nibble on the sandwich, he felt better. He took another glass of tea and his pie into the sitting room.

His dad caught his eye. "Tough day, son?"

Coop nodded and slipped into the chair closest to him.

He didn't want to talk about it, and his dad didn't press him.

Instead, Coop escaped to Australia and the show Aunt Camille and his dad were engrossed in that featured a middle-aged couple sharing a small motorhome while they stumbled upon adventures.

The two people who meant the most to him, along with the escape on the screen, were the remedy Coop needed after one of the worst days he remembered.

12

Coop woke early Friday morning, anxious to find out more about the status of the case. It was a rare Friday that he didn't go to breakfast with Ben, but he had the day off and was taking Jen for an early Mother's Day escape and wouldn't be back until midweek.

The house was quiet when he wandered into the kitchen wearing one of Gus' favorite t-shirts, sporting a smiling golden retriever and lettered with DON'T STOP RETRIEVIN'. He poured a large cup of coffee and retrieved the newspaper.

He scanned the front-page headlines and saw nothing new about Alyssa's case. At least Detective Mitchell had managed to keep the crime scene from the media overnight. Today, Coop anticipated a press conference to announce the grim discovery.

He fed Gus breakfast and finished off his coffee before quietly locking the door behind them and heading to the office.

AB was already at her desk and welcomed Gus with a thorough belly rub. "Morning, AB," Coop said as he wandered by on his way to his office.

He checked his email, then opened the secure system to check on Alyssa's case.

Anger bubbled to the surface as he read the report outlining the state of Alyssa's remains. She'd been found buried in a hole, naked, and shot in the chest and head. The caliber of gun was listed as nine-millimeter. They recovered only one casing, which was buried in the dirt under Alyssa's body.

The medical examiner suspected she was killed late Saturday or early Sunday.

They had confirmed it was Alyssa using dental records and a preliminary DNA match. They were awaiting full DNA results. Detective Mitchell must have called in a favor since the medical examiner completed the autopsy late last night. They had collected DNA samples from the body and were awaiting results.

He had sexually assaulted her prior to killing her.

Bile rose in Coop's throat.

The technicians collected the burnt remains of what appeared to be clothing and personal items, along with some sort of tarp, and analysis was underway.

The tire tread marks matched Alyssa's Honda, but there were no usable fingerprints to link to Stanton. The detectives surmised he wore gloves at the site.

Trace evidence from Stanton's truck tires was being compared to the soil and dirt at the mine and that collected from Alyssa's tires. They already knew the truck had been at the abandoned barn site next to where they found Alyssa's car. Coop only hoped they could tie it to the mine site as well.

With Stanton in such a hurry to get rid of the tires, it only made sense.

As Coop read, a notification came through on his email. It was from Anne.

She asked him to call as soon as he got in. She had some information to share on the location data he suggested.

He pulled out his cell phone and scrolled until he found her name.

She answered on the first ring. "Hey, Coop. I wasn't sure you'd be in this early. Mitchell said you were at the scene with them yesterday."

"Yeah, it was a tough day."

"We're all dealing with the grief, but we're focused on making sure we take down Stanton."

"I'm all in on that front."

"You had a theory about the site of the first date he had with his girlfriend. I thought that was a worthy idea and dug into those records from that timeframe. We found the date with the help of the girlfriend, I found the location."

Anne went on to give him the specifics on the location, which was a rural area in Rutherford County between Kittrell and Big Springs.

Coop tapped the keys on his keyboard and brought up a map of the area. "I wonder if we took Christine there whether she could remember more and pinpoint the spot he took her?"

"Probably depends on her level of cooperation and her mental state. Once they charge him with murder, she might change, putting things together."

"Thanks, Anne. I'll run it by Detective Mitchell and see what he thinks. Are you able to check his history for other times he visited that area?"

"Already on it. I should have those results soon. I'll give you a call the moment I have something."

He thanked her and disconnected.

AB came through the door with her laptop and two steaming mugs. She set his in front of him. "I read the latest report from the crime scene. It's horrific."

He reached for the mug and took a long swallow. "I know. I can't stop thinking about Alyssa." He darted his eyes to the sticky note with his mother's inmate information. "Before I forget again, could you add it to your calendar to do a weekly deposit to my mom's jail account? I got an angry call from her last night and with all that was going on, it slipped my mind. You're better at keeping track of those things."

AB nodded. "I'll put it on my calendar and do it. No problem, Coop."

He thanked her and smiled at the woman who had the ability to organize anything. He would be lost without her.

Coop pointed at his notepad. "Anne was able to figure out the location of Christine's first date with Stanton. It's outside of Kittrell. I'm still convinced he's killed others, and I think that could be another burial site. She's checking his history to see when he visited that area outside of the date with Christine a year ago."

AB nodded. "That makes sense. I haven't checked the working file on missing women from Tennessee lately. If Anne comes up with some timeframes, that will make it easier to cross-reference and see if any of them fall into a plausible window."

"Exactly what I'm thinking. Roane County is going to have this piece of human scum in their jail, and now that they've found Alyssa, the evidence will be undeniable. I'd still like to nail him for any others we can link to him. We can't examine each place he visited since he's been living in Tennessee for three years, but this feels like a good place to start."

As they strategized their next steps, Coop's cell rang.

"Deputy Bennett, what can I do for you?"

"Hey, Coop. Detective Mitchell is having a briefing this morning before they do a press conference late this afternoon to announce that we found Alyssa. They're adding murder charges, plus sexual assault, and few others. We know you can't get here in time for the briefing, so I just wanted to update you."

Coop listened as Bennett explained they had Stanton's DNA on Alyssa and on the casing from the bullet they found under her. No match on a gun yet. They also hadn't found the gun when they searched Stanton's house or vehicles. He wasn't permitted to have a gun due to his ex-felon status.

"We're sending a team down to Georgia to search the mother's place. We've got a record of her owning a nine-millimeter. It's not that far of a drive, and he could have used that gun or disposed of the one he used there or any number of places between the crime scene and his house."

Coop wrote on his notepad as Bennett gave him details. The click of keys on Bennett's keyboard filled the background as he checked for the latest information.

"They're going through Stanton's truck with the hope of getting location data from it and found he'd disabled the GPS system. From what I've learned from the dealer and the guys at the lab in Knoxville, it takes some doing. He had to take apart the dash and remove a computer board."

Coop's brows rose. "That's interesting. Definitely someone who's trying to keep his movements private."

"Ah," said Bennett, as keyboard keys clicked in the background. "Anne just reported that her search of Stanton's location history shows him in Clinton at another park-n-ride location with the same supermarket chain. It's about forty miles from the one Alyssa used. He was there early in the morning, two weeks prior to abducting Alyssa."

Coop shook his head. "He was hunting."

"Right. That's what we think." Bennett sighed. "We interviewed him again last night, and he continued to deny knowledge of Alyssa or the kidnapping. We'll take another run at him today once the charges have been added. He'll have a court-appointed attorney."

Coop tapped his pen against his desk. "He thinks he's smarter than all of us. He never thought we'd find Alyssa. It'll be interesting to see his reaction when he learns we found her and faces the new charges."

"We're hoping it shocks him enough to confess."

Coop cocked his head. "I wouldn't count on it. He's calm and calculating. I'll watch the interview later, but we're going to look back at his past. I have a theory about that place he took Christine on their first date, and Anne is checking his old location history."

The sound of more keys tapping filled the air. Bennett asked him to hold on. He wanted to put in a request to get any camera footage from the Clinton location before it was overwritten.

A few minutes later, Bennett's voice came back on the line. "Yeah, that's a good line to follow. I never had time to do much digging on any Tennessee cases. We're focusing on all the evidence related to Alyssa right now, but it would be great to link him to other cases. I'll keep you posted if we get anything new here. Talk to you soon, Coop."

After he disconnected, Coop went back to the map on his computer and zoomed in on the area surrounding Kittrell. There was a large expanse of wooded land with no buildings or housing nearby. He suspected Christine's first date with the man Coop believed was a serial killer to be somewhere in the midst of the uninhabited land.

AB CALLED Joe from the mining company, and he sent over a work history for Stanton. It showed the days he worked and those he had off for leave over the course of his employment.

Coop and AB studied the list and made note of the times when he was on leave from work. Coop was especially interested in times surrounding a weekend. That was the time he chose to abduct Alyssa, and Coop suspected Stanton had a routine.

They found several long weekends with him taking off

Thursday and Friday or Friday and Monday. As they made a list, Coop's email pinged.

Anne alerted him to another report she posted in the secure case file and hoped the historical location information would help.

Coop logged in and checked her latest report. There was only one other time Stanton had visited the area Christine described. It matched the location data from their first date, and his visit to that same area was about fifteen months ago.

What was interesting, and Anne drew attention to it in her report, was the fact that Stanton's phone showed him there one day, then about a week later, his cell phone reported no movement for four days. Much like when Alyssa had been kidnapped, and Stanton had left his phone at home.

Coop explained all this to AB as he wrote down the date of Stanton's activity and the lack thereof. He made a note to discuss that with Anne. He wondered if there was a way to pinpoint periods of inactivity. It was rare for a cell phone to be inactive over a few days. That might be the easiest way to identify when Stanton had been hunting and killing women.

AB checked Stanton's work history and nodded. "He was on leave over that period of time when his phone was inactive."

Coop tapped more keys and said, "Let's check the missing persons reports for that time period and see where that leads us."

After several minutes of looking through the reports, which weren't sortable or searchable, AB looked up from her laptop. "This could be it. Elizabeth Rogers, a twenty-five-year-old young woman, was reported missing from the Fall Creek Falls State Park area. She was known to hike there and disappeared without a trace. No ransom, never found. She was reported the first day Stanton's phone went dark, late February last year."

Coop keyed the information into the cold case file Bennett established and asked him to get the case file from Pikeville. He looked up from his screen. "I think Pikeville is in Blesdoe County, right?"

AB nodded. "This is horrific to think her family is still searching for her and has nothing. It just makes me sick." She turned her laptop so Coop could see the photo that had been posted on social media. Elizabeth was a beautiful blonde with a happy smile.

Coop sighed. "It might not be her. This is my working theory. I'm just thinking Stanton has a method of leaving his phone behind as part of his strategy of being untraceable. We can use that to our advantage."

Despite adding the note to the cold case file for Bennett, Coop reached for his cell phone and hit the button to connect with the deputy. He wanted to get someone working on Elizabeth's file. The area where Coop suspected she might be buried was in Rutherford County. They needed to search that area where Stanton bragged about being able to hide a body where nobody would ever find it.

13

Over the next few hours, Coop and AB studied maps and reports, while they waited for further updates and the complete file from Blesdoe County on Elizabeth. Coop's computer pinged with a notification. There was a new upload from the team who executed a search warrant at Stanton's mother's property. Coop and AB watched the bodycam footage with mouths agape and eyes wide.

Stanton's mother, a woman named Delia, with stringy, gray hair in need of blond dye, a constant scowl, and a mouth that never shut, spewed foul words at the police the entire time they were at her property. An older bloodhound, who rose from his ratty bed on the porch of the trailer, howled at the intruders.

The officers held it together and were respectful but firm when Delia tried to block them from entering her trailer house. Her live-in boyfriend, who wasn't Stanton's father, as he'd died long ago, at first tried to calm her, but then joined in on the tirade and made disparaging remarks as the local officers made them wait in an outdoor area while the others began the search.

The property looked to be at least five acres and housed not only the trailer and outbuildings, but corrals for horses, sheep, and goats, along with a few rusted-out vehicles and horse trailers.

The officers provided a receipt for over a dozen guns and several boxes of ammunition, all of which Stanton's mother claimed were hers and left her and her boyfriend at the gate, where they were still slinging insults and profanity, claiming the police were always out to get Roy and harass him.

AB rolled her eyes. "She's lovely."

Coop tilted his head at a file on his desk. "I printed out stuff on Stanton's earlier arrest when he went to prison at eighteen. I think his loving mother was deeply involved in that whole incident. The murder took place on her property, in her driveway, and her own car was used to lure the victim to stop and try to fix the disabled car."

As AB reached for the file, he continued, "Stanton committed a few armed robberies, including robbing a gun store, with two of his friends and the girlfriend of the murder victim. They were looking for money to buy drugs, and the girlfriend wanted to kill her then boyfriend, who was a known drug dealer. The three young men offered to help and set up the plan to lure the victim to the area to purchase drugs from him, then allegedly, the girlfriend shot him in the head with a shotgun. The gun belonged to Mrs. Driver."

AB frowned. "Did they charge her with anything?"

Coop shook his head. "No, it's just my own theory. She may not have been there, but I think she had full knowledge. She tried to protect Roy then, and she's still trying to protect him now."

AB scanned the printed pages. "Stanton wedged the dead guy into his own trunk, then he and the other two drove some fifty miles away, buried the victim, drove another twenty-five miles, and torched his car."

Coop sighed. "He did all that at eighteen. Imagine what he's capable of now."

As AB read more, Coop's email pinged with a notification. "It's from Bennett," he said.

They both rushed to check the system and found the file on the missing young woman from Pikeville had been uploaded.

Elizabeth Rogers hiked the park often and was familiar with it. Last February, she set out to spend the day there and when she didn't return home in the late afternoon, her parents grew worried. She didn't answer her phone or texts, and they drove out and found her car, where she always parked, but no sign of her.

They contacted the police, who were quick to mount a search. As the days wore on, the search for what people thought might be an injured Elizabeth turned into an urgent missing person case. The police and volunteers conducted numerous searches throughout the area where Elizabeth disappeared. The park was over thirty-thousand acres, but they had armies of searchers. They even used drones and dogs and came up empty.

The dogs followed her scent to the hiking area where she was known to go and didn't deviate from the trail between the area and Elizabeth's vehicle. The vehicle, on visual inspection, was undisturbed. The police fingerprinted it and found no other prints.

The report on Elizabeth's phone showed no activity after the early afternoon on that day she went for a hike. Coop looked up from reading. "He took her when she was back at her car, getting ready to leave."

AB shook her head. "It sounds a little like that old case from Idaho. The girl's car was found, but she was never seen or heard from again."

"Exactly. He has a definite MO."

AB sighed. "No cameras where she parked. From what it

says, it was a backcountry area, not a real draw for tourists, so not much traffic. No witnesses saw her. Two other hikers saw her car before noon, but that's it."

Coop pointed his finger at the map. "This area where Stanton took Christine on their date is about seventy miles from there."

With her eyes fixed on the screen, AB said, "They put out a state-wide alert and plea for information, but I suspect it was too late. They were focused on Elizabeth being injured from a fall and not abducted."

Coop's phone chimed. "Looks like the press conference is set for five o'clock."

AB glanced at the time. "Wow, that's just a little more than an hour. It feels like we just got here. I'm worn out mentally, but time flew by today."

"Outside of driving out to that area I suspect where we might find Elizabeth ourselves, I don't think there's much more we can do tonight. They've got to be swamped with the new charges and the press conference. Let's call it a day, and you can come over for dinner. We can watch the press conference with Dad and Aunt Camille."

At the mention of several of his favorite words, Gus bolted from his chair, ready for the ride home.

AB gathered her mug and notepad. "I won't say no to that idea. I'm beat."

Coop gestured to the files and his computer. "This is definitely depressing work. I can't imagine the stress Detective Mitchell and his team are under right now."

After locking the door behind them, Coop loaded Gus in the Jeep, and they led the way to Camille's.

Despite not knowing AB would be joining them, Camille welcomed her with a warm hug and added an extra setting to the table. "Charlie and I were just talkin' about the press conference for that missing girl."

AB and Coop looked at each other.

Aunt Camille gasped and put her hand over her mouth. "Oh, no. I can tell by the way you look this is bad news."

Charlie came from the kitchen with a pitcher of iced sweet tea. "Hey, you two." He smiled, then his forehead creased when he glanced over at Camille. "What's wrong?"

"Just the case, Dad. It's not a good outcome." Coop took the pitcher and set it on the table."

Charlie's eyes filled with sorrow. "I'm so sorry, Coop. I know how hard you and AB have been working on this one."

The four of them gathered in the sitting room nearest the dining room. With Gus nestled at Coop's feet, they watched as Sheriff Lawson's image filled the screen. Standing next to him was Detective Mitchell.

Sheriff Lawson read a short and factual statement announcing the sad discovery of Alyssa's remains in Smith county and the new charges filed against Royce Stanton. He expressed his sincere sorrow and condolences to Alyssa's family and friends. His voice cracked as he spoke of the young woman with a bright future and the senseless and heinous actions of Stanton.

He thanked Detective Mitchell and the other members of his department for their outstanding work and dedication. He assured the members of the community that there was no further threat, as young women especially, were fearful.

He also thanked the other law enforcement agencies who had assisted in the investigation and apprehension of the suspect. He reminded the reporters that he couldn't provide specifics related to their ongoing investigation; they would have to wait for court proceedings to learn more details.

When he concluded his prepared statement, he took a few questions. Coop grimaced as the vultures from the media shouted out a barrage of questions. Sheriff Lawson held up his hand and shook his head. "This isn't a free for all. I would ask that you conduct yourselves in a calm and professional manner. I'll call on a handful of local media and will be looking for those who are respectful and cognizant of the enormous loss for our community and Alyssa's family."

That dulled their exuberance, especially of the national media who had descended on the small town. After answering a few questions, most of which dealt with when they found Alyssa, Sheriff Lawson thanked them for coming and left the room, while some of them shouted more questions at his back.

Charlie shook his head. "And folks wonder why nobody likes the media or believes anything they say. They're like a pack of wild dogs."

With a nod, Coop met his eyes. "I know that's the aspect Ben dislikes about his job the most. I couldn't do it."

Camille sighed. "I'm just sickened by this. What a horrible loss. I want to do something to help Alyssa's family." Tears filled her eyes.

Coop reached over for her hand and squeezed it while Gus inched closer to her and leaned against her legs. "I know her mom doesn't have much. It'll be expensive to get Alyssa transported back to Oklahoma. Let me ask Ben if he knows what they're doing."

As Camille dabbed at her eyes, she nodded. "I'd be happy to cover those costs to get her back home. Just let me know. I want to do it anonymously, if possible."

Coop's heart filled with admiration for the woman he thought of as his mother. She never failed to impress him with her giving spirit. "I'll get all the information and put it into motion."

He and his dad ushered the ladies into the dining room where they sat down to a quiet dinner. Coop didn't feel like talking, and neither did the others.

After seeing AB to the door, he and Gus said good night and

padded down the hallway to their suite. For once, when he slipped beneath the sheets, Coop wasn't worried about the insomnia that plagued him. He recognized the sheer physical and emotional exhaustion that would guarantee sleep.

14

On Saturday, Aunt Camille organized a cookout in the backyard. It was a vast space, meticulously maintained by Mr. Henderson. Coop smiled at the memory of her winking at him when she announced his favorite cheeseburgers, deviled eggs, potato salad, and her decadent chocolate cake were on the menu. As she'd smiled at him, Coop knew what she was doing. She'd always been his shelter in a storm, and she was still trying to cushion the harsh reality of the world with her sweet distractions. If truth be told, she'd done it for Uncle John, too. He remembered her coming up with outings and activities after he'd worked on tough cases.

Between her and his dad, he had a wonderful weekend of fun and excellent food, which along with their company, filled his soul and helped ease the sense of loss he'd felt since working on Alyssa's case.

After a restful weekend, comforted by the people Coop loved most, he and Gus made their way to the office on Monday morning. Coop and AB spent most of the week focused on cases and projects they ignored the last few days. The usual lighthearted chatter and fun they had was missing, though.

Both of them were mourning the outcome of Alyssa's case and focused on work to keep from dwelling on the overwhelming sadness.

Late Thursday, Bennett called from Roane County and reported that they'd attempted to talk to Christine to see if she were willing to help guide them to the area of Rutherford County that they suspected Stanton had taken her on their first day. He relayed that her earlier cooperation with them had evaporated, and she was stonewalling any efforts on their part.

After a long sigh, Bennett added, "She visited Stanton in jail and from watching the video, he convinced her he was being railroaded and was innocent. I put the video up on the shared system, so you can watch it. It's creepy to watch how he manipulates her. Bottom line, she's not going to be helping us."

Coop shook his head. "Understood."

Bennett's exhaustion seeped through the phone line. "We've got a massive amount of work to complete on this case. I promise I'll get back to the Rutherford County location as soon as I can, but we just got a lead on our arson suspect, and I'm working that, too. Now that Alyssa's been found, and we've arrested Stanton, all the extra help from our neighbors has dried up. They've all got new cases, too."

"I'll let you get back to it," said Coop. "If you and Jim are okay with it, I'm going to work some contacts I have here in Nashville and see if I can get some resources to help search that area in Rutherford. I've got a nagging feeling and can't let it go until we check it out. I'm willing to dedicate some time to it free of charge."

Bennett chuckled. "I talked to Jim before I called you and predicted you might propose continuing on it. He said you have his blessing. You, like our other outside resources, have been cut off, per the bean counters. If you find anything though, Jim said he'll make sure you're compensated."

"Fair enough. I'll keep you posted." Coop disconnected and

glanced across his desk at AB, who'd come in during the conversation.

With her brows raised, she pointed at the phone. "Roane County, I take it?"

He nodded and gave her a quick recap. "I'm going to talk to Ben tomorrow morning at breakfast. I'll see if he can talk to his counterparts in Rutherford County and pull some strings to get us permission and some help to search out there. Maybe Blesdoe County will help since it's their cold case."

AB glanced at the map on the whiteboard. "Yeah, that's a pretty big area to search on your own."

"I know we've got a snowball's chance in hell of finding it, but I think there's a good chance Elizabeth is there. I have to try."

"You're a good person, Coop. I'll do whatever I can to help."

"That will probably mean holding down the fort here and making sure we make enough money for me to be so cavalier in my willingness to work for free." He winked at her.

She grinned and rose from her chair. "That's what makes you one of the good guys, Coop. One of the reasons I love working with you."

As she left the room, Gus gazed after her, then turned his eyes upon Coop. "I know, bud. I know. She's the best and the glue that holds us all together."

ON FRIDAY, Coop woke feeling more rested after another night of sleep that came easily. His exhausted body finally overrode his busy mind and after the stress of the last week, he felt almost human again.

Dressed in one of his favorite soft t-shirts lettered with LESS IS MORE UNLESS IT'S COFFEE, Coop loaded Gus in the Jeep, and they headed to Peg's Pancakes. His faithful friend's tail thumped against the seat as he hung his snout out the window, sniffing in all the spring scents. Coop was convinced Gus could tell time and knew exactly where they were going.

With the sun shining on a gorgeous morning, Coop led Gus to the table he preferred, tucked into the corner of the outdoor patio. Before he sat, Myrtle was at the table, pouring him a large mug of their excellent coffee.

"Howdy, Coop," she said, pushing the sugar container closer to him. "And my sweet friend Gus." Gus raised his brows at her and flicked his tail across the cool concrete.

She smiled and rattled off the special of the day. The blueberry pancakes she mentioned sounded good. Coop pointed at the chair across from him. "I'll wait for Ben and think on that special."

Myrtle left them with a quick nod and took her coffeepot to the next table.

A few minutes later, Ben arrived and, before he took his seat, bent over to ruffle Gus' ears. "How's it going, Gus?"

Gus thumped his tail and swiped at Ben's hand with his tongue. Coop relayed the blueberry pancake special.

Ben slipped into the chair and sighed. "Blueberry pancakes sound like a good way to end such a horrible week."

"You can say that again."

"They're having a candlelight vigil for Alyssa tonight. Erica, her roommate, organized it. It's at a park near her house."

Coop nodded. "I'll be there. AB has family visiting, so I'm not even going to tell her. She'll feel guilty if she doesn't go."

"You can ride with us. I told Jen we're not staying long."

Coop nodded. "That would be great, thanks."

Myrtle returned and filled Ben's cup. "What'll it be, boys?"

Coop raised his brows at Ben. "I think we're both going to do the special and get one to go for AB, please."

She pulled the pencil from behind her ear and wrote down

their orders. With her waiting on them for years, she knew how they ordered their eggs, and they both liked bacon. She didn't need to ask. "Be out in a jiffy." She topped off Coop's coffee before heading to the side door of the restaurant.

"Speaking of Alyssa. Two things. First, Aunt Camille would like to cover the costs of getting Alyssa back to Oklahoma. She doesn't want to make a fuss about it. Just wants to anonymously supply the money for the transport. Whatever the family needs to happen."

Ben finished his swallow of coffee and smiled. "She's a true angel. You know that, don't you?"

"I do. I'm very lucky to have her in my life."

Ben pulled out his phone and tapped in a note. "I'll find out what Mrs. Morgan needs and be the go-between." He put his fingers to his lips. "I'll never divulge who's paying. Not even to Jen. I love her, but she can't keep a secret."

Coop chuckled. "Good plan."

"You said two things, what's the other?"

"Based upon Stanton's history, I think there's a good chance he's done this before. Probably multiple times. AB and I have been digging into similar missing persons cases from where Stanton lived. Found several, but the most promising and recent is a young woman who disappeared from Blesdoe County just over a year ago. Elizabeth Rogers went missing from Fall Creek Falls while hiking. Long story short, they suspected she was injured and searched, but then concluded she was most likely abducted."

Their breakfasts arrived, along with a plain burger patty for Gus, courtesy of Myrtle, and as they dug in, Coop lowered his voice. He explained the research done with the GPS data from Stanton's phone and his work records and the revelations from the girlfriend about their first date. "Bottom line, as much as the detectives in Roane want to link this scumbag to other crimes, they don't have the manpower or resources. I was hoping you might be able to get some help. I thought between Rutherford and Blesdoe, they might be able to come up with some resources. I'm willing to volunteer my time unless it turns into an actual find."

Ben cut another bite from his stack of pancakes. "That's some good detective work, Coop. I agree, it sounds very plausible. I know the sheriffs in both of those counties. Let me make a few calls. It may be Monday before I have anything."

As he reached for his coffee mug, Ben added, "It would be a good idea to match Stanton's lack of cell phone activity with other missing persons. I'm going to get one of our cold case detectives on that and see if anything pops from our caseload here in Nashville."

Coop leaned back in his chair, satisfied and hopeful. He couldn't bring Alyssa back, but if he were right, he might be able to help bring some level of closure to Elizabeth's family.

ON FRIDAY, Coop gave AB the afternoon off. Her sister and mother arrived for a short visit, and Coop shooed all of them out of the office and insisted they enjoy the Mother's Day weekend, which promised to be beautiful. May was in full swing, and the mild early summer weather was nothing short of glorious.

After Coop finished off some administrative work for the agency, he gave himself and Gus the rest of the day off, too. He took Gus to the park, where they spent almost two hours playing fetch and walking among the lush grounds. Nature always had a way of reminding Coop of the good and endearing parts of the world.

Gus, with his happy grin as he loped back to him with one of his favorite bright-blue spiky balls, never failed to lift his spirits. As hard as it was to work a case with an outcome like

Alyssa's, there was something healing about soaking in the fresh air and sunshine, with his loyal friend by his side.

Coop's habit was to work out the puzzles of his cases while he walked in the park, but today, he let his mind empty and immersed himself in the moment. After such a harsh couple of weeks, Coop craved the simple joys of the scent of grass, warm sunshine, and his best friend.

When he and Gus arrived home, Camille and Charlie were playing cards, surprised to see him. "We knocked off early today. Gus and I have been at the park. I'm going to run over to attend the candlelight vigil for Alyssa tonight. I want to be there for her mom."

Camille brought her hand to her chest. "Oh, yes. Do be careful driving home in the dark."

Her thoughtfulness warmed Coop's heart. "I will, and Ben is working on your anonymous idea for Alyssa's family."

She beamed. "He already called me, and it's in motion." She glanced across the table at Charlie. "I've got us tickets to Silverwood tomorrow. I thought we could check out the new summer garden displays."

Even though he wasn't feeling it, Coop tried to look happy. When she mentioned there would be a beer garden and a few local bands, along with the classical music she loved, his excitement increased. This weekend was all about her and what she wanted to do.

As Coop made his way to his wing of the house, he smiled. Mother's Day was a time when Coop always did something special to honor Aunt Camille. In addition to her Saturday concert, he had reservations for Sunday brunch at the posh place Aunt Camille always enjoyed. His dad had picked up the ice cream cake Coop ordered for her from Steve's and stashed it in the freezer. AB secured a coveted dinner reservation for the three of them at one of the oldest steakhouses in Belle Meade and a favorite of Camille's.

As easy as it was for Coop to think of things for Aunt Camille, it was beyond difficult to come up with anything for his mother. He wasn't sure what was appropriate to gift an older woman in jail? He opted for his usual gift and put a generic card in the mail to her at the jail in Vermont. He couldn't stand the hypocrisy of sending her a sentimental or mushy one. More often than not, the cards were returned to him with an imprint from the post office that her address was unknown. At least she'd get the card this year.

Marlene wasn't known to stay in one spot for any length of time. She had an unlimited network of losers and miscreants she called upon and with whom she couch surfed or worse. Coop didn't want to know.

Coop pushed her from his mind. He changed out of his t-shirt and into a more sedate button down for the vigil. After an early dinner of leftovers, he promised Gus he'd be home soon and left him lounging on the couch between his dad and Aunt Camille.

He hurried to the driveway and opened the passenger door of Ben's SUV. Jen smiled from the backseat. "I can ride in the back," he offered.

She shook her head. "Nah, I'm good back here. You and Ben will want to chat, and I'm just going to relax and sneak in a nap back here."

Coop slipped into the seat and shrugged at Ben. Not wanting to divulge anything about the cold cases in front of Jen, and happy to have a break from the talk of murder and cold cases, Coop steered their conversation to baseball instead.

They made plans to attend an upcoming home game with Charlie. He loved the game, and Coop was focused on spending more quality time while he was visiting. It seemed like work always managed to get in the way, and this case, more than others, reminded Coop of how fragile life was. He didn't want to waste a minute of the time he had with his dad.

15

On Saturday, after a large cup of coffee, Coop leashed Gus for an early morning walk through the neighborhood. Ben dropped him off before ten last night, so although he hadn't slept as good as he had the last couple of days, Coop managed to get a few solid hours before his insomnia had his mind working overtime in the wee hours of the morning.

The vigil had been emotional and difficult. The whole community turned out to support Alyssa's family and friends. He hugged Alyssa's mom, and his heart broke even more than the first time he'd met her. She felt frail and looked like she'd lost twenty pounds. She whispered her thanks to Coop, which only made him feel worse.

He hadn't been able to figure things out quickly enough to save Alyssa. At least she knew where Alyssa was and could have a proper funeral. Elizabeth's parents were stuck in limbo, hoping their daughter was still alive but imagining the worst.

Those thoughts plagued him in the darkest hours.

While Coop concentrated on inhaling the fresh air and watching Gus' happy swish of his tail, his mind quieted. With

Gus' pace slowing and his tongue hanging out, they made the last turn back toward Camille's house. As they arrived, Coop reminded Gus that they'd be gone for a few hours. He encouraged Gus to take advantage of his alone time and nap in his favorite spot, lying across the cool tile floor by the entry.

As Gus glanced up at Coop, he gave him a bit of side-eye. He clearly wasn't thrilled at the prospect of being left out of whatever adventure they had planned. Coop distracted him by plucking a ball from his pocket and throwing it across the huge lawn that graced the front of the house.

The dog hurried to it, returning it with what could only be described as a happy grin. Guilt made Coop throw it several more times before he ushered Gus indoors, where they were welcomed by the aroma of bacon.

Last month, Aunt Camille and Charlie watched a docuseries on dog health and now made Gus a homemade concoction using ground turkey or lean ground beef. As soon as Charlie added the meaty topper to his bowl of kibble, Gus rushed toward the bowl and licked it clean.

He then rested his head atop Coop's knee. All was forgiven when it came to the non-dog friendly outing they planned. Once the three of them finished breakfast, they left Gus to rest and set out for Silverwood.

ALTHOUGH THE GARDENS were more Camille's idea of fun, Coop had to admit it had been a great day. He and his dad enjoyed sampling beers and listening to a few local bands, hoping to make it big in Music City.

He delighted in seeing Aunt Camille, decked out in one her fancy tea dresses, grinning from ear to ear as she listened to the classical music she loved. The weather was perfect, and the gardens were filled with colorful spring blooms and plenty of happy mothers and grandmothers, lavished with attention.

Sunday, they all enjoyed a day of complete relaxation, stuffing themselves on a delicious brunch, playing cards all afternoon, and indulging in the restaurant's signature filet mignons for dinner. As Coop sliced the ice cream cake for them on Sunday evening, with his aunt and dad in the sitting room, ready to tune into their latest favorite mystery series, Coop's phone pinged.

He finished adding the last slice to a plate and returned the rest of the cake to the freezer before he checked his phone. Ben sent a message to let him know he received an email reply from his counterparts in Rutherford and Blesdoe County. They were both on board with the search idea. He promised to stop by Coop's office in the morning with details.

Relieved, Coop replied with his thanks and carried the dessert into the sitting room.

Before the program started, Charlie cleared his throat. "Uh, Coop, I wanted to let you know something."

Coop's forehead creased with worry. "What's wrong, Dad?"

He shrugged. "Nothing, really. Just that I decided I need to get back home at the first part of June. I want to spend time with your brother and the kids over the summer." He glanced at Camille. "I promised Camille I'd be back in the fall, in plenty of time for Thanksgiving."

Although Coop's heart sank at the news, it wasn't a total surprise. His dad couldn't stay forever, and he knew he missed his grandkids. With what he hoped was a genuine smile, he reached out his hand and put it on his dad's shoulder. "That sounds great, Dad. I know I speak for Aunt Camille when I say we can't wait for you to come back. Do you want me to make the flight with you, so you don't have to go alone?"

Charlie's face relaxed. "That would be wonderful, Coop.

You know how much I hate to travel, but I don't want to take you away from work."

With a shake of his head, Coop said. "Don't worry. It's easy. You figure out when you want to go, and I'll just block it out on the calendar. AB can hold down the fort." He winked at him. "Trust me, when she's gone is when the place implodes."

Charlie chuckled, and Aunt Camille smiled at Coop. The hint of pain in her eyes let Coop know she was also doing her best to mask the sadness the thought of not having Charlie around brought. "I insist on treating you to first-class seats. You might as well be comfortable."

"I've had such a wonderful time here and can't thank you enough for your hospitality and generosity, Camille. If it weren't for Jack and Molly and the kids, I'd take you up on your offer to stay here forever. Like Coop said, I miss them and the beautiful mountains. I need to check on the house and take care of a few things." Charlie pointed at his knee. "I can't use my knee for an excuse any longer."

"Just brace yourself for the biggest welcome back party you've ever seen." Camille smiled while her voice cracked.

Charlie nodded at her. "I'd expect nothing less from you, Camille."

Coop had gotten used to having his dad there. He didn't want to think about coming through the door after work and not hearing his laugh. No matter how old he was, there was something comforting about having his dad nearby and this summer wouldn't be the same without him.

As Coop reached for his first bite, he stopped and stared at his dad. "One condition. You can't chicken out when you get home and decide you're not coming back. I'll share you with Jack but insist I get my share of you here."

Charlie laughed, and his eyes glinted with tears. He nodded and squeezed Coop's shoulder. "Deal, son."

Monday, Coop woke with bit of lingering sadness at his dad's news. When Aunt Camille hugged Coop last night, she'd thanked him for a perfect Mother's Day weekend and squeezed him tight. She also whispered that she would miss Charlie too, but time would fly, and he'd be back before they knew it. He'd never been able to fool her, and she had an uncanny sense of his feelings and moods.

Despite the impending loss of his dad's company, with a renewed sense of anticipation, Coop focused on Ben's news. He was anxious to meet with Ben and get started on the search for Elizabeth. After a quick visit over a cup of coffee with his dad, who laughed at Coop's shirt lettered with I'M ONLY HERE TO ESTABLISH AN ALIBI, he and Gus drove to the office.

AB arrived bearing gifts. Along with Coop's cup of decaf, she delivered a box with a slice of Tennessee Waltz cake. "We took my mom to dinner last night, and they had this on the dessert menu. I thought after the week you had, you could use a little pick-me-up."

Coop eyed the cake that made the restaurant famous. He patted his midsection. "I ate enough for the entire week yesterday, but that looks delish." He couldn't resist digging into the layers of white cake and the decadent frosting encrusted in chocolate buttermilk pecan praline and decorated with bourbon espresso ribbons. "Oh, that's so good," he said, after savoring the first bite. "Thanks, AB."

As he sipped his coffee, he let her know Ben was coming by to fill them in on the latest related to their search for Elizabeth.

For once, Coop didn't work from home over the weekend and, between sinful bites of his cake, used the morning to get caught up on emails and the files for a few of their corporate clients.

As Coop tapped on his keyboard, Gus sprang from his chair

and moments later, Ben's voice filled the outer office. Gus led AB and Ben into Coop's office and resumed his position on his leather throne.

The three of them sat at the conference table. Ben sighed and tapped his finger on the table. "The detective in Blesdoe doesn't want to tell the family anything until they find something. He said they're shattered and hanging on by a thread of hope. He's anxious to help and is working on getting it approved to supply manpower and a drone with an operator if it might be helpful. Rutherford is fine with a search. Their detective is trying to see if they can supply a canine team to help search."

Coop's eyes widened. "That's all good news."

Ben nodded. "Yeah, it really is. They stressed it's going to take some time. They need to go through the red tape and get the budget approval to move forward. Since it's more of a recovery mission and not an active case, there may not be the sense of urgency you have for this, Coop."

"So, I need to cool my jets?"

Ben nodded. "Right. From their attitude, I'm sure it will happen; it's just a matter of prioritization. Elizabeth's family is well connected and has been there for generations, so that will help. The detective is going to speak with the sheriff, and he wasn't just telling me what I wanted to hear. He's sincere, just honest."

AB set her mug on the table. "Did they give you an idea on timeframe?"

Ben shrugged. "Not really. I tried to press but didn't get far. I think it will be at least the end of the week." His cell phone rang, and he glanced at the screen. "Sorry, I gotta run."

As he stood and reached for his phone, he glanced over at Coop. "I'll let you know as soon as I hear anything."

AB blew out a breath that made her bangs flutter. "Well, that's a letdown."

"Yeah, but at least they're interested and engaged. That's something. We're spoiled because we don't have to check with anybody up the chain to take a case and focus on it. I get it. It's the reality of limited resources and way too much demand."

With a nod, AB rose and took her mug. "I've got plenty to do to keep me busy."

Coop pointed at the mess of files on the corner of his desk. "Me, too."

As Coop considered lunch, his desk phone buzzed, and AB let him know Aunt Camille was on the line for him.

He suspected she might be dropping off lunch and smiled as he picked up the phone. "Coop, I'm sorry to bother you. I know how busy you are." Her tone was breathless and rushed.

"It's okay, what's wrong?"

"Oh, it's just dreadful news. You know my friend Clara?"

Coop remembered the older woman who lived in a house not too far from them, but Camille didn't give him time to reply. "Anyway, she hosted book club last week. She just called in an absolute panic."

"What's happened?"

"Well, we read this book about a valuable necklace. A family heirloom. It was historical fiction and quite good. We all loved the story, and it got us talking about family pieces we had and such."

Coop waited patiently for the dreadful part of Aunt Camille's news bulletin.

"Clara brought out a brooch that had been in her family for generations. It glittered with diamonds and emeralds. It was a bit gaudy for my taste but obviously valuable and a sentimental piece, as it belonged to Clara's great-grandmother."

With a sigh, Camille continued, "The brooch is missing.

Clara said she got to thinking about it and went to look at it this morning, and it wasn't in her drawer where she usually kept it. She's frantic."

Coop quit doodling on this notepad. "She thinks someone from book club took it?"

"Well, I hate to say that, but yes, I think she might. She called hoping you might be able to look into it for her."

"Did she file a police report?"

"No. She doesn't want to make a fuss. She just wants it back."

Coop rolled his eyes. "How much do you think it's worth?"

In a voice barely above a whisper, Camille said, "Around forty thousand."

With his brows raised, Coop wrote down the number and circled it. "Okay. I've got some time. I'll stop in to see her."

Camille rattled off Clara's phone number for him and reminded him of her address. "Thank you, Coop. You're a saint."

Coop hung up the phone and was about to see what AB thought sounded good for lunch, when she came through the door, toting a takeout bag from a place near the office. "I made an executive decision." She motioned with her head toward the kitchen.

Gus flew from the chair and followed at her heels. It took Coop a moment longer to react, and he met her in the kitchen, where she unpacked two containers. Over their steak salads, Coop filled AB in on the latest case Aunt Camille sent their way.

When he finished, he reached for his sweet tea. "The good news is I have some time to kill. I'm going to run over to Clara's to see what I can figure out."

AB glanced down at Gus, with his head resting atop her foot. "Gus and I can hold down the fort here." She slipped him a tiny bite of beef.

Coop tossed his container in the trash. "I shouldn't be too long." He shrugged when he noticed Gus focused on AB. "I don't think Gus will miss me."

AB chuckled and pointed at his shirt. "You should put on one of your polo shirts. I'm not sure Miss Clara would find the humor in that one."

After he changed shirts and grabbed his notebook, Coop hopped into the Jeep and headed back to Camille's neighborhood. When he made the turn for Clara's street, he remembered the house and turned into the long tree-lined driveway that led to the stately white mansion tucked far from the road.

After he pushed the button for the security gate and announced himself, it opened, and he parked under the shade of the portico along the side of the house. He climbed from behind the wheel and gazed across the estate. He wasn't sure what Aunt Camille had gotten him into, but he was about to find out.

16

A woman with dark hair, wearing an apron, answered the door. "Good afternoon," said Coop. "I'm Cooper Harrington. Miss Clara spoke with Camille, my aunt, and asked me to stop by."

The woman bobbed her head. "She's in the sunroom. Follow me, please."

She led him through the entry to an elegant space done in shades of beige with windows that provided a view to the patio and large pool.

Clara, her silvery hair piled on her head in a bun, glanced up from the book she was reading and met Coop's eyes. "Mr. Harrington, thank you so much for coming."

As Coop stepped into the room, atop the plush beige carpet, he hoped his shoes were clean. He extended his hand to Clara, and she gestured to a chair next to her end of the small sofa where she sat. "Please call me, Coop. Everybody does."

With a quick glance at the woman in the apron, she said, "Anne, bring us some cold drinks, please."

Without a word, the woman left.

He focused his eyes on Clara, who was staring after her housekeeper. "Aunt Camille shared your issue with me."

Clara brought her fingers to her lips. "Anne is leaving in a few minutes. Let's wait until she's gone, shall we?"

Coop glanced around the room and said, "Your home is lovely, Clara."

She beamed with pride and fingered the strand of pearls at her neck. "Thank you. It's been in my family for years and holds a special place in my heart."

Anne returned with a tray, glasses of ice, and a pitcher of tea, along with several cans of soda and two bottles of beer. Clara nodded her approval. "Thank you, Anne. That will be all. I'll see you tomorrow."

"Yes, Miss Clara. Have a nice day."

She turned and was gone before Coop looked up from the selection of drinks. He offered to pour tea for them, handed Clara a glass, and settled back into his chair with his own.

As he glanced out the window, he noticed Anne walking down the pathway along the back of the house toward a gate. He pointed out the window. "Looks like Anne is gone."

Clara nodded. "I just want to keep this as quiet as possible. I don't need her or anyone else gossiping about it."

"Have you considered contacting the police?"

Her mouth puckered, like she'd bitten into a piece of lemon. "No, no. I'm not doing that. I want this to be a discreet investigation."

Coop opened his notebook. "Okay, so tell me more about this brooch and what happened on Thursday at book club."

He let her ramble on with her version of events, which was much the same as what Aunt Camille told him. He asked her to show him where she kept the brooch and where the ladies gathered for the book club event.

First, she pointed out the window. "It was a gorgeous day, so we had our meeting on the patio."

Coop walked out the door of the sunroom and took note of the area. Another door led into the kitchen area, plus another that he surmised was off the main living room. The property was fenced, and he sketched a rough plan in his notebook, where he noted the gate Anne had used and kept walking around the house and found another gate.

A gate near the pool led to an exterior staircase, a few feet from the patio. The staircase connected to a balcony of what he presumed was a bedroom or upstairs sitting room. He tried the gate that led to the stairway and found it open.

He returned, and Clara led the way upstairs to her bedroom and showed him into the vast walk-in closet and the chest in the corner of it where she kept her valuable jewelry. Coop studied the space, which was only accessible via the stairs from the interior, but as he suspected, connected to the exterior stairs via the balcony.

"When did you return the brooch to the chest?"

Her lips trembled. "I've been trying to remember that. I keep thinking I must have returned it, but then I honestly can't remember doing so. I remember bringing it in from the patio. I put it on the table in the breakfast room. After that, I'm really not sure."

He tried the door leading out to the balcony and discovered it was locked. The bedroom and bathroom windows were also locked.

He turned to Clara, who was leaning against the doorjamb. "How long has Anne worked for you?"

"Oh, I'd say about five years. My old housekeeper retired, and she's been with me since."

"Do you have other help besides Anne, with access to the house?"

"I have a pool service and a groundskeeper. The pool service comes through the back gate, and I'm always home when they come. They don't have any access to the house and have never been inside it."

She sighed. "Ralph, my groundskeeper, takes care of my place and several others in the neighborhood. He's a wonderful guy, who has been with me for years. He comes and goes as he needs to and has access to all the outside areas. Of course, he's been in the house. We've chatted over tea or lemonade several times over the years."

Coop added his name to his notebook and that of the pool service company. "And you live here alone, correct? No guests have been in the house since the book club meeting?"

"I live alone. No guests."

"How about cameras? Do you have any camera coverage of the property?"

Her eyes widened. "Oh my, I didn't even think of that. I have a security service. I don't have any cameras in the house, but they installed some exterior cameras. Let me get their number."

"I just want to check all the windows up here," said Coop, wandering to the next room. It took him more than ten minutes to check all the windows on the huge second floor. All were secure, and none of them looked like they'd been jimmied.

He found Clara in the kitchen and investigated the breakfast room she mentioned, just off it, with a door leading to the patio area. He copied down the phone number for Ralph and the details of her security company. "If you can call them and let them know you've retained me to work on your behalf, it will make things quicker."

She nodded. "I'll do that right away." She closed her address book and glanced out toward the pool. "It's not really about the money. I just hate to lose that piece of jewelry that's been handed down to me."

"I understand. All the ladies in your book club are people I've known forever. Do you suspect any one of them would take it?"

She shook her head. "I don't really, but it's hard not to wonder. I'm hoping you don't really have to ask any of them as I would be mortified if they believed I thought that."

"I'll have to talk to them, but I'm not going to accuse any of them. Just gather facts and see if they noticed anything or remember anything."

With her eyes cast downward, she nodded. "I truly can't imagine anybody I know doing this."

"Hopefully, the camera footage will be helpful in ascertaining if anyone came to the house. I'm sure you left the house between Thursday and today, at some point?"

"Oh, yes. I was out over the weekend. I went to Silverwood. Camille mentioned you did, too. Had a hair appointment on Friday."

"Do you get many deliveries?"

She shrugged. "Sometimes the mail carrier brings packages to the house, but usually, my mail fits in the box at the end of the drive on the street."

"Do you order food delivered or any other local services that might bring you products?"

She shook her head. "No, I can't think of anything that's been delivered in the timeframe."

"I noticed the security gate across the driveway when I arrived. Is that something that's always used?"

Color rose in her cheeks. "I hate to admit it, but I've been very lax about that lately. I left it open on book club day last week, just because it's a hassle to open it each time someone arrives. Again, I didn't give it a thought until this morning when I found the brooch was gone. So, it's been left open since then and several times before that, too." She shook her head. "I've learned my lesson. It will remain locked from here on out."

Coop nodded as he added to his notes. "You might consider changing the entry code on it, too." With him living in the area so long, Coop knew most of the estates were several acres, fenced at the property lines, but not all the fences were of the type designed to keep out intruders. Many of them were more of a decorative nature. He pointed toward the backyard. "What's your property line fencing like?"

"It's white rail for the most part. The backyard proper is fenced for privacy and has gates, but the rest beyond is much more open. Ralph could tell you more about it since he maintains it all."

Coop nodded. "I think I've got enough of a start to go on. The only thing I'd like to get is a photo of the brooch. Do you have one?"

She smiled. "I dug one out this morning. I don't have one of it by itself, but I have one of me wearing it to a holiday party from years ago." I've got it in the sitting room.

Coop remained where he was while she hurried to fetch it. A few minutes later, she returned and handed him a photo of her wearing a fancy gown in a shade of green that matched the emeralds in the brooch.

"Perfect," he said, taking the photo. "I'll make a copy and get this original back to you."

"I'd appreciate that, Coop."

He plucked a business card from his notebook and handed it to her. "I'll be in touch if I learn anything. Please call if you think of anything else that might help."

"I can write you a check right now."

He held up his hand. "No need. We'll send you an invoice."

She followed him to the door. "I truly appreciate you coming so quickly, Coop. Your aunt speaks so highly of you and is quite proud of you. I can see why."

He grinned. "Aunt Camille is my biggest fan. You'll hear from me or my associate, Annabelle, when we have more information."

As he descended the steps, he turned and smiled at the

clink of the deadbolt. At least she was taking her security seriously now.

17

When Coop arrived back at the office, he gave AB the details for billing Clara and asked her to send a formal request to the security company Clara used for the video at her house from Thursday to Monday morning.

While he waited for that, he put in a call to Ralph. Coop had to leave a message and asked him to call regarding Clara. With him being employed by Clara for so long, Coop didn't anticipate he was a likely suspect, but he might have noticed something or have more information about visitors to the property.

Anne would be back at Clara's tomorrow morning for her shift. He wanted to talk with her in person. He added that to his calendar.

As he poured himself a glass of sweet tea, AB hollered out that Ralph Haynes was on the line. Coop tilted his head. "Let him know Clara is our client and see if you can set up a time when he can come in and talk with me as soon as possible. I can stay late or come in early, whatever works for him."

Coop wanted to observe Ralph and his body language and didn't want to divulge much over the phone.

As Coop brought AB her glass of tea, she was hanging up the phone. "He says he can stop by late this afternoon. He finishes up around five and will come by after that."

"Great, thanks, AB."

Between checking his email for any updates from Roane County or Ben, he spent the rest of the afternoon filing and getting his desk in order. It was hard to shake the failure he felt related to Alyssa's case. He was glad they had Stanton behind bars but would never forget the shattered look in Alyssa's mother's eyes after they found her body. He hated the helplessness such an outcome created.

That was part of the obsession Coop had with searching the area for Elizabeth. As hard as it would be for her parents to learn she was gone, he couldn't fathom living these last fifteen months not knowing where she was. The fear and suffering would drive him mad.

On her way out for the day, AB stopped by Coop's office to let him know she hadn't heard anything back from the security company yet and promised to see him in the morning. Gus watched her leave and tilted his head at Coop, as if asking him what he was waiting for, but when Coop kept working, Gus meandered back to his chair and sighed.

Less than fifteen minutes later, the front door opened, and Gus beat Coop to the reception area, where Coop found his dog wagging his tail while an older man wearing a large, brimmed hat petted him.

Coop extended his hand. "Mr. Haynes, thanks for making time for me. I'm Coop."

Ralph shook his hand and smiled. "Beautiful dog you have, sir." Coop smiled at his thick Southern drawl.

"That's Gus and please just call me Coop. Come in and have a seat. Can I get you a sweet tea?"

"I wouldn't say no to one."

Coop poured him a glass and had it in his hands within a few minutes. Coop gave Gus his serious look when he started to put his paws on the edge of the couch in preparation for leaping onto it so he could cuddle up next to Ralph. "Down, Gus."

Gus hung his head and slinked to the floor, resting as close to Ralph as he could get.

"Sorry about Gus. He's never met a stranger."

"Probably smells my dog, Little Bit, not to mention all the places I've been today. It's no bother; I love dogs."

"I saw Miss Clara today. She's a friend of my aunt's and has a problem I'm helping her solve. Something is missing from her house, and I'm trying to piece together a timeline of events starting on Thursday last week. When were you working at her house?"

Ralph nodded. "I was at Miss Clara's on Thursday and Friday this week. I did her yard early Thursday mornin' on account of her club meeting and visitors comin'. Friday, I went back to do some things on the property behind the house."

Coop jotted in his notebook. "She said you could tell me more about the fencing at the rear of the estate. It looks like it's just rail fencing, so not secure against someone gaining access that way."

After a long swallow from his glass, Ralph said, "That's right. It's more of a property line marker. I've never seen anyone nosin' about back there, though."

"Did you notice any visitors come to the property while you were there? Other than her book club ladies, of course."

"No, I don't recall anybody. I keep to myself and my head down workin'."

Coop sighed and tapped his pen on his notebook. "Do you have a crew that helps you and tends to Miss Clara's yard with you?"

Ralph smiled. "No, I wish. I'm gettin' too old to be doing this. My sons are smarter than me and have jobs where they work behind a desk. I enjoy my time outside in the sunshine. There's nothin' like the satisfaction of seeing a well-groomed yard."

Coop grinned. "I agree and from seeing Miss Clara's, you do fine work, Ralph. You didn't see anyone access the house through the backyard area?"

Ralph shook his head. "No, I'm sorry. It's usually very quiet there. The only time I ever saw anything out of the ordinary was when Miss Clara's granddaughter Luna was stayin' with her several months ago. She came in and out at all hours, sometimes not getting home until I was arriving in the morning to work there."

Coop quizzed him more about Luna and while Ralph didn't come right out and say it, from how he described Luna's behavior and her grandmother's dismay, Coop suspected Luna was a drug user.

"But you haven't seen Luna around the house recently?"

"No, not since the holidays."

"Does she live in the area?"

Ralph shrugged. "I don't know. Miss Clara is a private person. I don't know much about her family."

Coop gave him a business card and asked him to call if he remembered anything that might help.

Ralph petted Gus and thanked Coop for the tea before he sauntered out to his truck with a trailer behind it, laden with lawn equipment.

With a long sigh, Coop glanced down at Gus. "Let's go home."

∽

TUESDAY, after AB arrived at the office, Coop left Gus with her and drove over to Clara's. The security gate was closed, but as soon as he pushed the button, it opened, and he made his way to the house.

Anne met him at the door. "I'll get Miss Clara for you."

He held up his hand. "I actually came to speak with you. It will just take a few minutes."

The look of exasperation on her face did nothing to hide her displeasure. She led the way to the kitchen where she was in the midst of cleaning.

"Miss Clara said you've been working here for a number of years. I'm helping her with the hope of locating something that's gone missing from the house. Were you working here on Thursday when her book club came?"

Anne frowned and nodded. "Yes, I came to help get things set up for them, then returned Friday morning so I could do the dishes and clean up."

"Were you here when the ladies arrived?"

She shook her head. "No, sir. I left before anyone arrived."

"Do you remember any other visitors to the house when you were working since Thursday?"

"Only you, Mr. Harrington. Miss Clara doesn't get much in the way of company. Her kids and grandchildren came in December, but outside of that, her book club meeting is the biggest event of the year for her."

"What about her granddaughter Luna?"

Anne's eyes went wide. "Oh, she's a handful, that girl." She shook her head. "Miss Clara let her stay here several months ago, but I haven't seen her since right after Christmas."

Coop prodded her for more information, and Anne confirmed his suspicions that Luna had a drug problem. "Miss Clara doesn't talk about her, and I was here when Luna stormed out with her things and sped away. Miss Clara was distraught and weepy for several days but never explained anything more."

"Did you see anything out of place or out of the ordinary when you came in on Friday to clean up after the book club meeting?"

Her forehead wrinkled and a few moments later, Anne shook her head. "No, I don't recall anything. Miss Clara had a hair appointment, so I came early that morning to get everything done, and she left as I was leaving. It was just the normal dessert plates, cups, saucers, glasses. I took care of the dishes and wiped the patio table and furniture down, as well as vacuumed, mopped, and cleaned the bathrooms downstairs."

"Did you find anything left on the breakfast table or anything left behind from the ladies who attended?"

She shook her head. "No, I waxed the breakfast table. I don't think it was even used but made sure it was clean. I don't remember seeing anything on it and didn't find anything left behind."

Coop nodded. "Thanks, Anne. That's a big help. If Miss Clara is in, could I speak to her for a moment?"

Anne gestured to him to follow her and led him to the sunroom where he'd first met Miss Clara. "I'll go fetch her."

A few minutes later, Clara stepped into the room and rewarded Coop with a quick smile. She gestured for him to take a seat and settled onto the settee. "I didn't expect to hear from you so soon. Good news, I hope?"

With a shake of his head, he said, "Just a question." He took a breath before asking. "Can you tell me about your granddaughter Luna? I understand she stayed with you for a few months. Does she live in the area still?"

The slight lift of Clara's lips vanished, and sadness filled her eyes. "I honestly don't know. She left here at the end of December, and I haven't spoken to her since. I've tried, but she never takes my call or returns my messages."

Coop nodded. "I'm sorry to ask you this, but do you believe Luna might have an addiction problem?"

With a tear trickling down her cheek, Clara nodded. "I do. I tried my best to help her, not understanding at first. Luna had burned her bridges with my daughter, who I thought was being too harsh, so I offered to let her stay with me. I even bought her a car. Nothing fancy, but a nice, reliable car so she could get a job."

She took a sip from her cup of tea and sighed. "Luna was incorrigible, and I tried my best to get her into a rehabilitation program, but it's impossible to do with an adult. I talked to her until I became hoarse from it. At times, she acted normal and excited about going to a treatment center, but each time it came down to actually going, she had an excuse or would disappear. My son and his family and my daughter came for the holidays. It was lovely to see all of them, but Luna made things stressful. After Christmas, things got uglier, and I told her she had to leave. I'm just too old to cope with her antics."

"I'm so very sorry. Did Luna have a key to your house?"

Her eyes widened, and her hand, holding the tea cup, shook. "Oh, my. I don't think so, but I honestly don't know."

"I think it might be wise to get your locks changed on the house. We talked about changing the gate code, but I would add the locks, too. Just to eliminate any further issues."

With a slouch in her shoulders, Clara nodded. "I'll make sure it's done." With her hands still shaking, she wrote down Luna's full name and details, along with last phone number she had for her and handed it to Coop.

He thanked her and slipped the paper into his notebook. "I'll see myself out, and I'll be in touch if I learn anything."

18

With no word from Ben or his counterparts in the other counties on the search, when Coop arrived back at the office, he and AB dug into Luna Marie Mann. AB already called the security company and rattled their chain about the camera footage, but it had yet to arrive.

Luna's cell phone number was still active and with a bit of digging, they found a couple of addresses for her. Both were in areas with a much higher crime rate than where Clara lived. The car she mentioned was no longer registered to Luna.

Armed with a printout of Luna's driver's license photo, Coop wrote down the two addresses. "Gus and I will drive by and take a look at both places, then we'll pick up lunch. Be back in a bit."

As soon as Gus heard he was going somewhere, he leapt from his chair and rushed to the back door, eager for an adventure.

Their first stop was in Berry Hill, the closest of the two addresses. He pulled in front of a rundown apartment complex. He made sure Gus' leash was attached, and they made their way over the dead and dying bits of grass, strewn with abandoned paper and plastic wrappers. Coop scanned the apartment doors and found one with a faded manager sign on it at the back of the first level.

He knocked on the door, and a woman in a worn housecoat, a cigarette hanging out of her mouth, with smoke from it swirling about her, answered. "Yeah," she barked.

"Sorry to bother you, ma'am."

She looked down at Gus. "We ain't got no vacancies, and we don't take no dogs."

Coop nodded and produced his business card. "I'm not in the market. I'm a private investigator looking for Luna Mann. Could you tell me if she still lives here."

The woman glanced at the card and shook her head. "Nah, she wasn't here long. She came around the first of the year and left, oh, the end of February, I think."

"Do you know where she moved to?"

The woman took a long drag of her cigarette, then chuckled. "Don't know. Don't care."

"Do you remember if she worked anywhere, or do you have any paperwork from when she rented from you?"

"I don't remember her working. She was here, then just up and gone. I send all the old paperwork to the owner. He lives out of state."

Coop took out his pen, while Gus did his best sad eye impression in an effort to engage with Ms. Crabbypants. She wouldn't even look at him.

With his pen poised over the back of his business card, Coop asked if he could get the name and contact information to contact the owner.

She finished her cigarette and flicked it outside in the dirt along the worn concrete walkway. With an exaggerated huff, she turned and disappeared around the edge of the door. Moments later, she returned and handed Coop a card. "Here's his card. Good luck."

Coop didn't have time to thank her before the door slammed in his face. Gus looked up at him with a bewildered look on his face that matched Coop's. Coop patted his head. "It's okay, Gus. I'm not sure how she could resist your charming face, but clearly, she's not a dog person."

They hurried back to the Jeep, where Coop drove to Buena Vista Heights to a street near Rosa L. Parks Boulevard. The small lot held a tiny house, its shingles curled and siding deteriorated. Coop made a loop around the block and when he did, he noticed an even tinier building behind the house.

It couldn't be more than a few hundred square feet and in the same shape, or worse, than the house in front of it. His gut told him if Luna was living here, it was in the shack out back.

He parked and hurried to the front door of the house in front. After he knocked several times without a response, he climbed back behind the wheel of the Jeep and shrugged at Gus.

He called AB and asked her to research the owner of the property and let her know they were on their way to grab lunch. When he pulled in front of the deli, Kelsey, one of the servers who always made sure Gus got a treat, saw him through the door and rushed out with the order.

She handed Coop the bag with her signature smile, then went around to the passenger side and fed Gus a dog cookie. Coop thanked her, and Gus gave her a quick lick on the hand.

As they drove back to the office, Coop glanced over at his partner and grinned. "Glad to see you smiling again, Gus. We definitely need more Kelseys in the world and can skip the crabby, cigarette-smoking gals."

Gus tilted his head and winked.

Coop pulled behind the office and toted the bag into the kitchen, while Gus rushed to AB's desk, in need of comfort petting.

As they ate, AB filled him in on the property owner.

"Charles Freeman is his name. He's eight-two years old and has owned the property for decades. Current on his taxes, no liens."

"Maybe try to dig up a phone number on him, and I'll give him a call."

She finished the bite of her turkey melt and smiled. "Already done. I've got his landline number on my desk."

"I would be lost without you, AB. You're the GOAT."

She slipped Gus a bite of turkey, shook her head, and laughed as Coop cleared the table.

In the midst of wiping the table, he stopped and tilted his head at AB. "Are you up for some fieldwork?"

"Sure," she said with a grin.

"If Luna took the brooch, she won't admit it. I'm sure she didn't take it to wear. She most likely pawned it and would pick a place that didn't ask too many questions."

AB nodded. "Got it. I need to visit the less than scrupulous establishments."

"I'd go myself, but too many of the proprietors know me, and I want to see if we can find the brooch before they clam up and pretend they know nothing."

"I can handle that. I've got that list on the computer from the last time we had to visit the pawnshops."

"Just make sure to check in often. You're not going to be in the nicest neighborhoods."

"I will. I'll be careful, and I'm always packin' that Smith and Wesson you bought me."

He grinned. "Check in all the same and if you find it, let me know right away."

She winked at him and patted Gus on the head before collecting her purse and the list of pawnshops. "See you boys in a few."

Gus stood at the door and watched AB drive away, glancing up at Coop with his soulful eyes. "She'll be okay, buddy. Don't worry."

Once Coop caught up on emails from the morning, he put in a call to Charles Freeman. After several rings, he answered, and Coop introduced himself. "I'm sorry to bother you, but I'm looking for a young woman who goes by Luna Mann. Her grandmother hired me and from what I've found, I think she lives on your property."

With a shaky voice, Charles confirmed that he let Luna stay in the little shack behind his house. As Coop asked more questions, he learned that Charles met her at the local burger joint he frequents in the neighborhood. She works there on and off, and they got to chatting. He confirmed Luna didn't have a car and walked or used the bus.

"She was in a bad way. I think she and her family are on the outs. Lord knows that place isn't much, but at least she has a roof over her head. I don't charge her anything, and she comes and goes as she pleases," said Charles. "She's troubled but has a kind heart."

Coop scribbled more notes. "Thanks, Mr. Freeman. I appreciate the help. Please don't tell Luna I called. I don't want to spook her or make her leave the only safe place she has. I'll talk with her grandmother more and figure out the best way to approach her."

"I'll keep it to myself, Mr. Harrington. Hopefully, you can help Luna find her way back home."

Coop thanked him and disconnected. He sounded like a nice old guy, and he suspected Luna was taking advantage of his kindness.

He picked up his cell and opened the tracking application he and AB shared on their phones. It was a safety feature they used when working cases. While he checked her location, she texted to report no progress, and she was moving to a new neighborhood.

As he pondered the next steps, he checked the main email box for the video footage from Clara's security company. Not expecting it to be there when he saw the email, he sprang into action and downloaded the video to review.

He watched the screen and saw Ralph arrive early on Thursday morning, followed by Anne. They both left before Clara's guests arrived for her book club meeting. He grinned when he recognized Aunt Camille's arrival.

Once the ladies arrived, he sped up the footage and kept his eye on the camera at the gate in search of anyone else making their way onto the property. After the ladies left, nobody came by the gate camera.

It was getting close to quitting time, but Coop started on the footage from the other cameras on the property. One was positioned to detect motion at the front door of the house, and the other was in the backyard, covering the back gates and access through them.

As he tapped the mouse to view the front door footage, his phone chimed with a message.

AB reported she had a lead on the brooch. She was at Quick Bucks Pawn and Loan, which wasn't far from the Buena Vista Heights neighborhood where Luna lived. Coop read the whole message and learned AB would have to come back and talk to the manager tomorrow, since he was gone for the day. The guy behind the counter was sure they had what she was looking for, but it was locked in the safe, and he didn't have access.

She was on her way back to the office. Coop sent her a quick reply and went back to his screen.

By the time Gus hurried from his chair to greet AB at the back door, Coop's eyes were blurry and tired. He was still watching the front door footage from Thursday after the ladies left, but so far had nothing to report.

He doused the light and joined Gus and AB at her desk.

She finished reading an email and turned to Coop with a

smirk. "I feel like I need a shower after visiting those shops. Not the finest our city has to offer."

"Sorry about that, AB. I'll go with you tomorrow when you go back and wait in the car until you confirm the brooch, then join you. Buck Jensen, the owner, is as sleazy as they come."

She nodded. "That's a good plan. The guy behind the counter was creepy enough."

He pointed at her computer. "The video footage came in, so I got started on it. Let's call it a day, and we'll tackle the rest of it tomorrow."

With a happy smile, she gathered her purse. "You don't have to tell me twice. I've had enough field work for one day."

After he locked the back door, Coop glanced down at Gus. "I think we can squeeze in a walk at the park on our way home."

Gus' tail went into hyperdrive, and he rushed to the Jeep, more than ready for one of his favorite activities.

Coop opened the passenger door and let his partner in crime settle into the seat. The last week had been one of Coop's worst. Working on Alyssa's case and the heartbreaking discovery of her body had knocked them all for a loop. Gus, though, with his happy smile and his tongue hanging out could brighten the darkest of days.

19

Wednesday, as Coop and Gus arrived at the office, Coop's phone chimed. Once inside, he started his coffee brewing, then opened the text.

It was from Ben, assuring Coop he was working on the search project and hoped to have news by Friday. Detective Mitchell was helping as their case would be strengthened if they could link Stanton to another abduction. Coop tapped in his thanks and went about his morning routine.

By the time AB arrived, he'd drained the real coffee from his oversized mug and managed to spill some on his shirt that read SORRY I'M LATE. I DIDN'T WANT TO COME. Luckily, it was dark brown, and the coffee didn't even show. He ignored it and focused on finishing up the Thursday footage of the front door at Clara's.

AB poked her head in his office. "I'll start on the backyard. The pawnshop opens at nine, so we'll need to leave in about thirty minutes."

Coop nodded and stared at the screen, which was dark, since it was showing Thursday night's activity. Or lack thereof.

By the time they left, AB made it through Thursday's footage in the backyard, which showed nothing out of the ordinary, just Ralph doing yardwork early and Anne and Clara arranging things on the patio before the book club ladies arrived.

Like a true gentleman, Gus hopped into the backseat of the Jeep and let AB have his usual seat. Coop got them to Quick Bucks a few minutes before they opened and parked in the shade, a few spots away from the door and front windows so he wasn't visible from inside the shop.

AB pointed at her cell phone in the pocket of her purse. "I'll text you as soon as I see the brooch."

As soon as AB exited the Jeep, Gus bounded into the passenger seat, his head out the open window, watching after his favorite gal. Well, one of his favorite gals. Aunt Camille and AB were both at the top of his favorite list.

Ten minutes later, Coop's phone chimed, and he glanced at the text from AB. She had her eyes on the brooch. He adjusted his sunglasses and added a baseball cap.

He put Gus' leash on and guided him toward the door. He didn't look for any signage about dogs and didn't care. He walked past a wall of guitars and spotted AB at the counter toward the back of the store.

Coop and Gus joined her as she pointed at Coop. "This is my lawyer. As I explained to you, this is a family heirloom my daughter took from me. She's a drug addict, and we suspected she pawned it."

The man behind the counter, clad in a white button-down shirt that was no longer white, with a limp and frayed collar, its buttons straining from the force of his ample belly, chuckled. "Well, little lady, that's a good sob story. I don't know nothin' about all that, but if you want to buy it, the price is five thousand dollars." A shady smile stayed plastered between his shiny cheeks. Coop didn't want to know what he'd just eaten to leave such a mess.

Coop laughed and removed his sunglasses. "Well now, Buck, you and I both know you didn't give the young woman who pawned this five thousand dollars. We'll gladly pay you what you gave her, provided you have a written record of it, plus a very small administrative charge. If you're not amenable to that arrangement, we can just call the police and get them involved. I'm sure they'd be interested in taking a look at your records."

The sparkle went out of Buck's eyes, and his phony smile evaporated. He ran his shirt sleeve across his mouth and got rid of most of the shine on his cheeks. "Mr. Harrington, I didn't recognize you," Buck stammered as he took hold of the velvet box encasing the brooch.

He removed the lid from behind the velvet-lined box and fingered a piece of paper. Once it was freed from the box, he placed it on the glass counter, and the light from below illuminated the pawn receipt.

Coop leaned over and read it, noting Luna's name and the amount she'd received when she pawned it on Friday. One thousand dollars.

As Coop shook his head and glared at Buck, he removed eleven one-hundred-dollar bills from his wallet. "There you go, Buck. Ten percent for your trouble and you keeping it safe for four days. That seems fair."

Buck palmed the cash and pushed the velvet box toward AB. "Could you mark that paid with the amount we gave you and could we get a copy of that pawn receipt please?" she asked.

He added the amount to the receipt and signed it, then walked over to a small copier in the corner. Moments later, he returned and placed the copy on top of the velvet box. "There you go, ma'am." He glanced at Coop and added, "Sorry for the misunderstandin'."

AB slipped the box and receipt in her handbag and thanked him before turning for the door. Coop slipped his sunglasses back on and nodded at Buck. "Always a pleasure, Buck."

He led Gus behind AB, and they made their way to the Jeep. As Coop settled behind the wheel, AB turned to him. "Buck is a first-class jerk. I know you've dealt with him in the past, but I never met him. He's the definition of sleazeball."

"Yes, he is. The police have raided him several times. I think they're too busy with other crime to pay him much attention lately. If you're looking for stolen stuff, he's always a good bet."

AB sighed. "Well, I guess this proves Luna took it."

Coop nodded as he took the turn for Harding Place. "Yeah, I still want to comb through that footage and find out when and how she gained access. Then, I'll show Miss Clara when I take the brooch back. Just add the cost from the pawn receipt to her invoice."

"Will do. I'm sure she'll be pleased to have it back."

Coop let out a long breath. "It's a sad state. Her grandmother was willing to foot the bill for Luna to go to rehab. She could use this as leverage and get Luna into a program."

"Sometimes I wish I had kids. You know, the whole family life, white picket fence idea? My mom never misses a chance to remind me I'm not getting any younger and the clock is ticking and all that, but then these kinds of stories make me glad I don't have to worry about a kid. That would be heartbreaking."

"Your kids wouldn't be like that, I'm sure. You'd be a great mom." He smiled at her. "Trust me, I know what a loser mom is, and it's not you."

With a chuckle, AB grinned at him. "I can't argue with that point. Marlene is definitely not mother of the year material."

"That's an understatement."

He pulled into the parking lot behind the office and held AB's door for her. As soon as she was out of the Jeep, Gus bolted over the passenger seat and went out the door.

AB brewed them a cup of tea, and they settled in to review the rest of the footage before they wrapped up Clara's case.

Within moments of each other, Coop and AB hollered out that they found something on the Friday footage. Coop spotted Luna walking through the gate on Friday morning, after her grandmother left for her hair appointment and Anne and Ralph had come and gone. He continued to watch and spotted her again walking out about fifteen minutes after he saw her arrive.

AB found her on the front door camera, using a key to open it and go inside. She was in and out of the house within five minutes.

She was wearing a jacket, and they couldn't tell whether she had the brooch or not but printed off the frames of her using her key to open the door, so Coop could show them to Clara.

As Coop put together the photos in a folder, Gus rushed from his chair to the back door. Moments later, Aunt Camille's voice carried through the office. After several minutes, she, along with Gus, came down the hallway and peeked through Coop's open door.

"Oh, hello, Coop. Just me. AB's on the phone. I dropped off a platter of chicken salad sandwiches. I'm on my way to the ladies afternoon luncheon, and Mrs. Henderson made way too many, so I thought you and AB could enjoy them."

"That sounds great. I'm already hungry for lunch and was just thinking about what we could order. You saved the day."

She beamed at Coop. "I left you a container of chocolate chunk pecan cookies, too, and there are more at home." She winked and scurried out the door.

Coop struck out in the mom department but hit a homerun

in the aunt department. Aunt Camille was simply the best he could imagine.

After grabbing a cookie, Coop gathered his folder, changed his shirt without AB reminding him, and headed over to Clara's. The moment he arrived at the gate, it opened, and she met him at the door. "Morning, Miss Clara."

"Do come in." She led him to the sunroom where they met the first time and pointed at the tea service on the table. "Would you like a cup of tea or something else?"

"No, thank you." He patted the thick folder he held. "I got your brooch back this morning and wanted to get it to you."

She brought her hand to her heart and took the velvet box from his outstretched hand. As soon as she flipped the lid open, tears sprang to her eyes, and she smiled at Coop. "Oh, my. This means the world to me. Thank you so very much."

She removed it from the case and examined it carefully. "It looks none the worse for wear." She closed the case and held it to her chest. "Now, tell me how you found it."

Coop cleared his throat and removed the photos from the folder. "Your granddaughter Luna came to the house when you were out on Friday. She pawned the brooch at a pawnshop. My associate and I visited there this morning and bought it back."

The cup she held quivered in her shaking hands. She set it down on the table and stared at Coop. "When you asked if Luna had a key, I worried it was her."

"I found out where she's staying. It's nothing more than a shack behind a small house. An older man took pity on her when he met her at a local burger joint and let her stay there free. He was worried about her."

Clara used a napkin to dab at the tears on her cheeks. "Luna can be charming." She shook her head. "Hopefully, she doesn't steal from him. She tends to take advantage of kindness."

"From the looks of things, Mr. Freeman doesn't have much.

He gives her a roof over her head but admitted it isn't much. He says she comes and goes, and he doesn't see much of her."

With a heavy sigh, Clara nodded. "That sounds like Luna."

Coop slipped another piece of paper from the file and pushed it over to Clara. "This is her address. She no longer has the car. It was sold soon after she left here. We confirmed Luna works at Burger Alley, part-time. We didn't approach her, as I didn't want to spook her."

After she read the paper, Clara lifted her eyes to meet Coop's. "How much did she get for the brooch?"

"A thousand dollars. I paid eleven hundred to get it back."

She shook her head and stared at the photos of her granddaughter. "I have a locksmith coming later today to change the locks. You were right to suggest that."

"If you decide you want to talk with Luna about the brooch or anything else, I'm happy to host both of you at my office. Sometimes, it's easier with a third party there."

"That's very kind of you, Coop. I'll give that some thought. Something has to change, or Luna will end up in more trouble. Or worse." Her voice faded.

"You may be able to use the stolen brooch for leverage. I know you've tried to get her into rehab before, but if you threaten to contact the police, she could be facing felony theft charges. It might be a way to force the issue, and the court could mandate drug rehab."

Clara tilted her head at his suggestion. "That's not a bad idea. I'm going to call my daughter tonight and discuss it." She stood and said, "Let me get you a check."

Coop held up his hand. "We'll send you an invoice."

She led the way to the front entry and extended her hand. "I truly appreciate your help, Coop. I'm going to put that brooch away right now and with my locks getting changed, and my gate entry changed, I feel safer already." She paused and added, "I'll definitely be in touch if I decide to try with Luna again. I think you're right about a third party and stressing the seriousness of her latest poor choice."

"My door is always open for you, Miss Clara." He shook her hand and wished her a nice day.

Families, no matter what they looked like on the outside, were often filled with strife, dysfunction, and utter sadness. He wished Miss Clara luck with hers.

20

Thursday, with nothing pressing to distract him, Coop outfitted the Jeep with his backpack, water, chicken salad sandwiches, and cookies, plus some dog treats for Gus. When AB arrived, Coop announced he and Gus were driving over to Rutherford County to take a look at the area he wanted to search. AB looked up from her desk and gave him a quizzical look. "Are you sure you want to do that?"

"I'm tired of waiting. I've been studying the map of the region each night. I just want to take a look and see if I can narrow down the area. Get a feel for the place. You know?"

He glanced over at Gus, who was on his back, lounging on the couch in the reception area. "Besides, Gus deserves a long walk and loves to explore new areas. We can take a sniffari, and he can enjoy smelling everything."

"Well, be sure to check in so I know you guys are okay."

"Will do, AB. It's only an hour away. We'll be back before closing time."

After a quick stop at the Donut Hole for road snacks, which went well with his t-shirt boasting EXERCISE? I THOUGHT YOU SAID EXTRA FRIES, Coop set out on the highway with

Gus relishing the breeze from the passenger window. It was a gorgeous sunny day and if it weren't such a grim task, Coop's heart would be lighter.

Coop had the map of the region memorized. He took the exit onto a smaller road that would lead him deeper into the uninhabited area covered with trees and narrow dirt roads.

Stanton's girlfriend mentioned crossing a creek, and Coop homed in on the route he suspected they'd taken. Coop surmised Stanton wouldn't have taken her too far from the road, but that was only an educated guess.

He navigated to the first dirt road that Stanton would have crossed after the creek and slowed his speed, taking in the terrain. As he drove, he kept an eye out for anything that looked out of place.

He drove for about two miles before the road narrowed and became overgrown with underbrush. There were no tire ruts beyond where the Jeep sat, idling with Gus giving him an expectant look. Coop turned off the ignition and climbed from behind the wheel. Once he had his backpack attached, he opened the passenger door, and Gus leapt from the seat.

Before they set out to explore, Coop sent AB a text with his coordinates and let her know they were going to take a hike.

They backtracked along the dirt road, flanked by tall oak and maple trees, providing a canopy of shade. Gus sniffed at every tree and bush, and Coop kept his eyes peeled for any disruption in the soil or a worn pathway.

After an hour of walking and looking, Coop spotted a large rock and sat on it while he drank from a bottle of water. After he drank half of it, he poured the rest into a travel bowl for Gus, who slurped it up until the bowl was empty.

Coop gave Gus a treat and munched on one of Aunt Camille's cookies while he contemplated his next move. After consulting the map on his phone, Coop sighed and led the way back to the Jeep. He turned around and headed back to the main road. From there, he kept driving until he came to another dirt road and spotted fresh tire tracks on it.

He followed it, over rough spots, and parked at a clearing where a huge log sat alongside the road. He raised his brows and turned to Gus. "Looks promising. The girlfriend mentioned they sat on a log."

Gus raised his brows.

Coop slipped the backpack on and let Gus out. They hiked around the area, Gus sniffed, and Coop hunted for any anomaly on the ground.

As he moved deeper into the thick oak trees, Coop realized how vast the search area was and how big of an operation was needed. He wished Stanton's girlfriend had been more precise with the location.

Coop called for Gus, who was several yards away, and headed back to the log where the Jeep was parked. He sent AB another text to let her know they hadn't found anything and where they were. They had another water break, and Coop ate a sandwich while Gus stared him down. He shared the last bites of chicken with his drooling dog.

After their lunch break, they drove back to the main road, and Coop set out for the next dirt road shown on the map. Before he got there, he noticed a narrow road and pulled onto it. He stopped and checked his map again. It didn't show this road, which looked to be less used than the others they'd explored.

He steered the Jeep over the rutted road, which in some spots didn't resemble much of a road, being covered in brush and blackberry vines. After a mile, Coop pulled the Jeep to the side where there was a narrow clearing and another thick log, suitable for sitting.

He gathered his backpack and led Gus to the log, where they each gave it a thorough examination. He with his eyes, and Gus with his nose. Coop didn't spot any recent tracks around it or in the clearing. He and Gus set out for the trees across from the clearing and began the tedious task of searching the ground.

The air was quiet and peaceful, except for a few chirps from the birds dashing from branch to branch in the thick trees. The sun was muted by the canopy of trees, the slight breeze fluttering the branches of the giant cedars and tall pines wicked the sweat at the back of Coop's neck.

After an hour of walking, sometimes through thick vines and brush, Coop's spirits sank. He didn't see anything that resembled a makeshift grave. He turned to look for Gus and didn't see him. He whistled and called his name, as he began a slow walk back toward the Jeep.

He kept calling for Gus as he walked and minutes later, Coop spotted his fluffy tail, then smiled when he noticed the top of his beloved dog's head above a bush. "Come on, Gus. Let's go."

Coop stopped and waited and moments later, Gus rushed toward him. When he reached him, he set something at Coop's feet. "What are you up to, Gus?"

As Coop squatted down to look at Gus' treasure, he gasped. He stared at what looked like a human hand, or at least what was left of one. He resisted the urge to touch it and turned to look at Gus, who was watching him, his tongue out and proud smile on his face.

"Good boy, Gus. Now, where did you find this?"

Coop wanted to check out where Gus had been exploring, but first, he had to protect the remains. He didn't want to touch the hand and compromise it further. He reached for Gus' leash he'd clipped to his backpack and attached it to his collar. Then, he pulled out his cell phone and sighed with relief at the sight of two bars in the upper part of the screen. He hoped it was enough.

He scrolled to Ben and tapped his name.

The call didn't connect, and he tried again.

After several rings, Ben answered, "Hey, Coop."

"Ben, I'm out in Rutherford County with Gus. We decided to do some hiking in that area I wanted to search for Elizabeth. Gus just found a human hand. It's mostly skeletal and not all there. Can you send someone out here right now to collect it?"

"Oh, man, Coop. Let me make some calls. I'll get right back to you. Don't disturb anything further. Text me your GPS coordinates and wait there."

"Got it. Thanks, Ben."

Coop stood by the hand, and Gus, tethered by his leash, sat behind him while they waited. The desire to head over to where he'd seen Gus and look was hard to ignore, but the last thing Coop wanted to do was compromise the scene. He was already pushing his luck even being out here.

The important task was to find Elizabeth and bring her family some sense of closure and bring Stanton to justice.

A few minutes later, Ben called. "Rutherford County is enroute. Did you find a gravesite?"

"No, I was searching the area, and Gus was off exploring. When I called him, he dropped the hand next to my boot."

"They're rolling the medical examiner, a supervising detective, and a crime scene team from Murfreesboro. Should be there in less than thirty minutes. My contact there is Captain Martin. He's over the detectives. He's requested a cadaver dog."

"We'll be here. Thanks, Ben."

Coop disconnected and glanced down at Gus. "You're being usurped by a professional cadaver dog."

Gus tilted his head and stared at Coop.

"I know. It's not fair. You did a good job. You're an excellent sniffer dog."

Gus' tail swung back and forth in an arc.

True to Ben's estimate, twenty minutes later, Gus barked, and the sound of a vehicle perked Coop's ears. A man's voice echoed through the trees. "Rutherford County Sheriff's Department looking for Mr. Cooper Harrington."

Coop shouted out and did his best to guide them to where he was waiting. A few minutes later, a man and woman emerged from the trees. Coop smiled. "You must be Captain Martin."

The tall man with gray hair and a serious look on his face nodded. "Yes, and this is Detective Wright. She's assigned to cold cases."

"Nice to meet you both and thanks for coming."

The man continued to stare at the remains at Coop's feet. "We were organizing a search. Had a plan to start tomorrow or Monday at the latest."

Coop braced for the tongue-lashing he expected.

Captain Martin moved his head to look behind Coop at Gus and smiled. "Good-looking dog you've got there. He's obviously got a good nose."

"Gus is a curious guy, but thankfully, he has a soft mouth, and his nature to retrieve is strong. He even found an injured bird once and brought it to my aunt who nursed it back to health."

Detective Wright joined her boss in studying the remains. She took several photographs and placed a ruler next to it and took a few more. With gloved hands, she carefully placed the remains in an evidence bag and wrote on a label, which she affixed to it.

Captain Martin stood and said, "Where was Gus when he made the find?"

Coop moved and pointed at the area several yards away. "I wasn't with him, but he was in that general area. I saw his tail after I called him a couple of times, and his head was just above that tallest bush there."

"Okay, we're going to secure the area and start a search. Chances are, we won't finish before dark. I know from talking to Chief Mason you have a vested interest in this case. Ben says nothing but good things about you, so I'll give you a pass on your zealousness today. As soon as we know more, I'll make sure you're updated, but after you sign a statement about today, you need to vacate."

Coop shook his hand. "I appreciate that. Honestly, I didn't expect to find much of anything. I just wanted to have a look for myself. After finding Alyssa and working with Detective Mitchell, I'm convinced Stanton has done this before and suspected he used this area as a burial site."

Captain Martin nodded. "After talking to Mitchell this last week and working on coordinating a search here, I have to agree with you." He lowered his voice. "In all honesty, you saved us countless hours narrowing it down to this area. It still won't be quick, since oftentimes animals carry remains far from the actual dump site, but it gives us a place to start."

He motioned back to the road where Coop's Jeep was parked. "I'll walk you back and get you to sign a statement now."

He turned toward Detective Wright, who was assessing the perimeter and stringing police tape between trees. "Be back in a few, Darlene."

She nodded and continued her examination.

It didn't take Coop long to write out his brief statement. He had the coordinates of the other areas he'd searched and provided those in the report. After he signed it, he thanked Captain Martin, left him with his business card, and slid behind the wheel of the Jeep where Gus was waiting for him.

Once back on the main road, he put in a call to AB. "Hey, we're on our way back now. Gus found the remains of a hand at our last search area, so Rutherford County is here now and immersed in the search."

"Wow. Good job, Gus."

Coop grinned as his passenger's ears perked at the sound of

AB's voice. "Yes, he's a very good boy. At least they're looking at the area now." Coop eyed the bit of brush stuck in Gus' tail. "I need to give him a good brushing out from our searching escapades."

"He loves pampering, so I'm sure he'll enjoy it. I'll be gone when you get back. I'll see you in the morning."

"Sounds good, AB. I'm anxious to see what Ben might know at breakfast tomorrow."

"That would be great if he had some news by then, but realistically, I don't think they'll know much by morning."

"Yeah, it's going to take time to get their equipment in place. They're bringing in a cadaver dog."

"Here's hoping they'll work the weekend."

"See you in the morning, AB." He disconnected and focused on the road, his thoughts with Elizabeth's family. If he was right about the burial site, they were about to endure the second part of their nightmare.

21

Friday morning, Coop woke after a restful night's sleep. All the hiking and fresh air must have done him good. That and the fact there was progress being made let him rest easier than he had all week.

After a shower, he slipped into one of his favorite shirts, lettered with SORRY, I CAN'T. I HAVE PLANS WITH MY DOG.

His loyal friend, who he'd spent hours with last night, brushing and making sure he was free from any stickers and twigs, was already gone from his sleeping chair and no doubt looking for more of the roast beef he'd been rewarded with after their grooming session. Coop slipped his phone into his pocket and went in search of Gus.

He found him hovering over his food bowl, patiently waiting for breakfast. Coop obliged, and Gus inhaled it before they set off for Peg's and their weekly outing with Ben.

Coop and Gus settled into their corner spot on the outdoor patio, and Myrtle filled his coffee while they waited for Ben. The breakfast special was a strawberry French toast platter and after perusing the menu he knew by heart, he made up his mind to indulge in the special and order one to go for AB, who was a fan of anything strawberry.

As Coop gazed at one of the specials go by, piled high with whipped cream, Ben slid into the chair across from him. Moments later, Myrtle arrived and filled his cup. With her pencil poised over her pad, she arched her brows. "What'll it be today, boys?"

"I'll take the special and one to go for AB."

Ben took a long sip from his cup and said, "Make it one more for me. Sounds good."

Myrtle recorded their choices of scrambled eggs and bacon and splashed a bit more of the hot elixir in their cups before she set off for the kitchen.

Ben reached down and gave Gus a pet before meeting Coop's intense look. "I was late because I was talking to Captain Martin. They didn't get far yesterday but have a whole team enroute this morning, with the cadaver dog, and looking to borrow a ground-penetrating radar from the archeology department at one of the universities."

Coop nodded. "Good news. I'm hoping they'll be able to recover DNA from that hand."

Ben shrugged. "Always hard to know with decomposition, but I'm hopeful. From what you described, it sounds like they should. They've got it at the lab now and are working it, but no word yet."

"Does Detective Mitchell know about the find?"

With a nod, Ben swallowed another sip of coffee. "Yeah, he's excited about it. Told me to pass on his thanks. You definitely got the ball rolling."

Myrtle arrived with their huge breakfast platters and a plain burger patty for her favorite furry customer.

As they ate, they talked more, and Ben mentioned how thankful Alyssa's mom was for the anonymous offer to get her daughter back home for a funeral. "Be sure to let Aunt

Camille know how much it meant to her. She was truly touched."

"She'll be glad to know she helped her in some way. That case really got to her... and me."

In the middle of their meal, Ben's phone rang. After a few seconds of listening, he said, "I'll be right there. Give me five minutes."

Coop shook his head. "It's a sad day when a guy can't even enjoy breakfast."

Ben hurried to eat the rest of his eggs and a few more bites of the strawberry-covered French toast. "You're telling me. We've been way too busy lately. Not in a good way, either."

He guzzled down the rest of his coffee and reached for his wallet.

Coop shook his head. "It's on me. I owe you big time for keeping me out of hot water with Captain Mitchell."

Ben stood and smiled. "You're right. You do. Initially, he wasn't very happy but came around when I explained how much you work with our department and the stellar work you did for Roane County."

Myrtle came by and frowned. "Leavin' already?"

"Work calls," said Ben. "See you next week."

He left with a quick wave and jogged toward the sidewalk.

"That man works too hard," said Myrtle, refilling Coop's cup and handing him the check along with AB's takeout container.

"He's definitely one of the best. We're lucky to have him on the job."

"Have a good day, Coop. See ya next week."

Coop finished his coffee and left cash on the table before he led Gus to the Jeep. He set AB's breakfast on the floor of the passenger seat, and Gus' nose went into overdrive, sniffing at it.

When they arrived, Gus hurried to AB's desk, where he settled in for his share of her breakfast. Gus was also a big fan of strawberries and never turned down an opportunity for a lick of whipped cream. Coop wandered to his office and dug into his emails.

AROUND MID-MORNING, Gus woke from his first nap of the day and rushed from his chair in Coop's office to the reception area. A few minutes later, AB came through Coop's door. "Miss Clara is here and would like a few minutes."

Coop glanced down at his shirt and shrugged. "Sure, send her in."

AB kept Gus with her and offered to bring in beverages, but Miss Clara declined. "I'm on my way to the hairdresser. I just have a few minutes but thank you."

Coop stood and welcomed her to the chair in front of his desk. "What can I do for you, Miss Clara?"

She plucked an envelope from her purse. "I received your invoice in the mail yesterday afternoon and just wanted to bring this by." She smiled and handed it to him. "Your price was much too low, so I added a bit to it."

"That wasn't necessary but thank you," he said, taking the envelope from her.

"I've also given some thought to your offer of serving as a mediator for me and Luna. I think I'd like to take you up on that."

"That's great news. I'm happy to help."

Clara sighed and nodded. "I'm hoping with your help, she might be convinced. I talked with my daughter, and she agrees that your idea has merit. I fear Luna's running out of chances before something very bad happens. She won't take my calls, so I'm hoping you might be able to set up a meeting here at your office."

Coop assured her they would think of something.

Miss Clara stood and said, "I'm very flexible all next week, so whatever time works for Luna, I can be here. I have nothing scheduled I can't cancel."

With a nod, Coop walked her to the door.

As she reached for the handle, she turned and added, "Of course, I'll pay you for your time. I should have made that clear before."

"Not to worry. We'll figure it out when the time comes. We'll be in touch as soon as we have something set up."

"Thank you, Coop. I truly appreciate this."

She waved goodbye to AB and made her way to the sidewalk, where her shiny Cadillac waited.

Coop watched as she pulled away, then sauntered over to the couch to join Gus. He leaned back and locked his hands behind his head. "I just promised Miss Clara we'd get Luna to come in for a meeting so I could play mediator at an intervention."

AB wrinkled her nose. "Oh, boy. That might be harder than you think."

"Yeah, I know. I made the offer, so now I need to make good on it." He thought for a few minutes. "We could ask her to come in to discuss her grandmother's will. Luna needs money, so that might spark her interest."

AB shrugged. "It wouldn't be a total lie, I guess. That might be another carrot and stick situation where Miss Clara could promise her a bequeathment provided she completes a program."

Coop's eyes widened. "I like how you think, AB. I thought Clara might want to threaten her with the police for stealing the brooch. Of course, that wouldn't entice her to a meeting but might have to be used to prompt action."

"I can call Luna and try to set something up." AB pulled up the calendar on her computer.

"Early next week, just in case they make progress on the search, and we know more about Elizabeth."

She nodded and pointed at Monday. "We could do it Monday. It's pretty open."

"I'll leave it in your hands. You'll have better luck with the granddaughter than I would." He stood and took a few steps. "Oh, she paid us, too. I'll grab the check. From what she said, she padded the payment."

He returned with the envelope and found Gus curled into the spot Coop had vacated on the couch, looking quite pleased with himself. Coop grinned at his goofy dog and slid his finger under the flap of the envelope.

Coop's eyes widened when he saw the amount of the check. He handed it to AB.

She gazed at it and grinned. "Wow! A five-thousand-dollar tip. I'd say that was more than padding."

"That should more than cover a meeting with her and Luna."

"I'd say so." AB stuck it in the drawer where she kept the deposit slips. "I'll get in touch with Luna today and see where we stand."

Coop wandered to the kitchen and filled his cup with decaf. He sighed as he spotted the time on the clock. It wasn't even noon yet. Time was crawling like a snail through a puddle of honey. Waiting for word on the search for Elizabeth weighed on him.

He could only imagine how her parents felt. He wasn't sure how they survived this long but assumed it was due to a tiny thread of hope. He feared that thread was about to be snipped, and they would be left with nothing but horrific and unbearable loss.

As he walked by AB's desk, she handed him a stack of background check requests from one of their corporate clients. "These just arrived, and you need something to do."

He grinned. AB knew him like the back of her hand.

He trudged to his desk and got to work, keeping himself occupied as he searched the records of prospective employees.

Between working on files, he and AB polished off the rest of the chicken salad sandwiches at lunch and in the late afternoon, AB came through the door, smiling.

"I got in touch with Luna and set up a meeting here on Monday at eleven o'clock. She thinks she's coming to go over her grandmother's will and, like we suspected, seems eager. Clara will be here early so we can discuss a gameplan with her."

They celebrated with one of Aunt Camille's cookies, and Coop carried the two remaining ones into his office to enjoy with a cup of tea.

At four thirty, Coop had had enough. He closed the file he was working on, gestured to Gus, and turned off his lights. "Gus and I are calling it a day. Feel free to leave early yourself, AB. It's been a long week."

She grinned as she went about closing the windows she had opened on her desktop. "I agree, and I'll be right behind you."

As soon as Coop pulled into the driveway of Aunt Camille's house, his phone rang. He noticed Ben's name and hurried to press the green button.

"Hey, Coop. Just got word from Rutherford County. They found a grave, but it's not Elizabeth."

22

Coop was speechless. After a few beats, he asked, "So, who is it?"

"They just have a preliminary match at this point, so not for publication. They matched jewelry and an old injury to a young woman from Coffee County. She's been missing for over two years. The hand Gus found belongs to her."

"Oh my gosh. That's not what I expected."

"It's a shock for sure. I just wanted you to know. They're continuing the search. If I hear more, I'll call you."

"Thanks, Ben."

Coop disconnected and led Gus into the house. The dog hurried to the kitchen, where the aroma of dinner cooking filled the air.

Still processing Ben's news, Coop opted to head to his home office. As soon as he stepped into his wing of the house, the fresh smell of the citrus cleaner Mrs. Henderson used greeted him. She'd worked her magic and tidied his space today.

He slipped behind his desk and pulled up the file on the missing persons from Tennessee he and AB had researched. He found the suspected victim. A twenty-two-year-old named Brittany Wells. Like so many of the others, she'd gone out jogging on Labor Day weekend and was never seen again. Her car was found but no clues as to what happened to her.

As Coop gazed at her smiling photo, his stomach knotted. Like Alyssa and Elizabeth, she was pretty, with a friendly smile. The thought of what they'd all endured made Coop's stomach clench, along with his jaw.

He pulled up Stanton's historical cell phone data and scanned it for that time period. There was nothing showing on the data to indicate he was at the grave location. His phone placed him at home that weekend and with it being a holiday, he was already off work for Labor Day.

He and AB looked for inactive periods with his phone off, but this time, if it was Stanton, he left his phone at home and had used the holiday weekend instead of leave from work.

The only other possibility was two such killers, and both of them liked the uninhabited area where the latest body was discovered. The chance of that reality seemed slim.

Coop's shoulders slumped. He berated himself for the sloppy error in not looking for times where Stanton's phone was stationary at his house for an extended period of time. He sent Anne an email to see if she could run another report on the GPS data and search for consecutive days where Stanton's phone was on but idle at his house.

With it being Friday, he didn't expect a response until next week, but moments after he sent it, he received an out of office autoreply. Anne would be out until the following week.

He hated to share the sad news about the remains with AB but promised he'd let her know. He tapped her name in his contact list, and she answered after the first ring.

"What's up, Coop?"

"I just heard from Ben. It's not public knowledge, but they located the remains that go with the hand Gus found. It's not Elizabeth."

She gasped. "You're kidding. We missed a victim?"

He explained about the phone data and let her know he asked Anne for another report, but she was out of the office. "I just wanted you to know. They're going to continue the search of the area."

"Keep me posted, Coop. I hope they find Elizabeth."

"Me too."

He disconnected and wandered into the dining room where his dad was adding a bowl of fruit to the table. Charlie looked up at him. "You look beat, son."

"It's been a day. A week. I just got word that the hand Gus found on our hike belongs to another missing girl. It wasn't Elizabeth."

Charlie's face fell. "That's horrible. I can't imagine the poor parents."

Coop lowered his voice. "Let's not tell Camille. This is all too much."

Charlie gave a quick nod and went about pouring tea in their glasses.

Aunt Camille came from the kitchen with a platter of pulled pork sandwiches. The three of them settled into their chairs and after a long sip of sweet tea, Aunt Camille turned to Coop. "You look exhausted, dear. I think we need a distraction from all this sad work you've been doing."

She winked at Charlie before she gazed over at her nephew. "Charlie and I stopped by the senior center for bingo today. Enid let us know her grandson and his band are playing tomorrow night at The Bluebird Café. She had tickets, and we snagged four of them. What do you think about joining us and inviting AB?"

Coop couldn't resist the twinkle in her eye, and he needed a night off from work and worrying. "I think that sounds like an excellent idea." A night at The Bluebird would soothe his tired soul.

Listening to his dad and aunt banter back and forth about bingo and the possible cheaters at one table made Coop smile. His heart was filled with joy. He wasn't sure how he would handle his dad going back to Nevada. His presence and the ability to spend time with him was a treat. Coop pushed the sadness he felt creeping over him to the back of his mind.

As he chuckled, listening to the two people he loved most in the world, he couldn't help but think of Alyssa's mom, Elizabeth's parents, and now Brittany's family, who would soon learn the horrific news of their daughter's death.

Family.

It was the root of so much happiness and love but could be complicated and messy and often filled with sadness and regret, but the absence of it was beyond tragic.

AFTER A FUN EVENING of dinner out and listening to Enid's grandson sing at The Bluebird, and the weekend almost over, Coop carried a tray laden with plates of fresh peach pie, topped with vanilla ice cream to the sitting room.

It was Sunday evening and time for one of his aunt's new favorite shows about a group of ladies who were determined to solve several murders in a quaint English village. He had to admit, it was a great show, and he and his dad enjoyed watching it with her.

Camille tapped her pen on her notepad. "So, we're all set for Florida. I'm so glad we can squeeze in a vacation there before Charlie goes back to Nevada. You and AB deserve some time away from the office, too."

Gus, wedged between Camille and Charlie, flicked his tail across Charlie's lap as he gazed at Camille, his pink tongue sticking out, and his lips raised in a smile. Coop laughed and said, "I think Gus agrees. He seems to know he's going on a road trip."

Coop's fork hovered over his next bite of pie. "Did you find a pet friendly hotel for us to stay in Georgia?"

With a tilt of her head, Camille grinned. "I made an executive decision and booked a charter flight for us. That way, poor Gus won't have to be cooped up in a car for two days."

Coop shook his head. "You're something else, Aunt Camille."

Charlie pointed at his knee. "She also didn't want your poor old dad's knee to be stuck in a car. I assured her I could manage, but you know how she is."

Camille smiled and stuck her fork into her slice of pie. "I told Charlie, I've got more money than I'll ever spend, and I'm not taking it with me, so I want to spend it making wonderful memories with my family." She sighed. "I'm so glad Jack can come out, even though it will just be him. It will be wonderful to see him."

Coop nodded. Past experience dictated arguing with his aunt was futile. "The flight sounds great and yes, it will be great to visit with Jack. Not only will we get to see him, but Dad won't have to fly alone, and I don't have to go. He'll have a capable wingman with him."

As he finished off the last spoonful of ice cream, Charlie grinned. "I'm so lucky to have two such wonderful sons who look after me. Not to mention, a sister-in-law, who makes sure I'm well fed and entertained. As much as I'm excited to get home and see the grandkids and spend some time with Jack and Molly and my friends, I'm already counting the days until I'm back here. My second home, I guess."

Camille smiled. "I'm so pleased to hear you say that. Yes, of course, I want you to think of this as your second home. You're welcome to stay as long as you want, whenever you want. It's been a boost to my spirits to have you here, Charlie. I miss John so much and love having Coop and Gus here, but you've filled my days with laughter and companionship. I treasure our time together."

Charlie reached across Gus' back and gripped her hand in his. "I'm very thankful for you, too. Not only have you been there for Coop since he started college, you've been a steady force in his life and provided the nurturing and love his mother couldn't for all those years, but you've also introduced me to a life outside the house. I'm grateful for your spunk, Camille. I tend to be a loner, so you inspire me."

Despite the beam of her smile, Camille used her hankie to dab at her eyes. "You boys know how to make a gal cry." After another bite of pie, she added, "When it comes to Coop, I've always thought of him as my own. So did John. He's always been the apple of our eyes. I can't imagine my life here without him. I'm very lucky he's still here and willing to put up with his old aunt."

She paused and petted the top of Gus' head. "He and this guy give me a reason to keep going. I love nothing more than being involved and part of his life, along with AB and Ben, and all their cases. It helps keep my mind sharp." She grinned and tapped her temple. "They've been my saving grace since losing John."

Coop's throat tightened. "Right back at you, Aunt Camille. Gus and I love you very much, and I don't say it enough, but I appreciate you more than you'll ever know."

Thank goodness the show they were waiting for filled the screen, and Coop was saved from blubbering further.

23

On Monday morning, Coop and Gus were in the office, with Coop finishing off the last few sips of the real coffee in his cup, when AB arrived.

Over her cup of tea, AB chatted with him, while she massaged Gus' ears. She was excited about the invite to join them in Florida before Charlie left to go home for the rest of the summer. "I can't wait to go but feel a little guilty for intruding on your family time. Especially with your brother coming. I wouldn't mind staying here to man the office while you enjoy a family vacation."

Coop wrinkled his forehead. "Nonsense. You must know we consider you part of the family. We wouldn't dream of leaving you behind." Coop took a sip from his cup. "Not to mention you work harder than anyone and deserve some time away at the beach."

AB blushed. "I appreciate that, Coop. I think of all of you as family, too. I'm going to miss Charlie when he goes back to Nevada. He's a sweetheart."

"It's not going to be the same without him."

"Aunt Camille has to be dreading it. She's blossomed with him here and their outings."

Coop chuckled. "He had no idea what he was in for. She's a social butterfly, and he's more of a homebody."

"Well, I'll sure miss him. Thank you again for including me on the trip."

"One thing you can do is make sure we're all caught up and employ that answering service we used to use. I'd really like to avoid taking any calls or working while we're there. I want to focus on Dad and Jack."

"Sure thing." AB rose and cradled her cup in her hands. "Miss Clara will be here an hour before Luna."

Coop nodded. "I'll be ready for her."

He followed her gaze to his shirt lettered with I'M NOT ARGUING, JUST EXPLAINING WHY I'M RIGHT. He nodded. "I know, I'll change before she comes. Promise."

AB WELCOMED Miss Clara when she arrived and led her back to Coop's office, where she settled her at the conference table before delivering a tray with tea and cookies. Gus remained on his leather chair, perched with his eyes fixed on the group at the table, poised to join them at the first hint of an invitation.

After a bit of small talk, AB explained Luna was coming to the meeting to discuss Clara's will. Coop outlined his proposed approach. As she took sips from her cup, Miss Clara nodded at his ideas.

She set her cup on the saucer. "As my will stands now, my son and daughter inherit the bulk of everything. I've named a couple of charities, but the children split the estate equally, and they in turn can provide something for their children or not. I didn't elect to name every grandchild in the will and thought it best to just leave that to my son and daughter to decide."

Coop nodded. "That makes perfect sense and is what most of my clients elect to do."

Miss Clara's forehead creased. "The suggestion you made about bequeathing something to Luna contingent upon her completion of a rehabilitation program and her staying clean, is an interesting one, but it would necessitate I bequeath my other grandchildren an equal amount. I try very hard to treat them equally, and I've already given Luna more than the others due to her problems."

"It's an easy change to make in your will and something we could do quickly. The other approach, of course, is to use the threat of turning her into the police for theft, which would be a felony theft charge and could very well result in jail time for her."

Miss Clara nodded. "The hard way or the easy way. Part of me thinks she needs to go to jail. She needs something big to wake her up before her entire life is a shambles. She's brought so much pain to my daughter." Her eyes welled with tears.

After another sip of tea, she sat up straighter in her chair. "As harsh as this may sound to you, let's start with the stick. Luna has had every carrot her mother and I could offer, and she squandered them all. I think she needs a shock. Something to jolt her to her senses."

Coop tapped his pen on his notepad. After all the escapades with his mother, Coop, more than anyone, understood being at the end of one's rope and the need for a strong shove into reality. "I can definitely present that and be the bad guy, so you don't have to be a party to it. If you would rather not be here, we can talk to Luna on our own and convey her options."

A slow tear fell from Miss Clara's eye. "That might be better. I tend to fold like a cheap tent when she lays on her woe-is-me attitude. This last Christmas, when I kicked her out, was the hardest thing I've ever done. She was beyond surprised, and I was hopeful it might wake her up, but even that didn't work."

"Okay, I'll take it from here and give you a call when the meeting is over."

Miss Clara rose from her seat. "Thank you, Coop." She glanced over to AB. "You too, AB. I hope neither of you judge me too harshly. As much as I would love the gentler option to work, I fear it won't, and we'll be back here in a few weeks anyway, so we might as well start with the biggest hammer."

AB rose and offered to walk Miss Clara to her car. She led the way out of Coop's office, with Coop following them. "We'll be in touch this afternoon and let you know where things stand."

"I appreciate that. Thank you again for all your help," said Miss Clara, as she let AB guide her outside.

While AB was outside with their client, Coop paced the reception area, rehearsing how he would approach Luna, who was due in less than twenty minutes. AB had researched the top in-patient treatment centers in the area and found three that were good candidates and had available space to take a new patient.

With Clara prepared to foot the bill, which was substantial, the only thing standing in the way was Luna.

AB returned and tidied the conference table, removing the used cups and tray and readying a new one in anticipation of Luna's arrival. Coop went back to his office to check his email while they waited.

At eleven fifteen, he wandered to AB's desk. "Still no sign of her?"

AB shook her head. "I left her a voicemail to remind her but haven't heard back."

Coop sighed. "Let's give her until noon and if she's a no-show, I'll call Miss Clara and let her know. If that's the case, I have a feeling we'll be talking to Ben about charges."

With a sad look, AB nodded. "Yeah, I think Grandma is done with her lies and crushed by Luna stealing from her.

That's such a violation and not something you expect from family."

Coop's jaw tightened. "The addiction, whether it be drugs, alcohol, gambling, whatever, really is the only thing that matters to addicts. It drives their whole life and destroys everything else. It's heartbreaking and wreaks havoc on everyone else."

Coop refilled his coffee and made his way back to his office.

At ten minutes to noon, the bell on the front door chimed and moments later, AB led Luna into his office.

Coop took in the young woman's thin frame, her stringy hair, and the almost wild look in her sunken eyes. With a frantic glance, she met Coop's stare. "I'm so sorry I'm late. I missed the bus and had to wait."

"It's fine. Come on in and have a seat. Would you like tea, coffee, sweet tea?"

"Sweet tea, please."

AB promised to be back with it and hurried down the hall.

Coop gestured to the conference table. "Have a seat, please."

Luna turned and smiled at Gus. "What a beautiful dog."

Gus thumped his tail across the leather chair.

"That's Gus. He's my office partner."

AB returned with the tray and set it on the table before handing Luna her glass and taking a seat next to her and closest to the office door.

Coop let Luna take a long swallow from her glass. "Luna, we've been working with your grandmother Clara."

"About her will?" Luna's eyes brightened as she posed the question.

"That and other things." Coop pulled a thick file folder toward him. "Your grandmother had a valuable brooch go missing from her home recently."

He pulled a photo of the brooch from the file and positioned it in front of Luna. "Do you know anything about that?"

Luna's eyes widened, and her leg bounced. "No." She shook her head back and forth.

"Clara hired us to find out who took it."

Luna stared at the photo and wouldn't meet Coop's eyes.

"The good news is we found the thief."

Luna bolted from her chair, but AB was quick and rolled hers to block the office door. Luna turned back to Coop.

"Sit back down, Luna. Your grandmother has asked us to discuss the situation with you."

The young woman plopped back in the chair and crossed her arms in front of her, while she glared at AB, then Coop.

Coop pulled a photo from the security camera showing Luna entering her grandmother's home and with the help of Buck from the pawnshop, showed her another photo from his security footage with a clear shot of her placing the brooch on his counter.

At the sight of the evidence, Luna turned on the tears. AB reached for the box of tissues and slid it closer to her.

"With the value of the brooch, you're looking at felony theft. Jail time." Coop's stern voice and direct manner elicited a new round of sobs from Luna.

"Your grandmother shared that she's encouraged you to seek treatment in the past, but you've never had success. She has a proposition for you. Rather than involve the police and have you arrested for theft, you can agree to an inpatient drug treatment center. Provided you successfully complete the program and stay in it for as long as the doctors deem necessary, she won't pursue criminal charges. If you don't agree or fail the program, you'll be arrested and face jail time."

In the midst of her sobs, Luna gasped. "She can't do that."

Coop raised his brows at her. "Yes, she can do that. You, of course, don't have to accept the offer. If you want to decline, I'll contact the police right now. My best friend from college is the Nashville Chief of Detectives. You'll be arrested, and I doubt you'll be bailed out. So, you'll await trial in jail and have a public defender, who will try to cut some type of deal for you. That deal will involve court-mandated drug treatment. If you fail there, you'll go to jail."

Luna used a tissue to swipe at her nose. "So, it's like I don't have any choice at all. This is like blackmail."

AB cleared her throat. "You exercised your choices when you rejected your grandmother's offers to help you, when you sold the car she gave you, and most recently, when you chose to steal from her. The brooch is worth forty thousand dollars. That's a serious felony. Sadly, the time for choices is over. You've used them all up."

Coop added, "Your grandmother could have just pursued the criminal charges and not given you any options, but more than anything, she loves you and wants to see you healthy, with a promising future. This is your last chance, Luna. Take the gift she's giving you and commit yourself to a better future where you've got lots of options and aren't living in a shack and working part-time at a burger joint. Your grandmother wants more for you."

After an hour, switching between consoling and admonishing Luna, Coop and AB had her signature on the dotted line where Luna agreed to enter an inpatient treatment program. She chose from the three her grandmother approved of, and AB offered to drive her to the facility.

Coop promised they would retrieve her personal items from where she'd been staying and deliver them to her.

While Luna was distracted petting Gus, who always enjoyed stepping into a therapy dog role, Coop whispered to AB, "I can go with you if you want. I don't want you to have to handle her on your own."

AB shook her head. "We'll be fine. I'll take her and get her something to eat, then drive her over. I think she's resolved herself to it. In fact, I think she might be relieved."

Coop glanced over at the young woman, smiling at Gus. "Maybe. I hope she succeeds. For her sake and Clara's."

After AB made a call to the treatment center, she and Luna left, and Coop stood with Gus at the back door and watched as they exited the parking lot. Coop glanced down at his faithful friend. "I hope this works, Gus."

They stayed at the door for a few minutes before Coop led the way back to his office. He blew out a breath and picked up the phone to inform Miss Clara.

24

After an emotional afternoon of getting Luna admitted and helping Miss Clara with the financial paperwork, on Tuesday, Coop elected to take Gus for a morning walk before work.

The strain he witnessed in working with Clara and the attitude of her granddaughter reminded him of his mother. It was a depressing topic that Coop did his best to avoid. Yesterday, it weighed heavy on his mind and lingered even after an evening of rest.

The beautiful blooms on the trees and the flowers that lined the walkway at Gus' favorite park, near Aunt Camille's, lifted Coop's spirits. Gus' tail wagged happily while they walked, and Coop let him sniff at everything he desired.

It was hard not to smile when walking next to a happy golden retriever.

Gus was also a chick magnet. Without fail, he attracted the interest of women of all ages, who stopped and asked to pet him or talk to him. Gus relished the attention and even winked at Coop, while one attractive woman petted him. She even chuckled at Coop's shirt lettered with YOU ARE ABOUT TO EXCEED THE LIMITATIONS OF MY MEDICATION.

By the time they finished their walk, Coop chuckled, and the burden from yesterday's case was forgotten, or at least shelved to a recess of his mind.

AB was at her desk when they arrived, and Coop couldn't sneak in another cup of caffeinated coffee. He filled his cup with the decaf she'd thoughtfully brewed and stopped to chat with her.

"Any word on Elizabeth or Brittany?"

She shook her head. "Nothing yet." She pointed at some papers on her desk. "Anne came through for us. She said she was off but saw your message and ran another report. I just printed the new report you requested on Stanton's phone."

Coop raised his brows. "Good news. I'll take a look at it right now."

He left Gus with AB and wandered to his office. After a quick look at his email, Coop perused the history of Stanton's phone.

As he made a list to compare to missing persons, his phone chimed. He hit the green button to connect with Ben.

"Hey, Coop. Just talked to Rutherford County. They've confirmed the identity on the hand and are analyzing Brittany's remains, hoping to find some link to Stanton. She was also shot, so they have that bullet, and it's a nine-millimeter, which is a good link. At the same time, they have a team in the field continuing to search the area for Elizabeth or others."

"What do you think the chances are on finding his DNA?"

"Hard to say. They might get lucky, but with remains that have been disturbed, it can be difficult. They know it's important and are taking their time to do it right."

"I really hope they find a link. I would like nothing more than to see that smirk wiped off his face if we can tie him to others."

"You and everyone across four counties are working on these."

"Thanks for the update. I'll try to be patient." Coop thanked him and disconnected.

He went back to combing through the dates of the missing persons from Tennessee and comparing them with the new report on Stanton's cell phone.

CLOSE TO FIVE O'CLOCK, Coop leaned back in his chair. His neck was sore from pouring over the tedious records. As he thought more about Stanton's habits and phone activity, he dug out the file on the Nevada cases and put in a call to Detective Sanford.

Outside of the Tennessee cases, those two were the most recent, and the authorities in Nevada might still be able to access GPS cell phone records.

After a couple of rings, he answered, "Sanford."

"This is Cooper Harrington calling from Nashville. We spoke a couple of weeks ago about your missing persons cases from 2019 and 2020."

"Of course, I remember. I received a quick update from Deputy Bennett. He sent me an email with the pertinent information on the suspect they arrested."

"I'm convinced this guy has done this before. I suspect numerous times. I've been putting in some extra time searching an area here for other victims and, with the help of my dog, ran across some remains. They're working on them now, but it looks like another missing young woman. One that wasn't on our radar."

"Interesting," said Sanford.

Coop explained about the cell phone data and what they'd learned about Stanton and his behaviors of visiting the dump site to ready it and leaving his phone at home or turning it off during the actual abduction periods.

"I understand why you like him for our cases. He's clearly not an amateur."

"Exactly. I just wanted to pass that along in case you can access his phone records from when he lived there. The number he's using now is one that he got when he moved here in 2021, so it's not the same one he was using when he lived in Nevada. I thought there was a chance that information might help you with your two cases or at least give you a place to start. The window is closing on how long you can get that data from the carriers."

"Good idea. We all hate these cold cases we can't solve. They leave the families with so many questions."

They chatted for a few more minutes, and Sanford promised to dig into the phone records, see what he could come up with, and take it from there. "Appreciate the tip, Mr. Harrington. I'll keep you posted if we make any progress."

"Sounds good. I hope it helps."

Coop looked at the two names he'd written on his pad and circled them. Two young women missing in 2021. Denise and Nancy. Both were blondes in their twenties. Their disappearance coincided with Stanton's phone being stationary at his residence.

Next, he would have to research where Stanton had been in the weeks leading up to their disappearances. He hoped there was a link that would lead to their discovery.

COOP HAD JUST FINISHED dinner and helped Aunt Camille tote a cake to her car, when his cell chimed with a call from Ben. With Camille off to one of her club meetings, he and his dad were on kitchen cleanup duty. He pointed at his phone and excused himself. Chuckling, he answered it, "Ben, you saved me from kitchen duty. What's up?"

"I just got word from Rutherford County. They found the remains of another body near the area you and Gus searched. It was at the end of another unmarked dirt road. They're in the process of recovery but suspect it could be Elizabeth."

The hair on Coop's arm stood on end. "Well, as bad as that sounds, it's good news."

"Yeah, it's horrific, but at least two families now will know where their daughters are instead of wondering. I'll never get used to telling parents such sad news. Anyway, keep it under your hat until you hear more, but I just wanted to pass it along."

"Thanks, Ben. I appreciate it. Talk to you soon." He disconnected and wandered back to the kitchen in time to dry some dishes, at least.

Charlie handed him a baking pan, freshly rinsed. "Bad news?" he asked, his eyes fixed on his son.

"Yes and no. Ben said they found another body where Gus and I were searching. Sounds like it could be Elizabeth."

"Well, at least you know you were on the right track. Good on you for lighting a fire under them."

Coop shrugged and put the pan in a cabinet. "Yeah, hopefully they really found her. I'm not sure how the officers who work these cases all the time deal with it. It's depressing."

"This Stanton guy really got under your skin, huh?"

With a nod, Coop reached for another pan. "It's not just the brutality of his crimes, but his total lack of remorse. He's pure evil. Killing for sport and fun. I want answers for the families of his victims." Coop finished the last pan. "I want justice."

"You've always been a seeker of justice and someone who stands for those who can't fight for themselves. That's admirable. Just don't let your quest overshadow all the happiness in your life. I remember having these same conversations with John. Especially when he had a case involving children. You remind me so much of him."

Coop noticed the tears in his dad's eyes.

"Uncle John was a great man, so I'll take that as a compliment. I miss him and his stories. His humor. Just his presence."

"I regret not visiting him enough. We talked often on the phone, but I should have made the effort to come here and see him much more. Time slips by so fast."

Coop put a hand on his dad's shoulder. "That's why I'm so glad you're here and coming back soon. I've missed seeing you and, like you, I regret not making the time to come back home more often. I think for me, it's the memories and all it stirs up with Mom."

Charlie's eyes widened. "Oh, believe me, I understand that. Your mother threw a grenade into our lives, and I'm not sure any of us will ever fully recover."

"She's the gift that keeps on giving."

With his arm wrapped around his dad, Coop laughed with Charlie. Coop squeezed his dad's shoulder and said, "You know Aunt Camille made two cakes and left one for us for dessert."

"She's a true gem. I tell you, Coop, I'm going to be lost without the two of you and Gus."

OVER THE NEXT FEW DAYS, Coop and AB stayed busy with their regular casework. All of this cold case work Coop was consumed with wasn't paying any bills and like his dad mentioned, obsessing over it wasn't healthy.

On Thursday afternoon, Coop found himself caught up and turned his attention to the folder he'd started on the two possible cases that could be linked to Stanton's phone being stationary at his house during their abduction periods.

Both were from Knox County. At the time they went missing, Stanton worked for Tennessee Valley Zinc, and they had operations outside of Knoxville and in neighboring Jefferson County. Coop found the number for Joe, who had helped them at the shuttered mine site.

He answered, and Coop glanced at his notepad. "Joe, hey, it's Cooper Harrington. You might remember me from the mine site where you helped us locate the missing young woman."

"Oh, yes. I'll never forget that. Just horrible."

"Well, I need your help again. I've been looking at some cold cases and have homed in on a couple of missing young women from Knox County. These are from 2021. Stanton was working for your company then at the sites you operate in East Tennessee."

"That's right. We've got two operational mines. One in Knox, then another just over the line in Jefferson."

"I'm working to create a timeline surrounding the abductions and wanted to send you some GPS coordinates to see if you could help me narrow down any areas that might be plausible for Stanton to have used as a burial site. I don't think he would chance using a working site, but I thought you'd know the area better than anyone and might be able to narrow my focus from the places I've gathered. Maybe even have records of where Stanton was working around the time in question."

"Of course, I'd be happy to help in any way possible. I'm just sick about this whole mess. Send me what you have, and I'll dig into it to see what I can do. I'll check his work schedule for that time period, too. It might be helpful."

Coop thanked him and promised to send him the coordinates and dates by the end of the day.

Soon after AB left for the day, Coop finished up his email to Joe, after distilling the information into a spreadsheet with dates and GPS coordinates. From the research he'd done, Coop suspected Stanton's work kept him moving between Jefferson City and the outskirts of Knoxville. Both of the mines were located off of Highway 11, and there were lots of coordinates to check.

Once he hit send, he and Gus headed for home and the dinner that was sure to be awaiting them.

25

On Friday morning, Coop and Gus found Ben waiting for them on the patio at Peg's Pancakes. Ben shook his head when he read Coop's shirt lettered with I MAY BE WRONG, BUT I DOUBT IT. Coop slid into his chair and after a few pets from Ben, Gus took his appointed position in the corner, atop the cool concrete.

Myrtle arrived with a full pot of fresh coffee and filled their cups. Coop couldn't resist the pecan and bacon waffles with maple butter, and Ben went with an omelet. Myrtle scribbled their order on her pad. "I'll be back with your food in a jiffy, boys." Myrtle left them with a smile as she dashed to the door.

"So," Coop said, his brows raised. "Any news on Elizabeth's remains?"

Ben shook his head. "Nothing official. Everyone is almost certain it's her, but they're still running all the trace evidence at the lab. Same with Brittany's. There's so much to sift through, and cold cases aren't exactly at the top of the list."

"I get it. I'm following a new lead on two more cold cases here in Tennessee." He went on to explain his thoughts about linking Stanton to the two cases from 2021.

Ben's eyebrows arched. "That's some excellent detective reasoning, Coop."

"I give credit to Anne for her ability to gain access to and sort the GPS records from the phone carrier. Without her, it would be beyond tedious."

Myrtle arrived with their orders and left them with refills of their coffees. Coop ordered AB's breakfast and dug into his waffle. He closed his eyes as he savored the first bite. "This is perfection."

"Well, it has bacon in it, so that's a no-brainer." Ben chuckled as he speared a bite of his omelet.

"Back to the two cold cases, I know it's a long shot. The chance of figuring out where they could be won't be easy."

"Well, it's more of a lead than anybody has had on the cases for several years. As much as we all want to close out cold cases, nobody has the time to dedicate to them. We even have a couple of detectives assigned to cold cases, but we often have to pull them to help on a current case. By the way, nothing popped up on our review of Nashville missing persons cases. Along with our lack of resources, there's the wait at the lab. The analysis is usually complex, and they won't prioritize a cold case unless somebody at the top gets a call from someone who matters."

Coop shook his head. "I remember reading about legislation and funding to try to clear the backlog of old sexual assault test kits. I couldn't believe how many thousands hadn't even been analyzed or added to the database."

"It's a sad testament to the state of things when our crime rates are overwhelming the lab resources. Nobody has money for more. Budgeting woes are never ending."

They continued to eat while Gus enjoyed the beef patty Myrtle delivered when she passed by their table. She never forgot him and insisted on treating him from her tip money.

Coop took a long swallow from his cup and sighed. "As hard as these cold cases are to stomach, I can't seem to let go of them. I'm going to squeeze in as much preliminary work as I can on them, between my paying cases, and if I can narrow down an area where we might find the two women, I'll let you know. Knoxville won't be excited to listen to some private detective with a wild hypothesis."

Ben chuckled. "If you've got something solid, I'm happy to contact them. You've proven yourself many times, Coop. I would never doubt your instincts. You were right about Elizabeth and ended up with another case they'll be able to close."

Coop nodded as he sipped the warm coffee laced with sugar. "I even called the detective in Nevada and told him about the cell phone data and Stanton's MO of leaving his phone behind or off. This guy belongs in prison forever, or worse. He's a true danger to society."

As Coop sipped his coffee, he frowned.

"I can see your wheels turning in there," said Ben.

"When you said nothing popped up to tie Stanton to any cases in Nashville, it makes sense. I think he purposely hunts in rural areas where he's less likely to be caught on camera or a traffic cam. He stays away from cities with more coverage. He lived in more rural areas in those other states, too."

Ben nodded. "That's a good theory. So far, everything you've found points to rural, out-of-the-way places."

"All with smaller police departments, less likely to be able to mount the resources necessary." He finished off his coffee and glanced down at Gus. "Ready to go?"

Ben swiped the ticket Myrtle left and smiled. "My treat. You and AB deserve it for all the effort you put in to find Elizabeth."

After he left some cash on the table, Ben followed Coop and Gus to the sidewalk, where Coop's Jeep was parked. "Are we still on for the game tomorrow night?"

Coop nodded. "Yep. Dad is very excited. We'll see you before the game for dinner."

Ben scratched Gus' ears. "You'll have to get Coop to take you on a Tuesday when they allow dogs to come to the park."

Gus answered with a low bark.

Coop smiled and laughed while he waved goodbye to Ben.

As Coop was getting ready to head home Friday night, Ben called. "Hey, Ben. What's up?"

"Good news. I just talked to the guys in Rutherford County. The lab matched a hair that was caught in Brittany's necklace. They were able to get DNA from it and match it to Stanton."

"Oh my gosh. That's excellent." Coop couldn't contain a smile at the thought of Stanton getting the news.

"I thought that would make your weekend. Nothing more on Elizabeth's remains, but I'll let you know when I hear anything. I'll see you tomorrow."

"Looking forward to it. Thanks, Ben."

With a spring in his step, Coop led Gus to the Jeep. They stopped at the park on the way home and while Coop's heart broke for Brittany's parents, he was relieved she'd been found and even happier that they'd discovered a definitive link to Stanton. He deserved all the punishment the State of Tennessee could muster.

Although Tennessee had a death penalty law on the books, executions had been put on hold per the governor, and reinstatement was awaiting a revision to the lethal injection protocol from the lawyers and the governor's office. Stanton was a definite candidate for it if there ever was one.

When Coop walked through the door, he found Aunt Camille adding a platter of cheeseburgers to the table. She winked at him. "Charlie insisted on grilling tonight."

A juicy burger with all the fixings, plus an easy conversation with Aunt Camille and his dad was the perfect way to wind down the week and kickoff the weekend. The brownie sundae for dessert didn't hurt either.

On Saturday, after lunch, Coop found his dad sipping sweet tea and wearing his new Nashville Sounds t-shirt. His nonstop grin broadcasted his love for the game. He was like a kid on Christmas morning, waiting to head downtown.

After a glass of tea, Coop turned to Charlie. "Want to go for a quick walk with us?"

"Sure thing." He swallowed the last sip of tea, and they slipped into their shoes while Gus waited patiently at the front door.

As they followed the sidewalk through the neighborhood, Coop set the slow pace, mindful of his dad's knee, which while improved, would never be perfect. "When is the last time you and Jack went to an Ace's game in Reno?"

"Last year," said Charlie. "We always make a point of going and taking the kids. They have several special events set up for youngsters each season. It gets a little crazy, but it's always fun. I hate driving in downtown Reno, or I'd go more often."

"Traffic is always an issue. I'm used to it around here, but gamedays are always busy. Hopefully, we can park close to the stadium, so you don't have to walk too far."

Charlie chuckled and patted his leg. "I've been walking extra this week to prepare. I'll be fine."

"I just need to finish up my notes on those cold cases from the Knoxville area. We'll head down around three o'clock, so we have plenty of time to meet up with Ben and eat before the game."

"Sounds great, Coop. I appreciate you taking me."

"Of course and thank Ben; he's the one with the fancy tickets. We've been talking about a guys' night of baseball for months, so I'm just glad we could squeeze it in before you leave for home."

"Speaking of that, I've actually been giving Camille's idea of moving here permanently some thought. I never imagined I'd ever leave, but Jack and Molly are pretty busy with work and the kids, so I don't see them as much as I could. The kids are getting older too, so they have their own lives. Most of the time, I putter around the house and occasionally meet up with some friends for coffee or a meal, but compared to here, my days are pretty dull."

"Wow, Dad, that would be awesome. I'd love it if you were here full-time, but I can't offer the lure of grandkids."

Charlie chuckled. "You might want to give that some thought, Coop. You aren't getting any younger."

Coop raised his brows. "I'm not sure that's in the cards for me, Dad. I don't have the best luck with women."

"Well, I'm no expert. Look at your mother." Charlie laughed, then quieted. "Seriously, though. I'm sure your mom's behavior has impacted your desire to marry and start a family. She's not a great role model."

Coop nodded as they turned the corner to head back to Aunt Camille's. "Subconsciously, I suspect that's part of it. Most of the women I've dated aren't marriage material. I've given up and focused more on work."

"You have an excellent work ethic, but I just want to make sure you have a full life. Someday, I'll be gone, as will your aunt. Trust me, being on your own, especially when you're older, isn't much fun."

With a sigh, Coop glanced at his dad. "I don't even like to think about that. I can't imagine losing you or Aunt Camille. The future isn't something I often contemplate. I might be more like Gus than I realize and live in the moment. He's taught me that, since for way too long, I was stuck in the past."

Charlie reached out to squeeze Coop's shoulder. "I've been there, son. Like you say, I spent way too many years reliving the horrors and regrets. I think that's what I've enjoyed most about being here with you and Camille. There are no bad memories. Everything is new here. It's an adventure."

As he slipped an arm around Charlie's shoulder, Coop grinned. "I would suggest you not mention you moving here until you know it's going to happen. Aunt Camille will be so excited and have a moving truck arranged for you before you know it. She'll also be way disappointed if it doesn't happen. You need to talk to Jack and figure things out back in Nevada before you even give her a hint."

Charlie chuckled. "Yeah, I figured I'd keep it on the down low until I talk to Jack. I hate to sell my house in case I get here and decide I want to move back." He sighed. "I might be too old for such a bold move. It's a little overwhelming."

"You won't need to worry about doing much. AB will pitch in and when she and Aunt Camille join forces, there's nothing those two can't do."

As Gus led the way to the front door, Charlie laughed. "You're right about that. Back to our original conversation about your future and the idea of finding the right person to make a life with, sometimes that person is right under your nose."

Coop tilted his head and stared at his dad.

Before he could ask him more, the front door opened, and Camille waved at them. "There y'all are." She petted Gus. "We're going to have to find something fun to do tonight, Gus. Maybe we'll find some mischief to get into."

∽

AFTER FEASTING on the best barbecue food in Nashville with Ben, and an epic game, with the Sounds winning, the three of them hurried to the street level, with the hope of getting out of the area before the traffic became unbearable.

As they walked toward the parking garage, two men came from the shadows, both wearing dark hooded sweatshirts. They targeted Charlie, who was several steps ahead of Ben and Coop and told him to hand over his wallet, or they'd kill him.

Ben and Coop sprang into action and tackled both of the thieves. Coop took the taller of the two, who hadn't said anything, but was helping the mouthy one to box Charlie between them. Coop used his leg to sweep across the tall guy's calves and knocked him to the ground, while Coop twisted and pinned his arm behind him. "You messed with the wrong guy tonight," he yelled.

While he was doing that, Ben announced he was the police, and he pulled his gun while he told the mouthy one to drop his weapon. The sound of a knife hitting the sidewalk made Coop flinch. He noticed his dad standing frozen, his eyes wide.

"It's okay, Dad. We've got it under control."

Ben, who always carried handcuffs and his weapon, even off-duty, had the smaller guy cuffed in no time. While the guy lay prone on the ground, Ben used his cell phone. As he slid the phone back into his pocket, he glanced over at Coop. "Patrol units are on the way to pick these two up. You okay?"

Coop nodded. "Yeah. If you can sit on this one, I want to check on Dad."

Ben relieved Coop from restraining the taller of the two men, and Coop hurried over to his dad, who was leaning against the edge of a building. "Hey, Dad. You okay?"

Charlie nodded, "I'm fine. Just a little shook up." His quivering voice confirmed that fact.

A small crowd had gathered by the time the patrol vehicle came to the curb, lights flashing, and two officers hurried to

Ben. Coop pointed at them. "I'm going to let Ben know we're going to head home."

Two more officers arrived before Coop walked over to Ben. Ben pointed at one of them and said, "Officer Keller, please escort Mr. Harrington and his dad back to his vehicle in the parking garage."

Coop nodded his thanks. "If you need a statement, let me know."

"Will do. I'll stop by later."

As the officer approached Charlie, Coop noticed his muscular arms stretched the limits of the sleeve of his shirt. He placed a gentle hand on Charlie's shoulder. "Are you okay, sir? Do you need any medical assistance?"

He shook his head. "No, I'm fine. Thanks to my son and Ben, of course. They took the brunt of it."

Coop waved off the officer's concern. "I'm fine, too. We just want to get home."

"I'll walk you both to the parking garage, or I can give you a ride, if you prefer."

"I'm fine to drive." He glanced at his dad who was still pale. "We'd appreciate the escort though."

With Charlie between the two of them, Coop led the way to the garage, and they made their way to the Jeep. As they walked, Officer Keller kept his eyes focused on their surroundings. "I'm truly sorry you were attacked tonight. We've been dealing with these young adult and juvenile offenders lately. They step up their activities when it's crowded like after a game. Usually, it's on the other side of the stadium."

"Luckily, we had Ben with us."

Officer Keller chuckled. "Yes, he's one of the best and a great chief."

Coop pointed at his Jeep. "This is us. Thanks again."

Officer Keller waited until Coop backed out of his spot, before waving and walking toward the exit.

As Coop made his way out of the traffic and to the highway, Charlie remained quiet. Once Coop merged and got up to speed, he glanced over at his dad. "You doing okay?"

"Yeah, just feeling old and useless. I don't know what I would have done if you and Ben hadn't been there tonight."

"When you're outnumbered like that, and they have a weapon, you give them your money. Typically, they take it and run. Don't ever risk your life for money."

He sighed. "Yes, that makes good sense. I just hate feeling so vulnerable. I need to rethink the idea of living here."

"Just remember, Camille has lived here forever and hasn't had a problem. Granted, she doesn't go downtown much, and Belle Meade is one of the safest places you could live. Truly, you have everything you need right there, and you've been all over with Aunt Camille and never had a problem, right?"

"That's true. I'm just rattled, I guess."

"You have to do what you think is best, but don't let tonight dictate your plans. Like any big city, Nashville has its share of crime and lawbreakers. You mentioned you don't go to downtown Reno anymore, and I suspect that safety factor is one reason, as is traffic. I wouldn't want you heading downtown on your own here, either."

"Yes, I mostly stick to Carson. It's still a small town, even though we've also seen an increase in crime."

"Have you ever felt unsafe before tonight?"

Charlie shook his head. "No, and I agree I don't see myself venturing downtown on my own."

"Bottom line, I want you to be happy, Dad. Whether that's here with us or back in Nevada with Jack. Whatever you decide will be fine with me. You can go back to your original plan of spending half the year here and half back home. Don't get stressed worrying over it."

Charlie reached over and patted Coop's arm. "Thanks,

Coop. After that dustup, it's not the best time to make the decision. I'll keep an open mind."

Coop exited the highway and turned onto West End Avenue. "I remember when I was worried about stuff, you'd always say, things will look better in the morning. You need a good night's rest."

Charlie chuckled. "I think you're right. Wise words."

"From a wise man," said Coop, smiling at his dad.

26

After a quiet Sunday, except for Ben coming by to collect their statements about the incident on Saturday night, which led to Aunt Camille fussing over Charlie the rest of the day, Coop and Gus were up early on Monday and ready for the work week.

The bonus of their altercation on Saturday night was a batch of Aunt Camille's chocolate chunk pecan cookies. She deemed them comfort cookies, and Coop was relieved to see his dad back to his usual jovial self, eating cookies and watching their Sunday series last night.

He put the platter of cookies Camille sent with him on the kitchen table and went about brewing a pot of real coffee. He had plenty of time to drink a couple of cups before AB arrived.

He chuckled as he stirred sugar into his first cup. Yesterday, just in case Coop hadn't caught on to his dad's hint at the perfect woman being right under his nose, Charlie mentioned what a great gal AB was. He went on to say she seemed like family and what a shame it was she was still single. He and Camille poured it on pretty heavily, and Coop suspected they had colluded but couldn't deny their observations.

He'd always had a special bond with AB, but he'd never given any serious thought to them being an actual couple. Like a romantic couple. He couldn't deny he loved spending his days with AB at the office and enjoyed her company away from work. The last thing Coop wanted to do was ruin his decades-long friendship with AB. He couldn't imagine not having her in his life and with his track record, he wasn't willing to risk such a fanciful idea.

Even if he did think she was the most perfect woman he knew.

Coop pushed the idea to the back of his mind and settled into his chair. He scrolled through his emails and stopped when he saw a reply from Joe. He apologized for not getting back to him sooner and included some ideas relative to Stanton's work area and sites he may have chosen to bury another victim.

Coop opened his file and brought up a map of Tennessee on his screen. The background report showed Stanton living in a trailer outside of Trentville in 2021, when the two women went missing. Stanton lived there until he was assigned work near Gordonsville and moved to the place where he lived with Christine.

Joe confirmed that most of the GPS data surrounding the weeks in question made sense with regard to Stanton's work assignments that took him along Highway 11 that connected the mining sites within twenty miles of each other. It also made sense that he would travel to Jefferson City or Knoxville for supplies.

As Coop continued reading, he discovered Joe flagged several of the GPS sites that could be suspect. He noted a few of them could be legitimate as there was an equipment repair place they utilized in New Market and various businesses Stanton would have had a reason to visit but highlighted a handful that didn't make any business sense.

All of them were remote locations near campgrounds or parks in the area or off the beaten path. When Coop consulted the map, several of them were in wooded areas, covered in thick trees, like the one he and Gus searched where they'd found two bodies.

Coop highlighted those coordinates on his list. It wasn't much to go on, other than a strong hunch and like Ben said, an excellent track record. He glanced over at Gus, perched on his leather chair, and contemplated a road trip. It would take almost four hours to drive to Jefferson City. That was a really long day.

It was after eight o'clock when he realized AB hadn't arrived. Coop pulled up the office calendar where AB always recorded any of her appointments and shook his head. It was Memorial Day.

His mind was so focused on these cold cases, he'd forgotten all about the holiday. He definitely didn't want to be searching around campgrounds and parks on a holiday. He'd have to do the best he could with online maps and see if he could narrow the search areas.

As he reviewed the maps online, Coop focused on the areas near Douglas Lake and Panther Creek. He zoomed in as much as the maps would allow to look for access to the wooded land that would be out of the view of other campers and hikers. He didn't know much about either area but doubted Stanton would risk taking a victim to an area close to public grounds or chance someone seeing him.

He suspected Stanton would pick an area more like where he and Gus discovered the remains. They hadn't seen anyone in all the hours they spent there.

As the hours ticked by, Coop's frustration grew. He needed to look at the potential areas in person. The details he searched for couldn't be found online.

With reluctance, he picked up his phone and texted Ben.

As he scoured an area near New Market, his phone rang. He smiled at Ben's name on the screen. "Hey, Ben. Sorry to bug you on a holiday."

"No problem. I'm just sitting here, enjoying the backyard. What's up?"

"I've been working on those two missing girls from Knoxville. I've got a list of a few places Stanton visited while working out there, that don't make sense for his work. Joe helped me out and reviewed them for me, since he's familiar with the mines and where Stanton's work would take him."

"Sounds like more great detective work."

"I've exhausted the capabilities of looking at online maps to try to determine if any of these could be possible burial sites. I'm convinced Stanton is involved based on his phone records and the fact that he left his phone in his trailer during the abduction periods. That's his MO. Either he turns the phone off or leaves it stationary so it can't be tracked."

Coop paused and took a deep breath. "I really need to see the area in person and wondered how you'd feel about a quick road trip this week to take a look with me. I don't think I'm going to get very far giving them my list and asking them to look. They won't have time and who knows when they'll get to it."

"So, you're talking Jefferson County, right?"

"Right. All the areas in question are in Jefferson."

"I know the sheriff there. Bob Holt. He's a good guy."

They chatted more, and Ben suggested they set out and find a motel for the night, then spend all day Tuesday searching the areas Coop had on his list. He offered to call Sheriff Holt in the morning, as a courtesy to let him know what they were doing.

If they found something promising, they'd be more apt to get cooperation from his department.

Relieved that Ben was willing to go, Coop sighed. "You're

the best, Ben. Such a pro when it comes to navigating the politics of it all. I appreciate it."

"Hard to say no to a guy I trust with my life and who's working for no pay to solve missing persons cases. I admire your tenacity, Coop. I'm happy to help pave the way with Jefferson. We often help smaller counties with cases, so it's easy for me to take a day or two and dedicate my time. We haven't been on a good road trip in a while."

Coop chuckled. "Yeah, the last time we headed that way was another one of my squirrely cases."

"I remember it well. I'll throw some stuff in a bag and come by to pick you up at the house in an hour or so."

"I'll be ready."

Coop disconnected and gathered his files along with the platter of cookies that would make excellent road trip snacks. He texted AB to let her know the latest and that he and Ben would be in Jefferson County to follow up.

He and Gus hurried to the Jeep, and Coop's heart broke at the sparkle in Gus' eyes. Something was up, and the dog was all set to be part of it.

As he drove to Aunt Camille's, Coop petted the top of Gus' head. "You'll have to stay with Dad and Aunt Camille. You need to watch over them while I'm away."

Gus tilted his head but thumped his tail against the seat.

When they got home, he threw some clothes and toiletries in a bag, choosing mostly polo shirts with his logo instead of his usual snarky t-shirts, and found his aunt and dad in the kitchen. Charlie looked up and pointed at his overnight bag. "Where are you headed, Coop?"

"Ben is coming by to pick me up in a few minutes. We're going to do some searching in Jefferson County. I think the guy who took Alyssa and the others is involved in the disappearance of two other young women from Knoxville. I've got a theory, and Ben is going to help me."

Camille sprang from her chair. "I could make you some sandwiches for the road."

Coop shook his head and pointed at the plate of cookies on the island counter. "We'll be fine. I have your cookies, remember."

She smiled as she slipped the cookies into a plastic container and added it to the top of Coop's bag. "There, that way they'll stay fresh."

"You boys be careful and check in so we know you're okay." Charlie stood and followed Coop to the door.

"We'll be fine and just call if you get worried." Coop ruffled the top of Gus' head. "You be a good boy and make sure these two are safe while I'm away."

Gus leaned against Coop's leg and wagged his tail. Coop pointed out the window. "There's Ben now. We should be home Wednesday."

He hugged both of them goodbye and patted Gus' head again before hurrying to Ben's car.

Ben stopped at a drive-thru, and they grabbed a couple of large sweet teas to drink on the journey. While Ben drove, Coop used his phone to search for a motel. He settled on one off I-40 near Strawberry Plains that put them about twenty minutes from both the Jefferson County Sheriff's Department and two of the promising locations he wanted to search. The campground and lake were a bit further but an easy drive.

During the drive, they chatted and snacked on cookies. After a long swallow of tea, Coop turned to Ben. "By the way, what happened to those two clowns who jumped us after the game?"

"They're both over eighteen and have a history. Plus, the one with the knife took a swing at me after I said I was with the police, so we added that to his charge. I think they're looking at jail time for sure. It's not their first or even second brush with the law. They've got a public defender who I'm sure will try some plea deal, but I think they'll get a custodial sentence."

"Good. I'm sick of the brazen way these criminals act, especially when they target our older population. Dad was really shaken."

"I'm sorry Charlie was targeted. That's another enhancement to their charges, and our judges take crimes against the elderly seriously."

"Dad was second-guessing his plan to move here. I tried to console him, but I also don't want him to feel unsafe."

"Aww, I hope he reconsiders. I know he's enjoyed his time here with you and Camille."

"Yeah, we talked about it, and I think it's just an overreaction to what happened. He and Camille spend most of their time in Belle Meade, which, as you know, is very safe. He admitted he's never felt in danger or at risk before. I tried to assure him, but I don't want to push him one way or another. He'll be home in a few weeks, and he can talk to Jack more about the idea and figure out the best approach."

"Well, I hope for our sake, he moves here. I think it's been good for you, and Camille is in her element. He's a great guy."

Coop chuckled. "He was even hinting I need to think about settling down with the right woman. Even went so far as to suggest she might be right under my nose."

Ben grinned and laughed. "Charlie is a wise man. He's not wrong, you know?"

Coop shrugged. "AB is my best friend, like you. I can't imagine a day without her. I would never want to lose her and not sure it's worth the risk."

"Sometimes the best marriages are built on long-term friendships. Might be something to think about."

Coop didn't respond and gazed out the window, surprised to see their exit come into view. With all their chatting, and despite a bit of a slowdown in the traffic around Knoxville, Ben made good time.

Ben pulled under the portico at the hotel, and Coop hurried inside to secure their room. The woman at the counter, who couldn't quit batting her fake eyelashes at Coop, gave him a free upgrade and after signing the credit card authorization, Coop thanked her and took the two keys.

They were on the second floor and opted to take the side entrance so Coop could avoid the reservation clerk. The suite was nice sized and held two queen beds, plus a desk area. They stashed their bags and while Coop texted his dad to let him know where they were staying, Ben glanced out the window. "Might as well head out and get dinner."

"Clarissa at the front desk was kind enough to give me a local map with their recommended restaurants." Coop scanned the paper map. "Fast food within walking distance and a Cracker Barrel on the other side of the freeway."

Both of them said, "Cracker Barrel," at the same time.

With a chuckle, they headed back to Ben's car and a meal as close to homecooked as the road trip offered.

27

On Tuesday morning, Coop was up early, having woken in the wee hours, contemplating their best approach to searching the area. He showered and went downstairs to check out the complimentary breakfast the hotel offered.

Concern about the day overrode his hunger, and he could only manage some toast. While he enjoyed his second cup of coffee, perusing the maps in his file, Ben joined him, his plate loaded with eggs and sausage.

"Good news," said Ben, as he wielded the plastic knife through his sausage patties. "I talked to Sheriff Holt. He's an early bird. I explained your sleuthing and research led to the discovery of the other two missing girls, along with Alyssa. He's happy to have you here and said we can rely on him for any assistance we need."

"Oh, that's great news. Thanks for paving the way."

"He suggested we stop by his office, and he would have someone from his department join us. They don't have a cadaver dog, but he said if we find something promising, come hell or highwater, he'll get one from Knoxville or elsewhere."

After a bite of his breakfast, Ben added, "Sheriff Holt thinks it would be a real feather in his cap if your hunch is correct, and he's able to be part of finding the two missing women. Those kinds of cases are always a positive when a sheriff is running for re-election."

"Sounds like a pragmatist. Can't argue with that and if it means some help and cooperation, all the better," said Coop. Feeling more positive, Coop wandered over to the baked goods case and took a donut to enjoy with the last of his coffee. They weren't like his favorites from the Donut Hole but hit the spot.

They finished their meal and opted to take a free bottle of water from the beverage station and set out for Sheriff Holt's office. When they arrived, Ben gave his name to the woman at the front counter and within minutes, they were led to an office near the back of the building.

Sheriff Holt, a tall, balding man with a generous midsection, greeted them at the door, shaking both their hands. "Pleased to meet you, fellas." He motioned them to follow him. "I've got some maps set up for us in the squad room."

He led them to a room, which reminded Coop of the squad room in Roane County. Sheriff Holt pointed out the coffee pot. "We've got sweet tea, water, juice, and soda in the fridge. You boys help yourself."

They both declined the offer and homed in on the maps that covered a large table. "Mr. Harrington, Chief Mason mentioned you had a few areas in mind. I've lived here my whole life and know this county like the back of my hand. Go ahead and point them out for me on the map, and let's see what we've got."

Coop smiled. "Call me Coop, please." He focused on the wooded land south of Highway 25 on the western edge of the county and another tree-covered area near one of the mines.

He used two sticky notes to mark the general areas. "These

are two areas that came up on the cell phone GPS records that don't match with any work-related movements."

Coop pointed at the area around the campgrounds and lake and added two more sticky notes. "He was also in these areas, but they seem too public to me. I think he would target a place that was untraveled, where he was unlikely to run into curious visitors."

Sheriff Holt nodded. "I would agree with you. There are some off-the-beaten-path areas around Douglas Lake, but even those get traffic. More traffic than you'd want if you're hiding a body."

Coop pointed at the area in question nearest the mine where Stanton had worked. "I'm also not convinced he would choose this area, so close to his work."

Holt nodded and drummed his fingers on the table. "Unless he was in a hurry. It would be convenient, and it's not an area people visit. It's not owned by the mine, so no direct link, but like you say, more of a chance there would be a connection."

He pondered the map some more and tapped the sticky note below Highway 25. "If I were a bettin' man, I'd start here. The only portion of this area people visit is this little sliver here by the lake. Locals fish there. There are a handful of dirt roads that lead into the area away from the lake, but it's not the place most people go. It's quiet and undisturbed."

Coop explained the other area where the two women had been found. "They weren't far from the end of pretty rough dirt road access points. I figured the burial sites would have to be within an easy carrying distance from where he'd have to park."

"Exactly. That's what I'm thinking about the dirt roads in this area. Did he have an ATV or anything like that?"

Coop shook his head. "We never found one registered or any record of one."

Sheriff Holt smacked his hand against the map on the table.

"Let's start there and see what we find. I've got the trailer with our side-by-side hooked up to the back of my truck. We'll have it in case we need it."

Ben's eyes widened. "You're going to go with us?"

Sheriff Holt smiled. "Sure thing. I'd love to get out of the office. It's a beautiful day for a hike." He pointed at his worn boots below his jeans. "I love nothing better than a search."

After letting his assistant know where he was going, Sheriff Holt led Ben and Coop out the back door of the building to the four-door truck waiting in the restricted parking area. Coop climbed into the backseat of the silver truck outfitted with blue and black stripes, sporting huge letters that spelled out SHERIFF.

Sheriff Holt turned from the front seat and pointed at the cooler in the back near Coop. "I've got plenty of cold drinks, sandwiches, and snacks if we need them. You fellas help yourself to one of our hats." He pointed at the stack of ball caps with the logo embroidered on them that matched the one he was wearing.

While he and Ben chatted in the front seat, Coop took in the scenery. Sheriff Holt was right. It was a gorgeous day with the sun shining. They traveled the interstate back the way they'd come, then took an exit that led them onto a county road.

Within thirty minutes, Sheriff Holt took a dirt road that led into the trees. Coop took in their surroundings and nodded. It was quiet and secluded. The place felt like the site he and Gus had searched. From behind the wheel, Sheriff Holt said, "No fresh tracks here, so nobody's been down here recently."

Sheriff Holt stopped the truck at the end of the dirt road. "We can take a look around here. I can't imagine he could carry a body more than a quarter of a mile or less. That will narrow our focus on where to look." Coop and Ben donned their free hats and followed the sheriff.

He lined up Coop between himself and Ben, and they proceeded to walk forward, taking slow and determined steps, searching the immediate area for any disturbances that could indicate a grave.

They searched one side of the road, then the other, noting nothing of significance. After a break for some sweet tea, they made their way back down the dirt road and headed to the next one.

By lunchtime, they'd searched three dirt road access points and driven to the fourth. As Coop took a sandwich from Sheriff Holt, he asked, "How many roads are there into this area?"

"About a dozen, I'd say. We're making good progress and only have a couple more that are as long as the ones we've seen. Many of them are short. My hunch was he would want to get as far away from the main road as possible."

Ben nodded. "That makes sense."

As Coop reached for a drink, his cell phone rang. He slipped it from his pocket and said, "It's Detective Mitchell."

"Hey, Jim," he answered.

"Hope I'm not calling at a bad time, Coop."

"No, I'm just here with Ben and Sheriff Holt in Jefferson County. I've got a theory on a couple of old cold cases out of Knoxville. We used Anne's cell GPS data to narrow down our focus to areas Stanton visited prior to the abductions. No joy yet, but we're in the midst of searching."

"Wow, you're one committed detective, Coop. If you ever need a job, I'd hire you in a New York minute."

Coop laughed. "Thanks, not looking for one. These cases just really got to me, and I'm convinced Stanton is a serial."

"I won't argue that point. I'm glad you're so dedicated. I'll make you a deal. If we ever need another private consultant, you're the first one I'll call. You're a legend around here."

"That's a fair deal. So, what can I do for you?"

"I've actually got some good news I wanted to share with

you. I've been working with my counterparts in Rutherford County. We just heard back from the lab. The second burial site you helped uncover was Elizabeth for sure. Based on the visual inspection and her clothing, we were all certain it was her, but they confirmed it this morning. They've been running all the trace evidence we found at Elizabeth's burial site. She was shot, like Alyssa. Along with the bullet, they found a casing under her in the dirt."

"Did they match it to anything?"

"I said it was good news, remember?" He chuckled before delivering the headline. "It's from the same gun used on Alyssa. They're hoping to find DNA on the casing. We're redoubling our efforts to trace Stanton's movements after his latest abduction of Alyssa in hopes of finding the gun."

"My money is still on his mother. Do you think he could have coerced his girlfriend into disposing of it?"

"It's possible, although I'm not sure she wouldn't have cracked by now. She's gone back and forth when interviewed. It seems dependent on if she's visited Stanton before her interview. I think he's very controlling and manipulative with her."

"He's definitely got a hold on her. I can't imagine too many women staying with someone after their first date experience."

"That's an understatement. My gut says she's not involved, but I'm not ruling her out."

Coop leaned against the tailgate of the truck. "Looking at Stanton's history and early criminal life, I got the distinct impression his mother was a willing accomplice or at least a shield for him. I can see her hiding the gun for him."

"We agree on that point, Coop. We're working with the authorities in Georgia right now. They're getting us some drone footage so we can compare it to our earlier visit where we videoed the search. We're looking for any anomalies. We're going to get another warrant for a more extensive search and hopefully get access to some ground-penetrating radar. If it's there, it's well hidden."

Coop nodded. "Yeah, as I recall, the officers did a very thorough search of the buildings, even getting under the house in the crawl space and up in the attic. I think they would have found it."

"Burial seems to be the method of choice for Stanton. It might be what he did with the gun, but we'll need to narrow it down if we can. Otherwise, we'll be out there for days, digging up the acreage."

"The problem will be if he buried it at some random place throughout all of his travels. That will make it impossible to find."

"Agreed. We don't think he'd risk hiding it on his own property or a work site. We actually dredged that pond at the old mine site where we found Alyssa. We thought he might have thrown it in there."

"I think he had plans to continue to use it. It seems to be his weapon of choice, and I'd bet he's used it plenty of times before Alyssa."

"As much as I hope not, I tend to agree." Jim sighed and added, "Anyway, I'll keep you posted. Give my best to Sheriff Holt. He's one of the good guys. If you have time to swing by the office on your way back to Nashville, please stop in. You're always welcome here."

"Thanks, Jim. Talk to you soon."

He disconnected and caught Ben's questioning look.

After a long swallow from his bottle of tea, Coop rehashed Detective Mitchell's conversation and shared the news about the match on the bullets and the casing.

Ben pointed at the truck. "That's great news that they can tie him directly to Elizabeth. That makes three direct links. Let's get going and see if we can find more."

With a renewed sense of hope and urgency, Coop and the two lawmen set out on foot to do another search of the area.

After a false alarm at finding a small mound of earth that turned out to be dug by a gopher or other animal, they finished without finding a possible burial site and headed back toward the main road.

The next road was much shorter than the previous ones and as they bumped over the rough terrain, Coop gazed out the window with the hope they might find something before dark. At this rate, he and Ben would be staying another night.

28

As Sheriff Holt parked the truck, Coop disconnected from chatting with Clarissa at the hotel. She was more than happy to extend his reservation for another night. He imagined her fluttering eyes as she tapped the keyboard.

As the three of them walked through the brush and trees, they kept their eyes focused on the ground and anything that resembled a disturbance, while they discussed their hope that Detective Mitchell would have some luck in Georgia and find the gun Stanton used.

As Sheriff Holt stood from where he'd bent to examine an area by a tall cedar tree, he grunted. "Detective Mitchell is top shelf. I've worked with him over the years, and he's one of the best. If that gun is there, he'll find it."

They found nothing at the site but kept going. As the sun dipped lower in the sky, Sheriff Holt suggested they call it a day and finish up the other locations in the morning.

Tired from the long day and disappointed in their lack of finding anything promising, Coop thanked Sheriff Holt and followed Ben to his car for their trek back to the hotel. They stashed their newly acquired Jefferson County Sheriff's Department caps in the backseat. Coop slid into the passenger seat and called AB to check in and report their lack of progress while Ben drove.

They opted to take the route that led to Trentville, where Stanton had lived during the abductions. With Ben behind the wheel, Coop remained quiet, focused on their surroundings and imagining Stanton making this same drive.

Coop pointed at a sign for the lake Sheriff Holt mentioned. Their route wound through the rural land on the other side of the area they'd spent searching all day. Tomorrow, they'd be making their way toward the lake side and with any luck, they'd find something.

Twenty minutes later, Ben pulled off the road and pointed at a dirt driveway that led to a mobile home. "There it is." The trailer wasn't in the best shape but was definitely off the beaten path, which no doubt suited Stanton.

"About what I expected," said Coop. "What do you say we try the pizza place Sheriff Holt recommended?"

"Sounds good. I'm starving. I'm not used to that much hiking."

"Same here. I hope we have better luck tomorrow."

Ben pulled back onto the road. "I can afford to stay tomorrow, even part of Thursday. As long as I'm in the office on Friday morning, I'm good."

"I appreciate you following me on my wild goose chase."

"You've never disappointed me yet, Coop. If we strike out in that first area tomorrow, we'll just move to the next spot on your list."

Coop sighed. "I had the same thought as Sheriff Holt. That area feels right to me."

Ben pulled into a gravel lot in front of Crossroads Pizza, where several cars were parked. It was as advertised. A hole in the wall. He shrugged at Coop. "Let's see if we can trust Holt."

With a laugh, Coop followed Ben to the front door of the worn wooden building.

The aroma of garlic and tomato sauce greeted them, along with the warmth from the pizza ovens behind the counter of the small dining area. A woman, wearing a red apron, and sporting a friendly smile, waved at them from behind the cash register. "Welcome in. What can we get started for you?"

Coop and Ben studied the menu board hanging above her. They both liked the sound of their meat lover's pizza and ordered a pitcher of sweet tea to go with it. Coop paid her, while Ben toted the pitcher and glasses and went in search of a table.

After slipping some bills into the tip jar, which made the cashier wink at him, Coop set out to find Ben. He figured he'd be in the back where he could watch everyone, and he found him at a table in the corner near the rear exit.

Coop slipped into the chair across from Ben and had just taken a long swallow of his tea when the cashier showed up at their table and set a basket in the middle of the table. "I thought you boys could use a snack while you wait." She removed the checkered cloth napkin to reveal knots of dough, browned to perfection. "These are our famous garlic and parmesan knots. Enjoy."

"Thank you, ma'am," said Coop, and Ben echoed his thanks.

After their first bite of the buttery dough, they both grinned. "Looks like Sheriff Holt didn't steer us wrong," said Ben, reaching for another one.

"I'm not sure if they're really good, or I'm just too hungry, but they taste delicious," said Coop. "If the pizza is anything close to these, we're set."

As they refilled their drinks, their number was called. Ben volunteered to retrieve the pizza and returned with it along with plates and silverware. He set the pizza in the middle of their table and raised his brows. "Looks great."

They dug into the cheesy goodness and in no time polished off the entire pizza. After finishing the last of the iced tea, they thanked the woman at the counter and made their way outside.

It was a short drive back to the hotel, where Ben took a few minutes to call his wife and check in with his office. Coop called his dad to let him know they'd be staying another day but would be back by Thursday night at the latest.

With their calls done, they turned on the television and stretched out on their beds. Coop tried to concentrate on the show, but his mind was busy calculating how much time they had to wrap up their search. The campground and Douglas Lake area were bigger.

The hope he had earlier in the day fizzled.

He closed his eyes and despite the images of the two missing girls stuck in his mind, willed himself to sleep.

On Wednesday, Coop and Ben were up early, ate breakfast, and were at Sheriff Holt's office by seven thirty. They found him ready to go, with his cooler restocked.

They started on the next access road, where they'd left off last night, and proceeded with their search.

After spending three hours striking out, Sheriff Holt drove down the last of the dirt roads before they reached the lake. He assured them there were plenty of places at the far end of the lake that could also be possibilities, and they would search them next.

He maneuvered over the bumpy ground and parked his truck in the widest spot where the road showed signs of wear from people turning around. After a quick break for a drink, the three of them, armed with colored flags they could use to mark the ground, took their appointed positions and began the painstaking search.

As they searched, they found a wider trail, one that a vehicle could fit through. Grass and low brush had grown over it, and it wasn't well used or worn, but it was easy to see the trail when compared to the surrounding area.

They focused their attention on following the crude trail and establishing a new search perimeter based off the end of it, where the large trees impeded it, and it came to a natural end. The undergrowth was heavier and the trees more numerous in this area than all the other places they'd searched.

Within thirty minutes of commencing the search, Ben hollered out, "Over here. Come take a look. I think I've got something."

Coop and Sheriff Holt jogged over to Ben. He pointed at the ground where he'd inserted a bright orange flag. "New growth here in the midst of all this old brush."

Coop nodded. "Looks about the right size to me."

Sheriff Holt took off his sunglasses and bent down to get a better look. He didn't say a word but stood and slapped Ben and Coop on the back. "I think we've found it. Good eye, Chief Mason. Good eye."

He used his cell phone to call into the office and asked for an evidence team to roll to their location. He also wanted a request sent to Knox County for a cadaver dog. "Try to keep it off the radio. We don't need everyone who monitors our channels yappin' about this."

He disconnected and grinned. "We don't need the media or looky-loos out here either."

Ben nodded. "Agreed. The fewer people who know the better."

Sheriff Holt pointed at the orange flag. "I don't want to disturb this area any more than we already have but will make sure the dog and the team go over every inch. We're looking for two, and I think we found one for sure."

Coop glanced up above them at the canopy of trees. "Too many trees to use a drone to help."

"Yeah, the dog will be our best bet." He pointed back toward the access road. "If you guys want to go back to the truck, feel free. I'm going to stay with the scene. The last thing we need is some lawyer saying we were sloppy and didn't adequately protect it."

Coop and Ben both shook their heads. "No chance. We've put in too much effort to take a break now."

They resisted the temptation to explore further and stood waiting for reinforcements. Within an hour, the sound of vehicle doors slamming and voices filled the air. Ben volunteered to walk back and guide them to the scene, so they wouldn't create a new path.

Within minutes, Ben appeared with four other officers, all dressed with protective suits and carrying evidence cases. Sheriff Holt introduced Ben and Coop to his lead detective, Dale Helton.

The sheriff explained their theory that there could be two burial sites in the area. "I'll leave you to it, Dale. Just call me the moment you find anything. We're going to need the lab folks to expedite this. If you need anything, you let me know, and I'll get to work on getting us any extra resources."

Dale nodded. "The canine team will be here within an hour. We'll get started on photos, video, and documenting the scene. I'll keep you posted, boss."

As much as Coop wanted to stay to watch the process, he followed Sheriff Holt to the truck. He slid behind the wheel and turned toward the backseat. "What do you say we go check those spots I mentioned by the lake, just in case, before I treat both of you to lunch?"

"I think that's a good idea. Then, we'll know we covered the entire area." Coop sighed. "I suspect we won't find anything. I'm not certain, of course, but with him choosing to bury Brittany and Elizabeth so close to each other, I tend to think your team will find the second site close to the one we uncovered. Not to mention, it felt pretty isolated and remote in there."

"I tend to agree, Coop. I just want to be thorough and scratch it off the list."

He drove the short distance to a well-worn dirt road and parked at the end of it. Coop climbed from the backseat and looked around. This section had the least amount of coverage from trees and brush. It was more open and exposed.

Sheriff Holt pointed out a few of the footpaths that led away from the road. They were littered with wrappers, beer cans, and bottles. Coop frowned. "Seems like this is a well-traveled spot. Not sure someone wouldn't have found a burial site if it were nearby."

Ben nodded as they followed the sheriff along the narrow pathway. As they traveled further from the dirt road, the trash dwindled and soon was nonexistent, leaving the trail covered in only grass and underbrush.

After several more steps, Sheriff Holt stopped and said, "I think this is about as far as he could manage carrying a body. Let's start our search here and see if we find anything promising."

Coop took out his cell phone and checked the map. He'd marked the GPS location of the possible site they found and when he checked the map, he realized they weren't that far from it. He caught Sheriff Holt's eye. "Any chance this trail leads back to where we just left? Looking on my phone, it sure looks possible."

He moved closer to let the sheriff see the map on his phone. He squinted at the screen. "I see what you're thinkin', Coop. Good point. He could have accessed that site we found from where we did or walked a bit farther on this trail. Let's keep going a bit more and extend this search area. I'm going to call Dale and let him know we're around the edges of his perimeter."

As they walked further, Sheriff Holt called his detective and gave him the GPS coordinates from Coop's phone.

Ben and Coop assumed their positions and waited for him to finish his call so they could begin the synchronized search pattern they'd been using. On their second full pass, Coop stopped and yelled, "I might have something here." He stuck one of his flags in a depressed area of soil. It was an area, much like the other site, where the old brush and growth was missing, but new sprouts of grass were evident.

Sheriff Hoyt squatted next to Coop, then turned to him and grinned. "I think this may be our second site. You've got a good nose on ya, son, and you just saved the search team a bunch of time. They would have reached this point eventually, but we can get the dog to check this immediately."

While the sheriff called Dale with the latest news, Coop and Ben stood under the shade of a tall pine tree. Ben smiled at his friend. "You were right, Coop. If not for your devotion to these old cases, I'm not sure either of these sites would have been found. They've escaped scrutiny for several years already."

Coop shrugged. "Well, it remains to be seen if they're really the burial sites. While I hope they are, for the sake of the families, it really makes me sick to think of that smug jackass and the utter depravity he's left in his wake. He's beyond evil."

"Can't disagree with that. These cases, while satisfying to close, are nothing but pure heartbreak."

Sheriff Holt finished his call and joined them under the tree. "Dale has the canine and his handler on scene at the first site. They're just starting their work. He's sending a detective our way to secure this scene, then we'll get out of their hair and let them process it."

They didn't wait long before two more people arrived, dressed like the others, and carrying heavy cases. After a short conversation, the sheriff motioned to Coop and Ben. "Let's get some grub, then we can head back to the office."

Coop had worked off his breakfast long ago, and the idea of lunch sounded great. The excitement of two possible sites overrode his stomach pangs. The reality of not finding Denise and Nancy had weighed on him since yesterday. He felt so sure about his theory until last night, but today's progress lifted that burden, and Coop let a hint of optimism replace the guilt he'd begun to harbor.

Sheriff Holt drove a couple of blocks past his office and pulled into the parking lot of Que's Café. "You fellas are in for a real treat. Que's has the best barbecue in Tennessee."

Coop and Ben ribbed him as they walked to the door, touting some of the most well-known places in Nashville that were famous for their sweet barbecue.

The sheriff waved at the waitresses and led them to a booth near the back of the restaurant. A friendly woman appeared with glasses of water and a basket of warm cornbread with honey butter. "Good to see you, Sheriff. Shall I get some menus for your friends?"

He shook his head. "No, Doris. We'll just take three of your large platters with everything and sweet teas all around."

She nodded and promised to be back with their teas.

As they ate the squares of cornbread, Ben said, "We've got to head home by tomorrow afternoon, regardless of the outcome."

Sheriff Holt finished his bite and nodded. "Understood. I've got a good feelin' about those two sites, and we should have some preliminary answers later today or early tomorrow. The lab results will take time, of course."

Doris appeared with a tray bearing long platters loaded

with pulled pork, juicy brisket, and ribs. The tangy and sweet scent made Coop's mouth water.

As they were about to dig in, Sheriff Holt lifted his glass of tea. "I'm not one to count my chickens before they hatch, but I dare say you fellas helped solve two very cold cases. Not to mention, you've made me a shoo-in for my next election. Eat up and enjoy."

Ben and Coop chuckled. Sheriff Holt was a good guy, but a realist, and he understood how solving high-profile crimes was an easy way to win another term.

Coop took his first bite of brisket and couldn't deny the sheriff's assessment of the food. He only hoped they weren't celebrating too early.

29

After their feast, with Ben and Coop admitting it was delicious and just as good as the places they loved in Nashville, they went back to Holt's office. While the sheriff took care of some business, the two of them hung out in the squad room, waiting for word.

Coop used the time to call AB and update her on their progress, while Ben checked in with his office. It was almost four o'clock when they finished their calls.

While they were twiddling their thumbs, checking out the framed memorabilia that hung on the walls, Sheriff Holt came in grinning. "Just got word. The dogs alerted us to those two areas we found, and they unearthed the first body. They can't tell much initially, but the medical examiner believes it is female. They're going to collect all the trace evidence, transport the remains, and hope to have the other site done before it's dark."

Coop slammed his hand on the table. "That's excellent news. If they're Denise and Nancy, their families will at least be able to put them to rest in a proper fashion."

"I've gotta get back to the phone and call Knox County. I

want them prepared as the remains will end up there at their facility since they have much better technology and more specialty technicians, which we'll need for these cases."

Coop nodded. "I think we'll head back to the hotel. If you get anything definitive, call us. We'll head out in the morning unless we need to stick around for anything?"

"I promise to keep in touch and let you know the moment we have an ID on either of them. I truly appreciate your help. It's a shame none of us have the resources to dedicate to these cold cases."

Ben shook Sheriff Holt's hand. "I doubt you would have found them where they were. It really took Coop's work in looking at Stanton's habits and our instincts that Stanton had done this before. Coop followed the thread that connected him to the other victims."

As the sheriff extended his hand to Coop, he smiled. "I agree, and I'm going to put in a request to pay you as a consultant on this one, Coop. The bean counters over at our county office will be hard-pressed to deny that once this hits the news. You just email me an invoice, and I'll see to it. Be sure to put your expenses on it." He handed him his business card. "My cell number is on the back. You call anytime. You've both got free barbecue from me anytime you're in Jefferson County."

They thanked him and made their way outside to Ben's car. They were back at the hotel before five o'clock and discovered free beer and wine, along with appetizers set up in the lobby of the hotel.

They each took a plastic cup of beer, along with some cheese and pretzels, and settled into a small table with a view out the windows.

As they relaxed, Coop's cell phone rang. He raised his eyes when he saw Detective Mitchell's name on his screen. He showed it to Ben and hurried outside, away from the other guests.

"Hey, Jim. I'm just walking outside right now. Give me a second."

"Are you still in Jefferson County?"

"We're leaving in the morning. We had some luck today and found two burial sites. They recovered the remains from the first one and hope to have the other one out tonight."

"That's excellent work. I just wanted to let you know, I've got a crew going down to Georgia, and we're going to be there to execute another search warrant at the mother's property. We've got equipment to excavate and plan to be there at first light tomorrow."

"More great news. We'll stop in on our way through and touch base. Sheriff Holt promised to keep us in the loop on the identification process of the remains, but we won't know anything for a few days."

"We'll have a live video feed from the search, so feel free to stop in, and you and Ben can watch it."

"We'll be there. I'll talk to Ben, but we can get out of here early. We'll be with you before eight o'clock. We can hang out until late afternoon."

"Sounds great, Coop. We'll see you then and congratulations on your finds."

He disconnected and walked back into the lobby, where Ben waited. Coop finished off his beer, and they headed upstairs to their room.

Once they were inside, Coop shared Mitchell's news. "I figured we could grab an early breakfast here and hit the road."

"Sounds good to me. Should be fun to watch."

"His mother is a real piece of work, so it should be eventful. She's got a mouth on her."

They were stuffed from their huge lunch and made do with the snacks from downstairs for dinner. They found an old series on television and sprawled on their beds, intent on an early night.

Just before eight o'clock, Coop's cell sprang to life. "Sheriff Holt, how's it going?"

"Good news, Coop. I just wanted you two to know they found remains at the second location, and they're on the way to the lab. Suspect they're also female, and we'll know more when they start their process."

"I'm glad they were recovered. We're stopping in to see Jim Mitchell on our way home but will be in Nashville by tomorrow night."

"Thank you again. I'll call you as soon as I hear more. You fellas have a safe trip."

Coop disconnected and glanced over at Ben. "Second site held remains they believe are female."

After a moment of jubilation, they both grew quiet. Ben shook his head. "Those poor parents are about to have their worst nightmare come true. Although, I think it would be worse not knowing."

"I won't be happy until I see that evil excuse for a human charged," said Coop, punching a fist into his pillow.

FOR A CHANGE, Coop slept soundly and woke ready to hit the road. He'd run out of his professional shirts and slipped into the dark-blue one lettered with BUT FIRST, DONUTS with a row of the pastries underneath. He figured Detective Mitchell and his crew wouldn't mind. They gobbled down a quick breakfast, checked out, and headed east to Roane County.

Knoxville rush-hour traffic slowed their progress, but they made it to Detective Mitchell's office a few minutes before eight o'clock. They were ushered into the squad room where the large screens were filled with live video footage from the team in Georgia. Coop poured himself and Ben a cup of coffee, collected a plate of donuts, and sat down to enjoy the show.

Detective Mitchell queued up the earlier footage when the team arrived and met Stanton's mother Delia. Coop and Ben watched as the officers knocked on the door and presented the warrant.

Their mouths fell open as she appeared, her bleached hair looking like squirrels nested in it and her housedress stained and spotted with burn marks from cigarettes. Her scrawny legs ended in filthy slippers. As soon as the officers spoke and explained they had a legal order to conduct an extensive search, including underground, she lit into them with a tirade of foul language that would shame an entire bar full of drunken sailors.

Coop raised his brows at Ben. "She's definitely not a morning person."

Ben chuckled and took a sip of coffee.

Along with her explosive language, when the officers spread out on the property and the trailer with the backhoe through the gate, she swung her fists. The lead detective from Georgia was beyond polite and did his best to diffuse the situation, but Delia wasn't having it. She hit his upper chest with her bony fists. He then advised her she could either be calm and stay for the search, or she could be arrested for assaulting an officer and booked into the county jail.

Her eyes bugged out at that news, and the vulgarities continued. The boyfriend appeared, dressed in jeans and a t-shirt, and tried to calm her down, but it wasn't working. The officers finally escorted her to a patrol vehicle, loaded her in the back, despite her screaming at them, and assigned a poor female officer to babysit her.

Once she was removed, the detective suggested the boyfriend might want to take her somewhere else for the duration of the search if he didn't want to be posting bail for her later.

"He looks like a beaten man," said Ben.

"Yeah. He's going to have a lovely morning with her, wherever they go."

While technicians unloaded a device that looked like an oversized lawn mower with a computer screen, the boyfriend gathered some clothes for Mrs. Stanton and coaxed her into a pickup. She was still shouting when he drove through the gate.

With her removed, the footage was much less entertaining. They stopped the playback and focused on the live footage where the camera followed the technician with the ground-penetrating radar to search the area before they dug. It was a slow process and a large plot of land.

While the technicians analyzed the radar data, a team of officers scoured the grounds, intent on inspecting every square inch of the acreage. Over the next few hours, they unearthed a few pieces of pipe and a metal fence clamp, but no sign of a gun.

As it neared the lunch hour, Detective Mitchell treated everyone to burgers, and while Coop ate his, his cell rang. He wiped his hands on a napkin and poked the button to connect with Sheriff Holt.

"Hey, Sheriff. Do you have some news for us?"

"I sure do, Coop. Just heard from the lab, and they don't yet have a confirmation on the identify of either of the remains but have the dental records from the two young women you suspect and are going to do the comparisons this afternoon. They did find a bullet in each of the remains. Looks like they were both shot in the head."

"That matches Stanton's method."

"We've got ballistics comparing the casings and bullets from the other scenes. I suspect we'll get a match that will tie the suspect to these two murders. It will take time to complete all the trace evidence, and they're looking for DNA, too. Just wanted you to know. Nothing is official yet, but it sure looks like your hunch was spot on."

"That's great news. We're here with Detective Mitchell now. If his team finds the gun, it would help the case."

"I'll keep you posted on our end. You and Ben have a good trip home, and I hope you come back to visit under more pleasant circumstances."

Coop thanked him and disconnected.

Ben raised his brows at Coop. "From the look on your face, I'd say it's good news."

Coop relayed the information about the bullets and the dental comparisons that would take place.

"That pretty much confirms your theory."

Coop hung his head, his appetite suddenly gone. He closed the lid on his takeout box. "Yeah, I always like being right, but it doesn't feel so great in this case."

"I understand. I had to come to terms with that grief and anguish that comes from being unable to save every victim. Once they're gone, it's about justice for the family and making sure I do everything in my power to provide all the evidence necessary for a conviction. Sometimes all we can do is lock up the monster after the fact."

With a sigh, Coop took a long swallow from his bottle of tea.

As Coop contemplated Ben's wisdom, shouting erupted around the table, and Detective Mitchell pointed at the screen. "They've got it."

The camera providing their view focused on a plastic bag a gloved technician lifted from the dirt. He noted it was discovered buried three feet down at the back of one of the horse corrals.

An officer hurried to inspect it, and he confirmed it was a nine-millimeter and slipped it into a large evidence bag. Mitchell's phone rang and after a brief conversation, he disconnected. "They're rushing it to the lab for analysis and comparison to the casings and bullets."

Coop raised his hand, and Mitchell nodded at him.

"Sheriff Holt from Jefferson County just let me know they found bullets in the remains they discovered this week and are running comparisons with the other two sites. He's confident they'll get a match."

Mitchell's grin broadened. "This will lock the case we have against that spawn of evil. And his lovely mother."

While those in the room celebrated the victory, Coop sought out Deputy Bennett. "Hey, can you make sure to forward the information related to the ballistics and the other two cases from Jefferson to the detective in Nevada? He was interested in the cell phone data angle, and I told him we'd update him with anything else we found. I'm pretty sure Stanton is involved in those cases, along with the others from Idaho and North Dakota."

"Will do, Coop. I feel the same way. The authorities in Georgia also have a renewed interest in looking into the missing women from ten years ago. Not sure they'll get very far, but their involvement with us at the mother's place has them digging into those cold cases."

"It will be interesting to see if he confesses to anything related to the other cases. He never expected us to find Alyssa, and I'm sure when these new charges get filed, he'll be shocked."

"I'll make sure the reports and new lab analysis go out to all of the detectives we contacted about their cold cases. I hope it helps."

Coop thanked him and found Ben chatting with Detective Mitchell near the door. Jim extended his hand to Coop. "Thanks again for everything. You really went above and beyond. Thanks to you, we have the prosecutors fighting about jurisdiction."

"I'd love to watch his trial. I just hope they don't make a plea deal with him."

"Sadly, I learned long ago, I don't have much control over

what the attorneys decide to do. I know the death penalty is on the table, but it's hard to say what they'll do. If anyone ever deserved it, it's this guy. Most prosecutors nowadays tend to go for life in prison without the possibility of parole because they're cheaper to prosecute and less risky."

Ben nodded. "I'll attest to that same fact. Most of them will tell you there's a greater chance of getting convictions overturned on a death penalty case, and the process is so long, it makes the expense not worth it. They tout they can get the same basic result with the perpetrator incarcerated forever, since most on death row are there for years and the appeals process is never-ending."

"I understand the argument. I just want to make sure he never sees the light of day, and I want the families to have the least amount of trauma possible during the trial."

Mitchell's jaw tightened. "Exactly. I think their wishes should be paramount when it comes to that decision."

He pointed at the officers gathered at the table. "I need to run, but I'll be in touch when we have the ballistics and know more."

They said their goodbyes and took a handful of the cookies they hadn't eaten from lunch, along with a couple of bottles of water for the road and set out for home.

30

When Coop walked through Aunt Camille's front door, Gus was waiting and couldn't stop wagging his tail. He wrapped his front legs around Coop's and wouldn't let go. "I missed you too, sweet boy. I'm sorry I was gone so long."

Coop left his overnight bag in the entryway and finally coaxed Gus to let go as the two of them made their way to the kitchen, where his dad and AB were gathered while Camille worked on dinner.

Camille hollered out a greeting, and Charlie pointed at Gus. "That dog has been sitting by the door for hours waiting on you."

"I'm happy to be home. Something smells delicious."

AB smiled at him. "I'm happy you're back." She eyed his face and touched his cheek. "Looks like you forgot your razor."

Coop smiled. "We were too busy for grooming."

AB laughed. "The office has been too quiet. Luckily, Charlie has been bringing Gus by to hang out for a few hours each day."

Gus thumped his tail against Coop's leg.

"I've got everything almost ready. Charlie, you can pour the tea, and Coop and AB can carry in the side dishes."

Coop took the rolls and potato salad, while AB carried the fruit salad into the dining room. Camille followed with a platter of sliced ham. She set it on the table and put her hands on her hips. "I think that's everything. I made a lemon meringue pie for dessert, so save some room."

At the mention of one of his favorites, Coop groaned, "Oh, you know how to spoil a guy."

As they ate, Coop filled them in on his trip. He explained their search and how they finally found the two burial sites. "I think we'll know more tomorrow, both about the identities and the ballistics report to see if the bullets are indeed a match to the other two sites."

Aunt Camille shivered and rubbed her arms. "My heart is broken for their parents. I can't imagine the pain. It's hard to imagine such evil exists."

AB put her fork down and glanced over at Coop. "I'm just glad you found them, and your hunch paid off. Cold cases are so hard to work. There's so much to piece together, and they take so long."

"Very proud of you Coop," said Charlie. "I hope with all this evidence, they put that guy away forever."

Coop nodded and winked at his dad. "My stubbornness turned out to be a strength for this case. I think they'll have more than enough to keep Stanton behind bars for the rest of his life."

As he glanced around the table and took in their solemn expressions, he opted to inject a little humor and related the story of Stanton's mother and her antics during the search.

By the time he was done, they were all laughing and smiling. "Now, don't tell that to anyone. I shouldn't have told you, but it was too fun not to share. She'll be facing charges, too."

In her wisdom, AB changed the subject to their upcoming

trip to Florida, asking a few questions Coop knew she already understood, but it shifted Aunt Camille from focusing on the murders to something happier.

They ended the evening enjoying pie while they played a game of pinochle. It was the escape Coop needed. Alyssa's case that started all of this and piqued Coop's curiosity was tragic on its own, but adding four more horrific and senseless deaths took a toll on Coop's spirit.

Surrounded by family, with Gus sleeping atop his foot, the depravity he witnessed over the last few weeks faded, and he embraced the joy and love that was so precious to him.

On Friday, Coop and Gus arrived at Peg's Pancakes before Ben, and Coop enjoyed a cup of coffee before his friend arrived.

As Coop took his first sip of coffee, his cell phone rang. He tapped the button to answer it.

"Sheriff Holt, you're up early."

"Hey, Coop. Just got word from the medical examiner. They made a positive identification. The first site we found was Denise, and the second one was Nancy. Just wanted you to know. With Detective Mitchell's team finding the gun, they're running ballistics now on what we recovered at our two scenes. Should have more on that later today."

"Thanks, Sheriff. I appreciate you letting me know."

"It's just what you thought, Coop. Excellent work. Talk to you soon."

Myrtle arrived within seconds of Ben taking his chair and filling his cup. They both went with the ham and cheese scramble special, served with a short stack of Peg's famous pancakes.

After a long swallow from his cup, Ben sighed. "I've been at work already. It's amazing how many things pile up in just a couple of days."

"I appreciate you taking time away to be my wingman. Only wish it hadn't been for such a grim task. I did just get a call from Sheriff Holt. They identified the remains. They were Denise and Nancy."

"What we expected, but good to have it confirmed. You did good, Coop."

Myrtle arrived with their plates and refilled their cups. "I'll have that takeout for AB in a jiffy."

Ben added some homemade jam to his toast. "I've got meetings all day, but if you hear anything on the ballistics, send me a text. I'm curious."

"I'm anxious to hear, too. Thankfully, I have enough work piled up to keep me occupied, but I'll text you when I hear anything."

Myrtle brought AB's breakfast along with a burger patty for her favorite four-legged customer and left the check for them. "Y'all have a nice weekend."

Coop insisted on paying the check. "I owe you, Ben. With Sheriff Holt offering to pay my fees, I'm feeling even more generous."

"I like that idea. Sounds like I'll be eating free breakfasts for a few weeks."

"We head to Florida next week, so I'll catch up when we get home."

"Oh, that's right. I hope you have a great time. I'll make sure we keep an eye on your office and the house while you're away. Do you need me to do anything else?"

"If you wouldn't mind grabbing the mail for us, that would be a big help."

"Consider it done," said Ben. He finished the last of his coffee. "I gotta run, but I'll talk to you before you leave."

Coop left some cash on the table, and he and Gus followed

Ben to the sidewalk. As he loaded Gus into the passenger seat, Ben waved and drove away from the restaurant.

Within five minutes, Coop and Gus came through the back door of the office and delivered AB's breakfast. She stopped typing and pointed at Coop's office. "I left you a stack of files on your desk and a few messages that came in while you were gone. One from Miss Clara."

"I'll get right on it. Thanks for holding down the fort, AB. Sheriff Holt just called, and they confirmed the identities. Nancy and Denise."

"I'm glad and sad at the same time."

"Me too, AB."

He wandered to his office while Gus remained next to AB's chair, eager for a morsel of her breakfast.

Coop tackled the files first and got through the bulk of them before he returned a few calls. Feeling accomplished with his stack of tasks almost done, he tapped his finger on the message from Miss Clara. Worried that she might have bad news and need more help, he saved her for the last of his calls.

She answered on the first ring.

"Hello, Miss Clara. I just got back in the office this morning and wanted to get back to you."

"Oh, Coop. Thanks so much for calling. I don't want to bother you but just wanted you to know Luna is doing well and making good progress. We even had a family meeting with a counselor at the rehab center, and I finally feel like she's turned the corner. My daughter and I are both hopeful. It's only been two weeks, but there's been a big improvement. I wanted you to know, your help was a true godsend. Luna wanted me to thank you as well. When she gets out, she wants to come to thank you in person."

"That's not necessary. I'm just glad we could help you and Luna. That's great news. Of course, you and Luna are always welcome to stop in and visit with us, but she shouldn't feel obligated."

Clara chuckled. "I don't think it's an obligation. For the first time in years, I think Luna sees a future filled with hope, and she equates your intervention with giving her that gift. As do I. I wanted you to know you and Annabelle really made a difference in her life. In my life." Her voice wobbled as she finished her sentence.

The image of Alyssa buried in a hole at the abandoned mine flashed in his mind. His throat tightened. He couldn't save them all, but he'd managed to pull Luna back from the brink. For her sake and Clara's, he hoped this time Luna was committed and serious about changing her life. When it came to Luna, Clara was shrewd and if she was convinced there was a real change, it gave Coop hope.

"That's wonderful to hear, Clara. I'm so happy for your family. Give Luna our best, and we look forward to seeing you both soon."

He disconnected and wandered into the reception area, where AB was finishing up something on her computer.

He leaned against the edge of her desk. "Just talked to Clara. She called to thank us and said Luna is making progress on the right track. She thinks Luna is serious."

"Wow, that's great news. Unexpected, if I'm honest, but wonderful to hear. Miss Clara deserves a break."

"That she does, AB."

They were both quiet for several seconds. AB pointed at her computer screen. "I just finished adding money to your mom's account. She'll be released a couple of days before we get home from Florida."

Coop rolled his eyes. "Don't remind me. That's another good reason to use that answering service."

"Any idea where she'll go?"

He shook his head. "Nope. I'm sure wherever she goes, it

won't be long before I know about it and get a call that she needs money, or she's in jail again."

AB nodded. "She's definitely a handful. I just wanted to alert you, since I know you've been so busy."

"Thanks, AB. I appreciate it. Truly, I do. It's just all beyond my control. She does whatever she wants, then when the situation is out of control, and she's in a bucket of crap, it becomes my mess. I'm just tired of it. Tired of her."

She reached over and patted his arm. "Don't worry about it. Whatever she does, we'll figure it out. We've handled worse, right?"

He laughed and smiled at her. "Yeah, we have, AB. Much worse."

He wanted to tell her that with her by his side, he was certain they could weather any storm, but the phone rang, and the moment was lost.

As they finished their late lunch of sandwiches from the Pickle Barrel, Coop's cell phone rang. He hurried to tap the button to connect with Detective Mitchell.

"Jim, you must have news."

"That I do, Coop. We just got the ballistics report back on the gun we excavated from Mrs. Stanton's place. It's a match for the two bullets and the casing we found at Alyssa's site. I don't want to steal Sheriff Holt's thunder, but just got off the phone with him, and the ballistics also match the two sites you helped find in Jefferson County. Same with Elizabeth and Brittany in Rutherford. We've got everything we need to tie Stanton to the four cold cases and Alyssa's."

"That's excellent news. I'm so glad you recovered the gun. That will make the case airtight."

"Those new charges will be filed most likely next week, but

I wanted you to know first. We're also charging his charming mother. Turns out that gun was reported stolen in North Dakota during the time Stanton lived there."

"Interesting tidbit. I imagine I'll be able to hear Delia yelling all the way up here when she gets that news."

Jim laughed. "No doubt. I can't wait to see Stanton's reaction when he gets hit with the new charges and learns we recovered the four others."

"I wish I could be there to watch that."

Coop thanked him for calling and disconnected. Nothing beat triumphing over evil. A sense of gratification came over him. He loved being a small part of bringing justice to those who deserved it.

EPILOGUE

Florida and the white sand beach never looked so good. Coop settled into the lounge chair, with an epic view of the blue water and sighed. He adjusted the brim on his hat to make sure his freshly shaved cheeks and chin were in the shade and relaxed against the padded headrest.

AB was stretched out in her chair next to him and beyond her, his dad and Camille were getting up to take Gus into the airconditioned condo. Camille's giant pink hat couldn't be missed as Charlie helped her from her chair.

He waved at them as they stepped through the sand, his dad keeping hold of Gus' leash. The sight of the three of them made Coop grin.

He closed his eyes and rested under the warmth of the sun. In a couple of days, Jack would arrive, and he looked forward to spending time with him. Coop was intent on making the most of their time together. Then, in less than a week, his dad would fly home to Nevada.

As much as Coop loved spending time in Florida, this was a bittersweet visit. He would miss his dad like crazy. At least he had his work to keep him occupied. Poor Aunt Camille would be lost without her sidekick.

Voices drew his gaze, and he focused on a group of young kids playing at the edge of the water, building sandcastles. As he watched the mother, who urged them to stay on the wet sand and not venture into the water, his thoughts drifted to Alyssa's mom. All she had were memories of her sweet girl. Coop wasn't sure he'd ever forget the heartbreak of Alyssa's case. Not to mention the other young women they'd found.

Ben sent Coop a text a few hours ago and said the story was going viral all across the state. The sheriffs of all the counties involved in the cases had appeared on television, discussing the cases and the hard work of their departments and the consultants who had worked on the cases. They were resolute in their condemnation of Stanton and vowed to seek more funding to tackle other cold cases.

Along with the news brief, Ben let him know the lead prosecutors used the death penalty as a tool, and Stanton agreed to plead guilty to the charges in exchange for a life sentence without the possibility of parole. He also took the blame for burying the gun at his mom's place. Oddly, he wouldn't admit to stealing it and said he found it along the road in North Dakota. Although all the detectives suspected Delia was involved and an accessory after the fact, their main objective was getting Stanton sentenced and sparing the families a trial.

Incarcerating Delia, who was in her seventies, was an easy position to give up if it meant Stanton would never see the light of day again. He would die in prison.

There wasn't a punishment harsh enough to fit what he'd done, but to know he could never hurt anyone else was a consolation. And if the families were satisfied, Coop was too.

Elizabeth's parents, along with those of Brittany, Denise, and Nancy, all wanted to meet with Coop when he was back in Nashville. The detectives on the cases made sure they all knew

Coop was instrumental in finding their daughters, and they were grateful for his help.

Coop couldn't imagine such a meeting and pushed it from his mind. He needed to decompress and enjoy his vacation. He'd deal with all of that when he was back to reality.

A waiter delivering Arnold Palmers interrupted his thoughts. AB thanked the server and slid her sunglasses down her nose as she turned to Coop and lifted her glass. "Here's to a week of doing absolutely nothing and drinking our weight in rum runners, hurricanes, and mojitos."

Coop returned her grin and clinked his glass with hers. "I'll drink to that as long as I can add coffee from that little beach hut Gus and I found this morning and ice cream that Dad discovered last night. You also may have to amend your toast. Aunt Camille has all of us signed up for ballroom dancing lessons this afternoon."

She flung her head back and laughed. "I can't believe you agreed to that."

He shrugged. "What can I say? I adore her, and she knows it."

"Well, I guess you won't mind that I made a reservation at the place down the beach. Line dancing tonight and this weekend."

Coop shook his head and took a long swallow from his drink. He'd also do anything for the woman smiling at him. "I could get used to these kinds of problems."

DEADLY PURSUIT IS the sixth book in the Cooper Harrington Detective Novels. You'll discover a new case in each book in the series, but the characters you've come to know will continue throughout the series. Tammy plans to continue this series until she runs out of cases for Coop. The books don't have to be read in order but are more enjoyable when you do, since you'll learn more about Coop's backstory as the series unfolds. If you're a new reader to Coop's books, you won't want to miss the other novels in the series. They are available in print, digital, and coming soon in audio.

If you've missed reading any, here are the links to the other books in the series, in order.
Killer Music
Deadly Connection
Dead Wrong
Cold Killer
Deadly Deception
Deadly Pursuit

ACKNOWLEDGMENTS

I have so much fun writing Coop and his cases. Mysteries have always been at the top of my list when it comes to books I enjoy reading. I love crafting the puzzle aspect of mysteries and enjoy sprinkling in a bit of family life and drama when it comes to Coop and all the other characters.

Many thanks to my editor, Susan, for finding my mistakes and helping me polish *Deadly Pursuit*. She does an awesome job, and I'm grateful for her. All the credit for this cover with handsome Gus goes to Elizabeth Mackey, who never disappoints. I'm fortunate to have such an incredible team helping me.

This case, like so many that make the headlines across the country, is heartbreaking. Criminals, like the one portrayed in this story, are often difficult to catch, especially if they move around and commit crimes across several states. In fact, this story was inspired by an abduction and murder that took place close to my hometown. Since Coop is driven by justice, it's easy to imagine him delving into what seems hopeless and finding the threads that connect clues and result in catching the culprit.

I so appreciate all of the readers who have taken the time to tell their friends about my work and provide reviews of my books. These reviews are especially important in promoting future books, so if you enjoy my novels, please consider leaving a review. I also encourage you to follow me on Amazon, Goodreads, and BookBub, where leaving a review is even easier, and you'll be the first to know about new releases and deals.

Remember to visit my website at http://www.tammylgrace.com and join my mailing list for my exclusive group of readers. I also have a fun Book Buddies Facebook Group. That's the best place to find me and get a chance to participate in my giveaways. Join my Facebook group at https://www.facebook.com/groups/AuthorTammyLGraceBookBuddies/ and keep in touch—I'd love to hear from you.

Happy Reading,

Tammy

MORE BY TAMMY L. GRACE

COOPER HARRINGTON DETECTIVE NOVELS
Killer Music

Deadly Connection

Dead Wrong

Cold Killer

Deadly Deception

Deadly Pursuit

HOMETOWN HARBOR SERIES
Hometown Harbor: The Beginning (Prequel Novella)

Finding Home

Home Blooms

A Promise of Home

Pieces of Home

Finally Home

Forever Home

Follow Me Home

Long Way Home

Come Home for Christmas

CHRISTMAS STORIES
A Season for Hope: Christmas in Silver Falls Book 1

The Magic of the Season: Christmas in Silver Falls Book 2

Christmas in Snow Valley: A Hometown Christmas Book 1

One Unforgettable Christmas: A Hometown Christmas Book 2

Christmas Wishes: Souls Sisters at Cedar Mountain Lodge

Christmas Surprises: Soul Sisters at Cedar Mountain Lodge

GLASS BEACH COTTAGE SERIES

Beach Haven

Moonlight Beach

Beach Dreams

WRITING AS CASEY WILSON

A Dog's Hope

A Dog's Chance

WISHING TREE SERIES

The Wishing Tree

Wish Again

Overdue Wishes

One More Wish

SISTERS OF THE HEART SERIES

Greetings from Lavender Valley

Pathway to Lavender Valley

Sanctuary at Lavender Valley

Blossoms at Lavender Valley

Comfort in Lavender Valley

Reunion in Lavender Valley

FROM THE AUTHOR

Thank you for reading the sixth book in the Cooper Harrington Detective novels. If you enjoyed it, I hope you'll post a review and tell your reader friends about it.

If you're a fan of women's fiction, readers love my bestselling HOMETOWN HARBOR SERIES, filled with characters who feel like old friends. You'll also want to try my GLASS BEACH COTTAGE SERIES, set in Driftwood Bay, or my newest series, SISTERS OF THE HEART. You can even start this one by downloading the first book, GREETINGS FROM LAVENDER VALLEY, for FREE!

The two books I've written as Casey Wilson, A DOG'S HOPE and A DOG'S CHANCE, both have received enthusiastic support from my readers and, if you're a dog lover, are must reads.

If you enjoy holiday stories, be sure to check out my CHRISTMAS IN SILVER FALLS SERIES and HOMETOWN CHRISTMAS SERIES. They're small-town Christmas stories of hope, friendship, and family. I'm also one of the authors of the bestselling SOUL SISTERS AT CEDAR MOUNTAIN LODGE

SERIES, centered around a woman who opens her heart and home to four foster girls one Christmas.

You'll want to check out one of my latest projects, the Dragonfly Cove Dog Park series. I wrote HEARTS UNLEASHED and you'll find Coop and Gus in cameo roles in this story, set in Florida.

I'm also one of the founding authors of *My Book Friends* and invite you to join this fun group of readers and authors on Facebook. I'd love to send you my exclusive interview with the canine companions in my *Hometown Harbor Series* as a thank you for joining my exclusive group of readers. You can sign up by following at my website here: https://www.tammylgrace.com/newsletter

I hope you'll connect with me on social media. You can find me on Facebook, where I have a page and a special group for my readers and follow me on Amazon and BookBub, so you'll know when I have a new release or a deal. If you haven't yet, be sure to download the free novella, HOMETOWN HARBOR: THE BEGINNING. It's a prequel to FINDING HOME that I know you'll enjoy.

If you did enjoy this book or any of my other books, I'd be grateful if you took a few minutes to leave a short review on Amazon, BookBub, Goodreads, or any of the other retailers you use.

ABOUT THE AUTHOR

Tammy L. Grace is the *USA Today* bestselling and award-winning author of the Cooper Harrington Detective Novels, the bestselling Hometown Harbor Series, and the Glass Beach Cottage Series, along with several sweet Christmas novellas. Tammy also writes under the pen name of Casey Wilson for Bookouture and Grand Central. You'll find Tammy online at www.tammylgrace.com where you can join her mailing list and be part of her exclusive group of readers. Connect with Tammy on Facebook at www.facebook.com/tammylgrace.books or Instagram at @authortammylgrace.

- facebook.com/tammylgrace.books
- x.com/TammyLGrace
- instagram.com/authortammylgrace
- bookbub.com/authors/tammy-l-grace
- goodreads.com/tammylgrace
- amazon.com/author/tammylgrace

Made in the USA
Las Vegas, NV
06 March 2025

19141493R00157